PENGUI
THE MINISTER'S WIFE

Amaresh Misra is a film-maker and freelance journalist. His previous books include *Lucknow: Fire of Grace,* a best-selling biography of Lucknow.

He lives in Delhi.

THE MINISTER'S WIFE

Amaresh Misra

PENGUIN BOOKS

Penguin Books India (P) Ltd., 11 Community Centre, Panchsheel Park,
New Delhi 110 017, India
Penguin Books Ltd., 80 Strand, London WC2R 0RL, UK
Penguin Putnam Inc., 375 Hudson Street, New York, NY 10014, USA
Penguin Books Australia Ltd., 250 Camberwell Road, Camberwell,
Victoria 3124, Australia
Penguin Books Canada Ltd., 10 Alcorn Avenue, Suite 300, Toronto,
Ontario, M4V 3B2, Canada
Penguin Books (NZ) Ltd., Cnr Rosedale and Airborne Roads, Albany,
Auckland, New Zealand

First published by Penguin Books India 2002

Copyright © Amaresh Misra 2002

All rights reserved

10 9 8 7 6 5 4 3 2 1

This is a work of fiction. Names, characters, places and incidents are either the product of the author's imagination or are used fictitiously, and any resemblance to actual persons, living or dead, events, or locales is entirely coincidental.

Typeset in *PalmSprings* by SÜRYA, New Delhi

Printed at Thomson Press (India) Limited, New Delhi

This book is sold subject to the condition that it shall not, by way of trade or otherwise, be lent, resold, hired out, or otherwise circulated without the publisher's prior written consent in any form of binding or cover other than that in which it is published and without a similar condition including this condition being imposed on the subsequent purchaser and without limiting the rights under copyright reserved above, no part of this publication may be reproduced, stored in or introduced into a retrieval system, or transmitted in any form or by any means (electronic, mechanical, photocopying, recording or otherwise), without the prior written permission of both the copyright owner and the above-mentioned publisher of this book.

Contents

	Prologue	1
1.	The Man	2
2.	Kanpur, 4 October 1990	7
3.	A Question of Paradise	9
4.	Allahabad, 3 September 1992	16
5.	Mumbai	20
6.	The Lover	29
7.	Bihar	37
8.	Benaras, 26 January 1993	63
9.	The Return	66
10.	An Affair to Remember	83
11.	Surprise	127
12.	A Way Too Long	137
13.	You Trusted Me	146
14.	The Minister's Wife	163
15.	Dhursal	174
	Epilogue	192

Prologue

The woman sat at the edge of the bed and bent down to smooth the crushed pleats of her sari. Her hands lingered awhile on the georgette. Then she lifted her sari, and the old-fashioned taffeta petticoat, to scratch her plump calf. She felt the smooth, rich flesh, and smiled.

She heard voices below—grunts, crude backslaps, nervous sniggers, faulty greetings.

She picked up a framed painting from the bedside table: a black stallion in an open field, beautiful and menacing, rearing up under a monsoon sky. She wiped the silver frame of the picture before putting it down again. She would find a wall to hang it up on. Someone had told her, long ago, 'This picture will always remind me of something sinister and seductive: our kind of love, my love.'

With the picture had come a mouth organ. She liked music, but not enough to learn to play that instrument.

In the mirror, she noticed a white patch on her neck, where she'd dabbed on a little extra Johnson's baby powder by mistake. She rubbed it into her skin. Everything was in order. She had to go down now.

The party was about to begin.

1. The Man

Slumped in his chair, rolling his second joint of another long and vacant day, Ajit watched the slim girl move around in his magazine and video store. She wore a short brown shirt over white gabardine trousers. She stopped before a display of VCD covers and bent forward to peer at something. 'Nice arse,' Ajit thought. He waited for her to approach him, and wondered if she was wearing anything underneath the trousers.

The girl turned around and walked up to the counter. She asked for the VCD of *Usual Suspects,* and he told her it wasn't available, she should find herself a DVD elsewhere. He couldn't keep the irritation out of his voice. It wasn't just her whiny, nasal tone. She had an insipid, oval face and thin lips; her arse had promised something much more interesting.

It was when the girl had turned away haughtily and he had lit the joint, that Ajit saw a tall, mildly overweight man in his mid thirties trudging towards him.

At the counter, the man did not ask for a VCD or a copy of the 'now-difficult-to-procure-in-India' *Playboy*. He sniffed, smelled grass and smiled—the friendly, gung-ho smile of good seniors in boarding schools.

'You belong to the joint family?'

'No, I live alone,' Ajit replied instinctively. The man laughed, reached across to pluck the joint from Ajit's hand and took a deep drag before handing it back.

'Anything special I can pull out for you?' Ajit asked to hide his embarrassment.

'I'm sure we can think of something special,' the man said, leaning against the counter. 'But can't we just chat a little first?'

He put his hand out for the joint again and asked Ajit about his family. On empty afternoons, small talk was a good way to pass time. So Ajit gave him vague details—parents, both retired doctors, who lived in Delhi; a sister, employed as a housewife in Ohio; no brothers; and him, alone in Lucknow, working in this store set up by his parents.

He was beginning to feel comfortable, seeing in this slightly older man an idle communicator.

The man was talking now about the streets of Lucknow. How he liked their energy, despite the fact that they were so humid and so busy, so narrow and so small, though the planners had given them big names. He wished he could visit Lucknow more often. It had been four years since his last visit. And he remembered seeing a shoot-out that time, right here in Hazratganj, between the police and two dreaded criminals. Ajit told him of a similar incident at Maulviganj where the police had shot down two boys in a fake encounter. Ajit said he knew one of them, a newspaper errand boy. There had been a big demonstration in the wake of that incident, which the police had lathi-charged brutally.

'Were you part of the demonstration?'

Ajit mumbled something incoherent in reply, and realizing that they had been talking like this, him sitting, the older man standing, for all this while, he stood up from his chair in an automatic gesture of respect. The man was almost exactly his height, but stockier. He had small, hooded eyes, a wide mouth, a square jaw, and a receding hairline. Up close he looked a little less amiable than he had just a moment before.

'So why don't you live with your parents?' he asked suddenly.

Ajit evaded a direct reply. The man dropped the joint to the floor and stubbed it out with his left toe. Then, leaning closer, he said, 'Is it because of what happened in Kanpur many years ago?'

Ajit looked away to hide his surprise. Copies of the latest issue of *Outlook* were lying in a heap in a dark corner. The slot fixed for the best video of the day was empty, as usual. Book markers and toffees, the free handouts meant for adults and children, were scattered on the counter. He picked up a marker and smiled weakly. 'The maid,' he said, 'she's lazy.'

'They're made that way, lazy and unscrupulous. But is yours sexy?'

Ajit looked sharply at the man.

'So what happened at Kanpur?' he said defiantly.

The man laughed. Ajit noticed that the upper portion of his incisors was yellow. He remembered his mother telling him that resulted from an extra dose of tetracycline in childhood.

'You are scared and you won't admit it,' the man said, still laughing.

Ajit reminded himself that looking nervous was the worst thing one could do when faced with a crisis. He walked round the counter and invited the man to sit down.

'Oh, I'm all right. I think you need that chair more than I do.'

'Do you have a name?'

'How about Poddar?' He picked up a large toffee from the table.

'That's a fake,' Ajit said with an imperious air.

'Maybe it is. But what happened in Kanpur on 4th October 1990—that wasn't fake, was it?'

Ajit began to sweat. He was reminded of his first ragging in hostel. The man now looked callous and sadistic, like bad seniors in boarding schools. Ajit watched him as he began to pace in front of the counter, looking intense and preoccupied and gesticulating like some lawyer in a movie, reconstructing a crime for the jury.

'On the evening of 4th October you shot a man, no, a boy, your best friend, inside the DAV College premises. The bullet came from a handmade pistol, and got him in the face, just above his left eye. He writhed for six seconds precisely. In that short time, before he died, he called out first for his mother and then yours.'

The short speech was delivered like an official report with easy precision. And the tone was impersonal, not icy. After a brief pause the man went on.

'You were arrested and kept in the lock up for a night. Your mother, who was then a famous doctor in Allahabad, came to get you out, and the inspector in charge came forward to salute her. You refused to go. You were then drugged and taken to Allahabad. The inspector was indebted to your mother. She had saved his wife's life during his Allahabad posting after a near fatal accident.

'You were locked up in your room for days, while the police hunted down the radical friends who had taken you to Kanpur. Some of them were arrested, some were let off with a warning. You finally came to your senses and accepted the exile in Lucknow. This store came as a bribe. Those are the facts.'

Ajit felt his head spinning. He felt cornered, and almost as a reflex action he grabbed the man by the shoulders. He wanted to shake him hard, to say that his facts were wrong. Then he wanted to correct parts of the story and explain things 'ideologically'. All he could manage was a weak question: 'What do you want?'

'I want you to do a job for me.'

'What kind of job?'

'There is a woman I want you to follow. She is the wife of Sunil Agnihotri, the new home minister of Maharashtra.'

'That's crazy.'

'I want you to peep into her closet. See whom she's meeting when she tells her husband she's going shopping or seeing a friend. I want you to follow her into her bedroom, note the expression on her face when she takes off her clothes. Note especially whether she has that look of having been screwed in some seedy Mumbai room.'

Ajit stared deep into the man's eyes for some hint of sanity before ramming a fist into his stomach. The man belched and opened his mouth, as if to vomit. Ajit landed another fist on his yellow incisors. The man asked Ajit to stop. Ajit positioned himself for a third blow and the man picked up a stool. The stool slammed against Ajit's left hip, and he crashed into a wooden store rack. He recovered quickly and charged at the man, head forward. He did not notice the .32 Webley Scot that the man pulled out from his trouser pocket. He staggered when the butt of the revolver struck his forehead. The second blow filled his head with a buzzing darkness and his mouth with the salt taste of blood.

2. Kanpur, 4 October 1990

DAV College stood at the far end of a broken cement road. The protesting upper-caste students had torn down portions of its crumbling walls to erect barricades. The police were ready to storm the college, when a rival procession arrived from the far end of the road. Walking in the last line of the procession, Ajit saw his friends from Allahabad behind the barricades. Anil Sinha, Sunil Agarwal and Rakesh Tripathi.

The boys manning the barricades started throwing stones at the procession. The police moved forward for a lathi charge but the hailstorm of stones and stray bottles forced them to retreat. The boys in the procession scattered into small groups, some of them picked up the stones that had landed around them and threw them back at the protestors. The air was thick with abuse and slogans.

It was a scene that was being played out in cities and towns all over northern India that year, ever since V.P. Singh's government announced that it would implement the Mandal Commission Report recommending reservations in government jobs for the backward castes.

The crowd behind the barricades called the procession leaders 'low-caste pigs'. The leaders shouted back that the 'Brahmin-Rajput-Baniya motherfuckers' had had their day; they were finished now.

The police became jittery. The Rajput officer in charge ordered a low-caste constable to go and talk to the leaders of the procession. He refused. The officer slapped him across the face, and the constable's caste brethren ran to his aid. One of them caught the officer by the throat. Another officer fired in the air.

Ajit was hiding behind a tree with a Yadav boy he barely knew, unsure about what he was supposed to do, now that he was here with the procession. And then he saw Rakesh bring up a country-made pistol and aim at the pro-reservationists. The shot missed a lower-caste student leader by inches. The pro-reservationists responded with a country-made bomb. There was pandemonium. A roar went up among the upper-caste protestors and they surged forward, having decided to storm the enemy ranks. Rakesh spotted Ajit behind the tree and shouted for him to come and join the protestors: 'Fuck leftism, you stupid bastard! You're not one of them, stop licking V.P. Singh's arse.' Ajit yelled back that he could go screw himself. Rakesh ran straight at him with the gun, and at first Ajit was confused. Then he heard Rakesh shouting at him to get out of the way—he wanted to shoot down the 'Yadav motherfucker'. Before Ajit could utter a word, Rakesh had fired his shot. The bullet grazed the Yadav's right hand, and the boy ran for his life. But Rakesh wasn't through with him. He ran in pursuit. When Ajit tripped him, the momentum made him fly forward, almost parallel to the ground. Rakesh's pistol went off even as he fell, blasting the left side of his head.

Ajit dropped to his knees to attend to his friend. Rakesh called out his mother's name. He then asked Ajit to give his last respects to 'Doctor aunty'.

3. A Question of Paradise

Ajit blinked. Even the late-afternoon light hurt his eyes. He saw the man standing next to the portable colour TV of his store, reading something. The TV was on, but the dancing images were hazy, and when he tried to focus on them, a sharp pain flared up in his head and he had to close his eyes. He was lying on the floor. Someone had put a cushion under his back and propped his legs up on a chair.

The man spoke—a languid but firm voice.

'Is shaam hum akelon ka kya hoga?
Urdu ke maaron ka kya hoga?
Sohbaten haseen hain
Samander nasheela hai
Maahaul mein kasak hai
Mohabbat mein shak hai—
Is shaam ek haseena ka kya hoga?
Usulon ke maaron ka kya hoga?'

(What is fated for us lonesome men tonight?
What is fated for those seduced by Urdu?
There is beauty by our side
And this ocean that is drunk
A sweet pain in the air

The twist of mistrust in our love—
What is fated for some enchantress tonight?
What is fated for the men of principles?)

There was mirth in the man's voice as he finished the poem. 'That's good. Yours?'

'How dare you read my diary!'

'*Is shaam ek haseena ka kya hoga?/Usulon ke maaron ka kya hoga*,' the man hummed the lines. 'Remember the job I talked about?'

'I still think you are crazy,' Ajit replied, but did not look up.

The man lit a cigarette, and went on, as if Ajit hadn't spoken.

'Her name's Rukmini. She lives in her husband's flat in Khar. Bombay's a slum, but her part of the city is nice. Small, clean roads, few encroachments. You might find the occasional authentic Bombaywala there—the kind who'll drive sensibly even late at night, and with his headlights down.'

His casual tone irritated Ajit. 'Who the *fuck* are you?' He shouted. The man stopped and looked at him. It was as if he had been woken from a dream.

'An agent from Paradise. Sign a contract and you will be taken on the most wonderful tour of your life. Remember the old Sufi saying?—Do not go unless you are sent.'

'You talk too much,' Ajit snapped.

'I do. All the more reason for you to do the job for me. If I talk, you're in trouble. I can have that case re-opened—'

'You can do no such thing,' Ajit shot back. 'The case is closed.' He sat up and felt his shirt pocket. He badly needed a joint.

The man winked. 'You will graduate to better things if you accept my offer.'

Ajit ignored him.

'You are a drifter, my friend, like me. But there's one difference, an important one—even we drifters need some direction. Not an ideal, but something to do that will keep us from thinking too much; I have that, you don't. I had a sister once. She died due to emotional causes. Emotional Indian causes. You don't remind me of her, but you could end up like her. Though your case would be a little different: Ajit Vajpayee—died of non-emotional Indian causes. Worse than emotional Indian causes.'

Ajit did not like the shift to intellectualism, and he asked the man to stop talking nonsense.

'I see that you are not impressed. But you will change your mind when you see Rukmini. All the pieces will fall into place, and you'll thank me for having made your life worthwhile. I've thought of everything—you'll have a side job as a *Times of India* corespondent in Mumbai. Good cover, and it also makes it easier for you to poke your nose in her affairs. Her most private affairs. You should carry lots of old thumris in your music collection. She loved thumris. Do you know what she did with them?'

The man was kneeling now, and whispering in Ajit's ear. Ajit felt the heat of his breath on his neck and thought of pushing him away, but found himself unable to do so. He could smell the man's deodorant.

'She made love to the voice of Siddheswari Devi. Her legs would go up over my shoulders during the *bol banav* and the climax at *laggi ladi* was always accompanied by a scream.'

Ajit felt a lazy stirring in his groin. The man sat down next to him.

'Rukmini was like a wet heroine from a Puranic text— does that sound strange? No, I'm sure you understand what

I mean. I still remember the first time with her. She faked virginity—if someone were to ask her about it now, I'm certain she'll say she did it for my sake. Because I was a virgin, you see, and it showed. My cock always slipped at the mouth, probably because I was too excited and couldn't get it up. Then suddenly, one day, it went in. It slid in nicely, and I lost all control over myself. I was a crazed young bull that day. But she was calm and there was no blood. Then later, after she'd gone home, she phoned to tell me that she had bled for more than an hour. The doctor had to be called. But it was a lie. One of her many lies.

'About the only thing she didn't lie about was her love of horses. She was a freak who dreamt of owning race courses. I gave her this amazing portrait of a black horse in a field, with a caption to match. The same day she gave me the crap about her mental illness.'

The man lit another cigarette.

'For seven years she told me that she was sick in the head. Electric shocks, straitjackets, shrinks, dark rooms. Then one day she told me she had cooked it all up because she loved me so much, and the thought of losing me was like a knife in the guts. I was good looking, and she imagined me screwing other women. With that mental illness story she had hoped to keep me with her always. I should understand, she said, because she was a wreck. Her brother-in-law had raped her when she was barely twelve. Then a few days later she said the rape bit was a lie too. She really *was* sick, but for another reason, and she wasn't sure she could ever tell me or anyone else about it.

'If her intention was to fuck me up, she did a good job. I stayed up nights thinking of her, feeling like a shit because I could do nothing for her. I told her about a friend of mine in Lucknow who was a shrink. I'd told him about her and he'd said he could help. He'd agreed to come to Allahabad—that's where the lies were taking place. And what happens the day he's supposed to board a train to Allahabad? He gets killed. In broad daylight.'

The cigarette had burned out. His voice had been even, almost flat, throughout the narration. His eyes were red, but he wasn't going to cry. Then he put his arm around Ajit's shoulder and lowered his voice, speaking slowly.

'When we made love, when I fucked her, she always lay down on her side with her face turned away from me. I used to take her slowly from behind, playing with her tits like a child. They were big. She did not know much about orgasms, she said, but told me that it felt good at times. She seemed so pure and pale, like a child. She applied nothing but Johnson's baby powder on her body. She was allergic to perfumes and creams, she said. She said she didn't like giving blow jobs, then one day she stopped in the middle of some story about her childhood nightmares and went down and gave me a BJ. She did it like a professional, taking her time over it, and when I came, my sperm trickled down her smooth face. She told me she'd used extra baby powder on her face that day, just before I'd come in.'

Ajit was beginning to get a hard on. He sat mesmerized. The man did not stop.

'And then it turned out that she was actually a whore. My smooth, fair, Johnson's-baby-powder-addict Brahmin girl screwed clients in the three-star hotels of UP. In retrospect, the liar was quite honest in her own way. She always told me about her fucks, she did that by saying they happened to her friend Anjali. She would call me up and cry over the phone.'

Ajit pulled up his knees to hide his hard on. The man pretended not to notice, and continued, now impersonating Rukmini. ' "You know what happened to Anjali today? Her driver laid her in the outhouse. She did it because he knew about her hotel visits and she wanted him to keep quiet about it. How could she! When she told me about it, I almost puked. He came today to fetch her and was eyeing me as well. He thinks I'm like her!"

'I'd always tell her there was no reason for her to be affected by what Anjali did. Anjali could lay the whole world if she wanted to. It was her business. But she never agreed. According to her I was too un-Indian, too Westernized, too much of a Marxist in my opinions.

'Then she told me Anjali was a sophisticated whore, one of those respectable middle-class girls who screw for money. Good for her, I said, and she went hysterical over the phone. I told her it was okay, these things happen, she should calm down. But she said I didn't understand anything, it wasn't okay—did I know what had happened just that afternoon? Anjali had gone to please a client in some hotel. The guy's friends had turned up demanding their pound of the hot flesh. She was gang banged by seven guys.

'"She must be pretty hard up," I said. "No," replied Rukmini. "She was laughing when she told me about it."

'It was Rukmini who laughed that day.

'The night she had my friend killed, it rained after months of fierce heat. I lay naked in her arms, hopelessly in love, almost fucked in the head myself. She had traumatized me beyond repair. And even as I surrendered all of myself to the fragrance of wet earth and the warmth of her body, an innocent man was being chased down a gali in Lucknow by men armed with six-inch knives. The body lay unclaimed for two days. All he'd wanted to do was to help. The fucking injustice of it! The bitch has to pay!'

Ajit felt a current run through his body. He heard himself ask the man how he could help.

'Does that mean you're game? Something's convinced you we're both of a kind—it's the sorrow in my story,' he laughed wryly. 'Or is it because of what happened on another date, at another place?

The man was almost breathing down his neck.

'Is it because of what happened in Allahabad on 3rd September 1992?'

Ajit stared at him in disbelief. He punched the man hard on the face. He did that again, and then a third time. When he stopped, he was trembling. The man's lips were torn and he was bleeding.

The man smiled. There was blood on his teeth.

'You're on the job. I'll pay you handsomely, over and above your *Times of India* salary, like a proper detective. But of course the money's only a minor inducement. I'm offering you adventure. We are both lost, distorted creatures—more than just alienated Westerners in a brown land, forced to run drug stores and shag out our obsessions. Our curse is greater than that ... But let's leave it at that. And don't even ask who I am. Or how I know so much. Know me as Sameer, the name Rukmini knew. Two sinners seek each other out. We all have our 4th Octobers and 3rd Septembers. Just try and come out unscathed. Women may not have loved you. But the country needs you.'

With this last, slightly arcane, almost improbable speech, the man winced and collapsed to the floor.

4. Allahabad, 3 September 1992

It was on a muggy September evening that Ajit heard about Seema's infidelity from his friend Ramesh. She had been sleeping with her history professor, a bright young Christian with a deep voice who was good in the dramatic arts and had a way with his female students. They were in a restaurant cubicle, drinking, and Ramesh made no attempt to keep the pity out of his voice.

When Ajit confronted her the next day, Seema said it was all in his head, she'd only had coffee with the professor a couple of times. They were sitting on the couch in her father's study, as they often did in the afternoons when there was no one else in the house. They had lain together here, naked, making love as the vendors and the neighbourhood maids and kids went about their business just outside the windows. Ajit asked if this was where she fucked the professor too. Seema snapped that he was imagining things. Ajit grabbed her by her long, thick hair, which he so loved, and bellowed that he wanted the truth, not stupid lies.

He yanked her by the hair till there were tears in her eyes. He saw the pain in her face, and then he began what he was best at—emotional interrogation, his tone soft and overly reasonable. She knew him well enough to sense the menace behind the pose, but he could think of no other approach that would make her talk. He told her that he was acting in her interest, that it did not matter even if she had slept with the professor. A liberal might have objected but he was a Marxist. At this last bit she smiled a bitter, mocking smile and his grip on her hair tightened. But he didn't want to hurt her. He wanted a confession.

He sat next to her. She would feel better if she told him the truth, he said in a low, calm voice. It was the right thing to do. He put his hand on her neck and moved it to her breasts.

Seema looked exhausted. She began telling him what he wanted to hear. It had started, she said, with a shared passion for Napoleon. And before she knew it, she was having long telephonic conversations with the professor late at night. Ajit felt a tinge of pain, for this was precisely how he and Seema had started off—marathon phone sessions at night, sometimes stretching to five or six hours. And yet, far greater than the hurt was the thrill he felt guessing at what she would reveal further.

He had stormed in expecting to shame her, end the relationship and walk out triumphantly. But the betrayal faded away before the prospect of her confession. He goaded her on and she began to recount the intimate details.

Seema told him that the professor had kissed her for the first time in the same suburban restaurant where Ajit often took her for a feel. Ajit asked whether the professor felt her too. Seema hesitated before replying. Yes, the professor did touch her. He was also in the habit of putting his hand inside her bra. A couple of days back, on this same couch, the professor had disrobed her. He took her salwaar to her knees. But she had kept her panties on that time.

Ajit was overcome with desire. He began opening her blouse and fondling her tight breasts. He lay her on the couch and pulled her loose skirt up. He slid his index finger in her cunt. And he asked her to tell him more. Hadn't the professor actually put his cock inside her? Hadn't he done what he was doing to her now? Seema tried to sit up, but Ajit pushed her back and slid his finger in deeper. She was wet, and Ajit knew that if he kept working her like this, she would tell him all that he wanted to hear. Yes, she said, the professor had done this to her the last time they met.

And what did he say to her when he did it?

Seema began to tell him, and as she spoke the professor's desperate, heated words, Ajit pulled out his cock and masturbated. When he was done, he pulled her up and made her an offer. He wanted to meet the professor. In his house, not here, and with her, not alone. He wanted her and the professor to finish what they had started.

There was suspicion and shock in Seema's eyes, but to Ajit it seemed faked. She looked away from him and shook her head silently. He told her she owed him this much. This was the only way they could both put it all behind them. She turned to face him—the look on her face confused him, it was as if she was in another world. Did she have a choice, she asked. He pretended not to understand the question. She shut her eyes and asked him to leave; he'd get what he wanted. Then he left her, shutting the door behind him politely.

Seema arrived in his house on 3rd September 1992, dressed in a green-and-blue sari. She looked aloof. He took her to his room and was about to make small talk when the professor too arrived. He was short, dark and stocky. He looked nervous.

Ajit locked them in his bedroom at 10 a.m. The professor was embarrassed. He requested Ajit to open the lock at 12 p.m. sharp.

Ajit walked out to his terrace. He wasn't sure of what he had done, or why. He walked round in circles, trying not to think of what he had set up. Perhaps there was nothing happening in there. Would that satisfy him? Perhaps he should drive off somewhere and return only when it was time to let them out.

But it was no use. He found himself imagining the professor's dark penis making a trail of pre-cum on Seema's warm white thighs. He saw her raise her hips to meet the final assault, and he could control himself no longer. He went into the room adjoining his bedroom. He stood by the connecting door, unzipped and began to masturbate. It was unnaturally quiet on the other side. He went down on his knees and put his eyes to the large crack he had cut into the door, almost exactly in the centre. He saw Seema on the bed, her arse in the air, slobbering over the professor's dark penis. Then, without a word spoken, as if they had rehearsed this sequence, she stopped sucking him off and turned around. The professor went up on his knees and caught her by her hips. He placed his cock, slick with saliva, just below her arse, and when he pushed into her in one swift motion, Seema hollered.

Later, Seema had called Ajit a coward. This was the first time the professor had touched her, she said. He never forgot the contempt in her voice, nor the image of her face buried in the professor's crotch. He had been unable to make love to a woman ever since.

•

The man was right. They had much in common. Both were condemned to a lifetime of voyeurism, to desperate, memory-driven shagging, and empty lives. The mission had to be undertaken.

A month later, he was in Mumbai.

5. Mumbai

Ajit saw two men taking position on the make-shift platform in the lawns of Sunil Agnihotri's house in Khar. They were both strong and would have beaten him hollow were he to take them on.

Rukmini appeared on the platform with folded hands. She was to address a small crowd of die-hard followers. Ajit was not particularly impressed. She was fair and of medium height; her tits bounced lightly when she walked, but she was plump.

Rukmini began talking to her followers. Her speech seemed rehearsed and there was an obvious attempt to please. 'An artificial style,' Ajit noted in his diary. 'Tries too hard to sound sincere—an Aishwarya Rai type.'

The other journalists present weren't interested in slotting Rukmini. They wanted to catch her on the wrong foot on the controversy surrounding her husband.

A weeping woman fell at her feet. Rukmini picked her up and Ajit noticed her smooth, soft neck. He was filled with a sudden urge to plant his teeth in that rich flesh.

'Don't worry, Sunilji will be out of this mess soon,' she told the woman.

'But, Mrs Agnihotri, Sunilji's employee Sudha was found dead in her car, allegedly just after some lover of hers who was with her in the car had left. She had marks on her body and the first autopsy did confirm rape. Sunilji was found near the scene of the crime exactly seven minutes after that, fixing his car. How do you explain that?'

This was Rishikesh Jadhav, Ajit's *Times of India* colleague, asking a planted question.

'You are mistaken. My husband was never there. He was at Hotel Sea Princess trying to help his driver get over a local problem. The bar owner has given his statement.'

As Rukmini replied, Ajit inched closer to note the expression in her eyes. They were impassive.

'But the bar owner is from Hardoi, Sunil Agnihotri's hometown!' screeched Shalini, the correspondent from *Indian Express*.

'That is precisely the point, dear,' Rukmini began, switching to light humour. Ajit saw her face break into a lazy, charming smile. 'People are jealous of us UP-ites making it big in Mumbai. My husband is the first UP-ite to get a state cabinet berth. Naturally the opposition is out to get him.'

The smile was intact when she finished.

Just then, two large Alsatians appeared on the lawns, led by a trainer. Rukmini's smile widened as they snuggled up to her. Ajit was not fond of dogs. His mind was elsewhere, occupied by the actions of a boy in the crowd. Ajit had noticed him earlier, some two or three metres away, fidgeting nervously. He wore a shabby cotton shirt, and from the vermilion on his forehead—three fingers twisted like snakes—Ajit presumed he was a Maharashtrian or a South Indian. Ajit watched him come forward now and shout, 'Your husband's a killer. Shiv Sena was the right answer for you UP-ites.'

Rukmini stopped patting her dogs and looked up. One of her body guards pointed the boy out to her, and for a while she was absolutely still. Then her face hardened and she threw a challenge to the crowd: 'Will you all allow this chit of a boy to get away with the statement'?

Immediately two men from the crowd lunged at the boy and caught him by the collar. He began to struggle. The strongmen flanking Rukmini looked on nervously. After a while the boy gave up fighting. Looking still at Rukmini, he pulled up his shirt and took out a pistol. The men assaulting him let go of him and staggered back. The journalists began retreating.

The boy levelled the nozzle of the gun in the direction of the platform and fired. The bullet caught the strongman standing to Rukmini's left. He fell, clutching his stomach. Someone from the crowd threw a knife. It planted itself on the grass beside the boy, who whirled around and fired thrice indiscriminately. In the noise and commotion Ajit saw Rukmini exhorting the other strongman to attack the boy. She was also shouting at the crowd not to panic; this was an attack on her party and the people of UP by members of the opposition party.

Ajit decided that his role there was to help Rukmini. It wasn't a considered reaction, rather an impulse—perhaps it was the effect of her husky voice when she shouted. In his mind such a voice was associated as much with courage as with sex. Taking advantage of his position—he was standing behind the boy—Ajit pushed the unsuspecting Shiv Sainik rugby style to the ground. The gun was still in the air when Ajit saw Rukmini grappling with the boy. She must have stepped down from the platform while Ajit played amateur football. Her sari had slid much below her navel.

Rukmini shook the boy's hand, to make him drop the

gun, but he was strong. He tried pushing her away and nearly succeeded, but she held on, and tried to pin him down. She wasn't a strong woman, and Ajit couldn't help marvelling at what he thought kept her going: not spirit or will, or any heroism, but a pure passion to put up a successful show.

Her strongmen were out of the reckoning—one was on the ground screaming with pain, the other had vanished. And Ajit could sense that no one from the crowd would come forward to help her. This was his chance.

Planting his right foot on the boy's shoulder, Ajit kicked his gun-toting hand with his left. In the process, he inadvertently kicked Rukmini in the hip and unbalanced her. The boy twisted his head and dug his teeth in Ajit's right leg. Ajit yelled, and before he could react, Rukmini was on her feet and kicking the boy viciously. One kick landed bang on target, just below the chin. The boy's tongue was ripped off. He was trying to say something at that very instant.

They were in Rukmini's drawing room. The crowd had thinned following the arrival of the police. Groups in khaki were mopping up after the performance. The injured strongman was bundled into an ambulance, the squealing boy, blood pouring out of his mouth and soaking his shirt, was handcuffed and driven off in a police van.

'Why did you have to hit me?' Rukmini asked, handing Ajit a glass of ginger ale.

'You came in the way,' Ajit replied.

Rukmini smiled. Ajit liked the way her face changed and softened when she did that.

'You've got courage. You're just a boy. You must be what—30-31? I'm at least five years older.'

She seemed pleased with her observation.

'You're right about my age,' Ajit conceded, and added, 'You have courage too. You surprised me.'

Rukmini smiled again and looked down at her body. She then got up to tidy the room. Ajit was reminded of something his lecherous granduncle used to say about what went on in a woman's head when she looked down at her body in the presence of men. Ajit held him responsible for some of his early hard-ons. He had to suppress one right now as he imagined his granduncle eyeing Rukmini.

'Will you write a story about Sudha's death?' Rukmini asked, having handed a maid a pile of old magazines.

'Yes, but give me an angle.'

'It was suicide. I think her lover wanted to ditch her and run off to the US. She compelled him to make love to him one last time and then she strangled herself.'

Ajit was surprised. He couldn't help asking whether that sounded logical to her.

'I know it's natural to think, "Ah, here's a murder." It is always tempting to think there's something murky under the surface. But reality is often quite plain and simple. You scratch the surface but there's seldom anything beneath it. It's a waste of time. But where would you media people be without hype and conspiracy theories.'

'And then there are politicians who spend half their lives hiding things. Much worse than creating a little hype, don't you think?' Ajit was beginning to enjoy this.

Rukmini laughed, clearly amused. 'You are a pucca media hound. Are you new to Mumbai?'

'Yes. I'm from Allahabad.'

Ajit thought he saw her pale for a second. But then she smiled again.

'I'm from UP too. What's your full name'?

'Ajit Vajpayee.'

'Oh, you're a Brahmin. Kanyakubja or Sarayupari?'
'Kanyakubja. All Vajpayees are Kanyakubjas.'
'I'm Kanyakubja too.'
'I don't believe in the caste system.'
'Are you a leftist?'
'No, a democrat.'

•

Ajit came out of the house, feeling a little dizzy. Sameer's whore was an intrepid character. She was politically astute and a show-woman to boot, which was likeable, but she was also a turn-on in the insidious fashion that his granduncle talked about. She could have been a perfect bitch.

Ajit realized he hadn't observed her carefully enough to make out if she still used Johnson's baby powder. There had been no obvious clues about her interest in horses or thumris either.

While he was leaving, Rukmini had told him she liked him. That hadn't sounded like a proposition to him. Sameer had warned him about her duplicity, her capacity to ensnare, but for the moment he couldn't think of her as a whore-murderess. He found her strangely romantic, fighting off a rightwing arsehole in a georgette sari on a humid Mumbai evening.

To get his mind off Rukmini, Ajit began mulling over the details she had given him about the Sudha case. He was about to ask his auto-rickshaw driver to turn the vehicle in the direction of Sudha's aunt's house, who lived in the suburbs, when he saw two heavily decked-up women standing on the Bandra-Santa Cruz Linking Road. They were both dressed in identical tight white blouses and blue miniskirts. Ajit wondered if they were twins. The driver slowed down. Even from a distance Ajit could see that the figures were handsome, and utterly self-assured. They seemed like European women out on a stroll.

The auto had stopped. Ajit was about to question the driver when he found two painted faces peering at him. It was when they spoke that he realized something was wrong. Speaking in gruff, manly voices, the figures identified themselves as *'chheh number ka maal'*. They asked him to take them to a hotel. They would charge Rs 300 each, and the hotel room would cost Rs 400 for an hour.

Ajit had never been this close to any eunuch before, and even as he thought of how to react, they had forced their way into the auto. He was informed that in fact he had no choice in the matter. He had to lay them or pay up without doing anything. Otherwise they would take him to their den where he would be robbed and beaten. Worse, they would insult him in public and hand him over to the police.

An incensed Ajit looked at the driver. He smiled, told him frankly that he was in league with them and that yes, Ajit really had no choice.

'I'm a journalist,' Ajit protested, and flashed his *Times of India* card.

The eunuchs were speechless for a while. Then the more handsome one began speaking in Bambaiya Hindi. In a rich and sonorous voice Ajit was told that he could use that piece of paper to plug his arse. It made no difference in Mumbai whether you were a journalist or even the PM. Sooner or later everyone got fucked. There was justice for all in this city. *'Asli* democracy,' said one of them and giggled.

Ajit almost decided to put up a fight. But he stood outnumbered two to one. And there was the driver to consider. But what really clinched the issue were the proud and painted faces. Ajit wanted to keep looking at them. The coarse words spewing out of their pink-lipsticked lips were hypnotic. And they had amazing legs, strong and shapely, lean with muscle, which he rarely got to see in the women of his choice. He had a hard on. He felt a hand moving up his thigh like a snake; after a pause it went for his balls.

Ajit could not scream. Another hand had sealed his lips. The driver kick-started the auto.

Ajit did not know how he reached the hotel room. He saw a cracked pink roof, soiled green curtains and a filthy mosaic floor. Great legs were sitting on either side of him on a narrow bed, showing off a pair of shaved chests. Ajit abused them hard. Complimenting him on his use of language, they laughed and then told him to undress. Ajit refused. Great legs pulled him off the bed and slapped him twice on the face. Ajit hit back, sending one of them reeling to the wall. The second one tripped him to the floor and climbed onto his chest. Ajit felt crushed. Two fist blows to his head told him that he was dealing with real men.

The great legs thrown to the wall came back and robbed Ajit of exactly one thousand bucks. He then stripped him with disdain, gasping only at the sight of his thick six-inch cock.

Ajit felt strong lips slide down his cock and then heard the lips tell the figure on his chest that he tasted good. The figure looked at him in wonder and put his lips on his. Ajit resisted, but the feel of an alien tongue inside his mouth, probing deep, tickling his palate, felt good. He imagined a strong woman laying him flat. He opened his mouth and kissed the figure as hard as he could. The figure responded with immediate effect. Ajit felt an intense pre-orgasmic wave pass through his body. He pushed the chest-rider back, catching him unawares, and urged the cocksucker to speed up, slapping him hard on the face. The cocksucker's head bobbed up and down in rapid-fire motion. His frenzied excitement made Ajit's head spin with an excess of pleasure. He yanked the eunuch's hair to make him stop and stood up and commanded him to open his arse. The cocksucker went down on his hands and knees. Ajit positioned himself at the crack of his arse and gave a hard shove.

Abruptly, he heard the sensational strains of a Hindi cabaret song. The feel was baroque, chic and heated. It reminded him of something he'd seen in a forgotten film, sweaty, half-naked bodies in a night club somewhere in Arabia. The chest rider was standing by a two-in-one, adjusting the volume. The number, from a 1960s' film, spoke of true grit in the heart and the value of taking and giving lives—

Kisiki jaan lete hain
Kisi par jaan dete hain
Vahi karte hain dilwaale jo dil mein thaan lete hain
Lagale jaan ya ya ya ya ya ya ya
Lagale jaan ya ya ya ya ya ya ya

Incongruously, Ajit thought of the lost glory of Beirut. He gave another deep shove. Great legs screamed. The curve of a plump, fair neck appeared before Ajit's eyes. Then the sight of long muscular legs dancing close to his heaving body. Ajit saw fierce warriors emerging from a deep lane, charging into the darkness. He speeded up against the weight of the howling figure. The chest rider began kissing the cocksucker as Ajit slapped his arse. He forgot the number of times he did that. In the end, when Ajit came, it was like a release from an old curse.

The battle had been won. Mumbai had done something.

6. The Lover

The fence had four horizontal wooden planks. The top one had been cut in the centre to make way for a wire which ran to a pole in the back garden. Ajit was unable to decide whether he had seen a scene like this in a Benaras Hindu University campus dwelling or during his last visit to London as a child in the '70s.

He had reached Sudha's aunt's house in Andheri after a one-and-a-half-hour cab drive. He wasn't quite sure where he had taken the cab from; after the eunuchs left, he was alone in the hotel room for a while, and even after he had walked out, his head was heavy. He had staggered into the first taxi he could spot. The evening had seemed unreal.

The cab driver belonged to Bhadohi in UP and recognized Ajit's accent. He told him to be wary of Marathi and Gujarati taxiwalas. Ajit wasn't paying attention. The eunuchs kept coming back to his mind. Tough, feminine faces, muscular legs, the sounds of abuse and love, the strangely seductive smell of semen and blood.

The cab driver kept abusing loudly, calling Mumbai a whorehouse.

At the wooden gate, Ajit remembered vaguely that when he paid the man, his metre showed twice the normal rate.

Sudha's aunt was in her forties and not good looking. Ajit had expected this from what he had been told about her. But he had forgotten to ask either Rukmini or his colleagues at TOI about her antecedents. So he asked the plain-looking woman herself, taking note of the untidiness of the drawing room. The room had three chairs, a couple of wooden stools and a dirty carpet, on which stood a table with a split surface. There were too many shelves around.

'We belong to Bihar.'

'Where in Bihar?'

'Why do you want to know? People don't ask these type of questions in Bombay.'

Ajit wanted to say he did not belong to Mumbai but checked himself.

'There is talk that Sudha had a lover. That he fled the scene after her death.'

He wanted to go on but saw the aunt hiding something in a drawer. She hid it more in the nature of putting it away.

'What are you hiding?' Ajit blurted out impulsively.

'What is it to you? You're being too intrusive. I know you are on Rukmini's payroll.'

At first Ajit was unable to grasp the connection. Then he realized he had not yet revealed his full identity.

'I am a journalist, from the TOI. Do you suspect Ms Rukmini's hand in Sudha's murder?'

'I don't suspect anyone. All I know is that the day before she died she was very happy. She told me that she loved a man. I wanted to know more but she would not tell me. When I persisted she mentioned a desire to be born again, so that she would not have to work under Sunil and Rukmini.'

She had barely completed the sentence when the bullet hit her. Bang on the chest, making a big, Hindi cinema-style hole in the middle. She was thrown off the stool with the impact and onto the dirty carpet.

Ajit was not shocked. He hadn't anticipated this, but now that it had happened it seemed somehow natural. He felt no fear. His attitude surprised him, but he did not question it. He also did not go out to check on the assassin. Instead, he began walking towards the table drawer.

Inside, he found a hair clip, a few five-rupee notes, and a crumpled piece of paper. He opened the paper out. There was something scrawled on it in Hindi, as if in haste, but someone had torn the upper portion off. What remained for Ajit to read was an address—it mentioned a *qasbah* of Darbhanga district in the northern part of Bihar. The note ended with a sign-off—'*Sudha, mera pyaar*' (Sudha, my love). There was no name below that.

Ajit looked around for a phone. He found one on a dusty stool near the door and dialled the TOI number. As he gave the details over the phone, he kept his eyes on the aunt's body. The pool of blood hadn't spread or thickened. Her mouth was wide open. Ajit could not help feeling that she was probably still thinking about Sudha's desire to be born again.

He realized that he had not even asked her her name.

•

'Mrs Dixit. She was a widow. Moved to Bombay after her husband's death on Sudha's invitation.'

They were sitting in Khar, near the Danai bookshop, under the tin roof of a makeshift restaurant outside a music shop. A day had passed since the aunt's murder.

'But you don't find Dixits in Bihar,' Ajit said.

'We're not talking of endemic wildlife here,' Rishikesh laughed. 'Why can't there be Dixits in Bihar? Maybe she married a UP-ite.'

'What was Sudha's surname?' Ajit thought this was an important question.

'Jha. She wrote Jha,' Rishikesh replied.
'Oh! Then she was a Maithali Brahmin.'
'Does that make her more of a victim?'
'No it doesn't.'
'Then?'
'Then what?'
'Then why these questions?'
'Well, normal curiosity.'
'Normal or caste curiosity?'
'I don't believe in the caste system.'

Rishikesh got up to stand near the restaurant entrance. His frame covered a film poster featuring the actress Saumya in a miniskirt, her legs clasped together tightly, in mock shame.

'Move. You're blocking my vision.'
'What do you want to see?'
'Saumya, and the way she's trying to look innocent and whorish at the same time. You know about her, don't you? She's a Maharashtrian who failed to make it big in Bombay but got her big break in the South with those Sati-Savitri roles. She's back in Bombay now, trying to be a glamour doll once again.'

Rishikesh gave him a dirty look.
'Don't you think you should mind your business?'
Ajit was puzzled.
'Why do you say that? Is she a relative of yours?'

Rishikesh turned his face away as two girls in baggy shorts and T-shirts, holding plastic bags and with a 'touch-me-not' attitude, walked up to the music shop.

'Scratch a Brahmin and you find a casteist,' he muttered.

The touch-me-nots twisted around to give him puzzled looks before handing their bags at the outside counter.

Ajit went and patted him on the shoulder.

'Come on, yaar, don't be such a prig.'

'I am not being a prig. It's just that I know the reality. And it hurts.'

'You're too emotional.'

'No. I'm a Jhadav.'

Ajit knew the Jhadav's love for a chicken roll with Fanta. He led Rishikesh back to the bench and ordered the items.

'Now tell me, what exactly are people saying about the aunt's murder? They're not blaming me, are they?'

'No, they're not blaming you. The police feel the shot came from outside and missed you by a whisker.'

'But it wasn't meant for me.'

'It could have been.'

'What do you mean could have? There are no could haves in this.'

'Tell me how much you talked to the police.'

'Nothing. Gave the usual spiel about going there on a journalistic exercise.'

'Sure you didn't find anything there?'

'Nothing.'

•

Ajit clutched the paper with the Hindi scrawl in his pocket. Rukmini stood two metres away, pouring coffee.

'So you escaped death by a whisker.'

'Yes. I almost died. You see, the bullet was meant for me.'

Rukmini stopped and stared at him in disbelief.

'No, seriously. The guy wanted to kill me.'

'But why?'

'Because I was in his way.'

'In his way to what?'

'In his way to covering up Sudha's murder.'

Rukmini stifled a laugh. 'That's nonsense,' she said, handing him his coffee. She sat down opposite him.

'Really? I'm not so sure. And I'm quite intrigued by this lover angle. Who the hell is he? Did you ever see him?'

'Why should you think I know him?'

'Did he belong to Bihar?'

'Why're you asking me? And what makes you think her lover had a Bihar connection?' she asked. 'Did you find something there? I think you should tell me, the murder could affect my husband's career.'

Ajit was struck by her unnatural curiosity. 'No I didn't—except a plastic bottle of Johnson's baby powder.'

Rukmini looked like a woman who had been slapped across the face in public. Ajit got up with a triumphant smile.

'That was meant to be a joke. What made you blanch?'

Rukmini lowered her head and said softly, 'It's nothing. I get emotional when I hear about the powder. Reminds me of my mother, this was her favourite powder. My first daughter died when she was barely four. Johnson was her favourite powder too.'

Ajit was amazed. Sameer hadn't said anything about Rukmini's kids.

'How many children do you have? I've never seen them around.'

'Two. They study in a boarding school. You haven't been around much.'

•

The street light had dimmed. In the half-shadow the street looked like a cross between a locale from a sophisticated horror film and a set for *New York New York*. This was how Ajit had come to see Mumbai after his first few days here. He was intrigued by the way people enjoyed life and its sensations here. And how little they cared when someone wanted to define the contours of life in the city.

He decided to take a casual walk to clear his mind. Rukmini had confused him again. He could swear that this time too her body had not smelt even remotely of the talc. Which meant that she did not use any. Or that she used some new variety of Baby Johnson that had no odour. And he was unsure about his relationship with her—he felt both free and inhibited in her presence, like a schoolboy in front of his favourite teacher.

The breeze blew in from the direction of the sea, carrying with it the sounds of two street urchins fighting a few metres away, swearing to tear each other to pieces. Ajit decided to ignore the boys and walk past them, when one of them pulled his sleeve roughly and asked for money.

Ajit stopped with a start, startled by the boy's hard tone. Then he shook his hand off and pushed him away. The boy lost his balance and fell on his backside.

'*Kya saab*. You push us poor to the ground.' The boy was up on his feet and smiling. Ajit found the situation funny. He imitated the boy.

'*Kya harami*. You push us rich off the road.'

The boy was confused for a second. Then he turned round and summoned the other boy. The two picked up pebbles and stones from the roadside and began throwing them at the row of middle-class houses near by.

'What the fuck are you two doing? Why're you throwing stones at those houses?' Ajit said indignantly and lunged at them. Eluding his grasp, the urchin who had demanded money flung a stone at him and ran. When he was at a safe enough distance he turned around and aimed another pebble at Ajit and laughed. Before he ran off the road and into an alley he yelled, 'That's why we were stoning the houses, harami, to get at you.'

The urchin warriors disappeared into the alley, leaving Ajit with a sore bump at the side of his head.

Walking back, he was struck by the street wisdom of the boys: to get at what eludes you, hit its source first.

Ajit had found a lead in the Sudha murder case.

But Sameer had not sent him here to handle a regular investigation. That wasn't his job. He'd been promised adventure.

Rukmini had shown a strange interest in the Bihar angle. There was clearly some connection between Rukmini's past and the case.

That connection was in the address in his pocket.

To hit her, he should hit Bihar first.

7. Bihar

The fat man in a safari suit had just stepped out of his compartment and off the train, but he was already impatient. He yelled for a coolie but there was none in sight. He saw a young boy in shorts and a flimsy vest loitering near the train and asked him to carry his luggage. The boy refused. Without another word the man pulled out a wooden ruler from his pocket and began beating the boy. The station master was busy in a discussion with some policemen and did not intervene. A few passengers gathered around to watch the show. Some of them laughed, as if at an amusing family affair.

Less than a minute into the beating, the boy had cuts on his face and his back. He was bent at ninety degrees at his hip and had his hands on his head. To straighten him up the man grabbed his hair. The boy screamed, and got a kick in his arse for the protest. Propelled forward towards the luggage by the blow, he picked up the VIP suitcase and the large cloth bag and began limping towards the exit gate.

Watching the incident from his side of the platform Ajit knew he was in Bihar.

The train had reached Narayanpur four hours late. Ajit had spent much of his journey thinking about his last visit to Bihar.

He could not recall the exact date, but he remembered the

year—1989, the year of the snake, when V.P. Singh was elected to office. It was raining when they entered a village in Bhojpur to perform their first radical play. Ram Prakash Yadav was ill that day, so Ajit had had to step in for the role of the Janata, the public.

Ajit had expected action because the play, *Janata Paagal Ho Gayi Hai*—The Public Has Gone Mad—was provocative. He had argued with the troupe leader, Anil, that real whips be used for the scenes where the main character, the suffering, eponymous Janata, gets beaten by the exploiters. After all, this was Bihar; subtlety would be absurd here.

The play had barely begun when Ram Prakash yelled something from his position ten metres away from the arena of the performance, behind the tight circle of the largely rural audience. He was shouting and waving the *gamchha* that he always carried thrown over one shoulder. Ajit thought he was improvising a distraction. And then, before anyone could move, six well-built youths with guns had muscled their way through the audience.

They asked the troupe to stop the performance. Anil bravely stepped forward to say that 'orders' would not be followed. The troupe was here on the invitation of the public, and they would leave only if the public asked them to.

A dark-skinned man with a thin moustache who stood to Anil's right shouted at his men, and they took positions around the troupe with their rifles. One of them, a thickset man in a lungi, pointed his rifle at Anil. The dark man then addressed the gathering. After an incomprehensible two minutes, he began shouting in clear Hindi—'*Kaun hai saali janata? Kaun hai kutiya ki saali janata* (Who is this public, who is this bitch of a public)!'

The public was quiet; only a few murmurs at the back.

Then a schoolteacher came forward and requested the men to go back. They refused, saying that the play was politically motivated. The public had by now broken off into groups, some supporting the intruders, others opposing them, but no one mentioned the play at all. Ajit found this odd—only a few minutes earlier they had all been watching the play quietly.

Something came over him, and locating a lone muscleman in a corner he went up and began arguing with him. The muscleman gave him a deadpan look and told him to fuck off. Ajit abused back. And immediately the tide had turned against the troupe. The public was now accusing the city boys of disturbing the peace of their village. Anil looked around for the men of the party who had brought them to Bhojpur. They had disappeared. The musclemen had by now lowered their rifles. Ajit saw their dark-skinned leader busy delivering an anti-Naxalite speech. The public stood around, just as attentive to his performance as they had been to theirs. Only a few of the crowd glanced disinterestedly at the departing city boys.

Ajit had informed Ram Prakash of his Darbhanga visit but the fair Yadav boy who used to talk with a squint in his eyes was nowhere to be seen on the platform. He had kept in touch with Ajit, writing to him occasionally about his escapades as a teacher in a local primary school, but they hadn't met in years.

'*Ajit ke bacche*—you haven't changed!'

Ajit turned around to face a tall, thin man in goggles, a Lacoste T-shirt and expensive blue jeans.

The man laughed.

'You too did not recognize me, you bastard!'

Ajit finally recognized Ram Prakash and stared at him in stupefaction.

Ram Prakash thumped him on the back. 'You expected to find the same old Yadav boy with his gamchha, the hanger on of the street theatre troupe? Didn't I write to you about my transformation?'

They were now walking towards the exit. The station master eyed Ajit suspiciously and then saluted Ram Prakash.

Ajit was flabbergasted.

'Why did he salute you?' he asked.

'The days of Yadav governence, son. We are respected nowadays.'

Ajit noted the casual insolence in his tone, which matched his new look. He'd always been a temperamental guy, easily swayed, perhaps that accounted for the transformation.

'I've arranged a guest house for you. My school is just a few kilometres from Narayanpur. What did you tell me you are here for? Actually it really doesn't matter. We'll have fun along the way.'

They set off in a rundown jeep, on a bumpy road. Seated in the back beside a man whom Ram Prakash had not bothered to introduce, Ajit wondered briefly what Ram Prakash had meant by 'along the way'. He asked about the other members of the long-defunct troupe.

'Anil is in Germany working for some newspaper. I don't know anything about Ramesh and Bholanath. Suhel died a few years back, killed in a road accident while driving his fiancée on the Meerut-Delhi road.'

Ajit remembered a snap of the six friends, taken in Allahabad. It had Suhel looking rakish in a stolen Himachali cap. He was good with his hands and a voracious reader and a bit of a dreamer. Now it seemed somehow natural that he should have died young.

The jeep stopped in front of a house with a thatched roof and a little hut next to it which looked like a kennel. A man ran out of the kennel like a well-trained dog to receive the guest.

'Take the babu's luggage, Budhiya, he'll be staying for some time.' Ram Prakash's tone was almost contemptuous, and his manner dismissive. He hadn't even bothered to look at the man he was addressing.

The house had two rooms and a surprisingly clean Indian-style bathroom. After ordering tea Ram Prakash asked Ajit about his job. He literally jumped from his chair when he heard that Ajit was working with the TOI.

'Arre, TOI!' Then he laughed. 'Remember the time when you were freelancing and a stray article of yours got published in TOI? You went around telling everyone after that that you were working for *The Times of India*.'

Ajit did not find that funny. It was so long ago.

He showed him his card. 'This is real. I really am working for the paper.'

Ram Prakash looked amazed at first but then regained his haughtiness. 'Working in newspapers is no big deal. Didn't people leave the print media for jobs in TV and the Internet?—hey, am I not up to date?'

Ajit said he was impressed. Ram Prakash then invited him to a function in his school. He was obviously in a hurry to leave.

'You rest here. Tell me about your story tomorrow. The car will be here at eleven sharp. You'll enjoy the show.'

Ajit thought a lot about friends and friendship that night.

•

He had hoped to get up early and look around for the Narayanpur address before leaving for the function. But Budhiya had let him sleep till late. By the time he had fully woken up, the car had arrived.

It was a white ambassador, something one would expect in Bihar, with the roof torn from the sides. Ajit reached the school premises about half an hour later, driven at reckless speed by a driver who stopped twice to buy *surtee*.

The school was a mere shed where students stood performing songs. The teachers sat in a pucca house looking condescendingly at their pupils and sipping tea. Ram Prakash waved. Ajit went over and sat on an empty chair beside him.

'You'll like it; I'm sure you'll like it,' Ram Prakash began, but he was interrupted by three Maruti cars that came screeching in down the passageway that separated the school from the main road. Before the school kids could disperse, the Marutis were inside the campus.

No one was hurt. A hefty man got out of the leading car and asked everyone to shut up. He was here on Ashok Singh's command to talk to Master Ram Sajeevan Gupta.

Ajit saw Ram Prakash fidgeting in his seat. He leaned over to ask a question, but Ram Prakash put a finger to his lips, indicating that he should be quiet. Ram Prakash was eyeing a figure slinking into the shed that was the school.

'That's him, Ram Sajeevan,' he whispered.

The doors of all the Marutis flew open. Ajit counted seventeen men, each brandishing a firearm of some kind—he wondered how they could all have fitted into the cars. One of them spotted Ram Sajeevan and fired. Soon the figure slinking into the shed was sprinting into the fields behind the school, followed by the men from the Marutis. The boys broke ranks and scampered to a small platform near the fields for a better view.

The men with guns, in pants and lungis, rushed through the paddy fields like seasoned athletes. They raced confidently past the wiry men working in the fields. The farm workers stood nonchalantly, squinting into the sun, a couple of them tying the dense tail of hair at the back of their shaved heads, as if in anticipation of some great happening.

The first question that Ajit asked Ram Prakash after they reached the spot was about the farm labourers. Were they Brahmins? Ram Prakash smiled and replied that no, they were Chamars—it was an ancient tradition in Darbhanga, the centre of Brahminism in Bihar, where even untouchables shaved their heads and sported thick *bodis*.

Ajit was still looking at the ancient Chamars when Ram Prakash started talking about Ashok Singh. He was a big Bhumihaar criminal of the area accused of over a dozen murders. He and Ram Sajeevan were running a school co-operative. It was blacklisted by the state's anti-corruption bureau as a bogus enterprise. Ram Sajeevan then blew the lid, implicating Ashok Singh in a rape case as well. He also went and joined the Rashtriya Janata Dal party.

Ashok Singh had sworn to kill Ram Sajeevan in broad daylight. He had even informed the police about this—they were there in the school till about 11 a.m. But had left soon after.

'So they're in league with Ashok Singh?'

'No, yaar—you see, in Bihar, where issues of honour are concerned the police prefer to watch from the sidelines.'

Their conversation was interrupted by a series of gunshots and a loud shout from somewhere far in the fields. Ajit knew that honour had been avenged.

He saw an ancient untying his tail.

It wasn't yet half an hour since the hunt, and the police had arrived. Sloppy men in khaki were swarming all over the place, barking orders in Bhojpuri and Maithili. But they did not go in pursuit of the culprits who had left the scene barely fifteen minutes before.

Everyone had been ordered out of the school campus. Ajit and Ram Prakash stood on a clearing about six metres from the school, drinking tea purchased from a nearby shop. They did not talk much about the incident. Ram Prakash didn't seem interested and Ajit suddenly felt drained of all curiosity. They stood in silence for a while, then Ajit pulled out the address he had brought from Mumbai and showed it to Ram Prakash. 'I need to find this place,' he said.

'Where did you get this address?' Ram Prakash asked, looking incredulous.

'In Mumbai—it involves a murder case I'm investigating.'

Ram Prakash looked at him, bemused.

'Look, don't get me wrong,' Ajit said. 'I don't mean trouble for you. I—'

'You're here to investigate the Sudha murder case?'

Ajit couldn't have concealed his astonishment even if he had tried.

'You think I'm just a school teacher? Come on, yaar, I was the smartest of you all.'

Ram Prakash had now thrown the teacup down. The tea stall owner asked a boy to pick it up but he did not bother.

'You think we Biharis are fools. The Hindi newspapers here have plants in the English newspapers of Delhi and Mumbai, they pick up even behind-the-scenes happenings connected with Bihar. In Mumbai you were commissioned by TOI to go to Bihar and investigate an intriguing angle to a sensitive murder involving a top politician. Here the story was out in every major Hindi newspaper the very next day.'

Ajit felt he'd been had. 'You mean people here know about my finding an address in Sudha's aunt's house which connects her mysterious lover to Bihar?'

'Oh, it was you who found the address in Sudha's aunt's house? And that address is the same as this one? Now that I did not know.'

Ram Prakash was smiling again.

Exactly thirty minutes after the primary school murder, Ram Prakash and Ajit were seated in the drawing room of a house which had a tiled floor and walls done up with synthetic paint.

Ajit had already asked about the Bihari opulence he saw. Ram Prakash revealed that he was working secretly with the Hindu Hitkari Sangh.

'It is an organization which protects Hindus. Previously we were targeting Muslims. Now we want to attack Christians,' he explained.

'You mean just like the Vishwa Hindu Parishad?'

'No, yaar, not that. VHP is the icing, we are the cake personified.'

Ajit sensed he was expected to be impressed with the answer.

'What about your leftist convictions?' he asked to embarrass the Yadav.

'What leftism? For us backward castes it is all the same. There was a train coming our way—it had the leftist label in bold written over it. Since all other trains were barred to us and we had to reach our destination we climbed on. Then another train came—it had Hinduvaad written over it. We saw some benefit and climbed onto that one as well. Simple.'

'But you were never that practical,' Ajit said, trying to bring in some irony into the conversation. 'You were in fact so rigid that we used to call you the Jehadi Marxist.'

Ram Prakash looked irritated.

'My Jehad concerns the rise and rise of the backward castes. Whether through Marx or through Ram.'

Ajit decided to get on with the job at hand.

Ram Prakash explained that the address belonged to

Dhananjay Jha, who was wanted in two murder cases. The leak published in Bihari newspapers gave no details about his residence. But it quoted an unnamed source establishing Darbhanga as the lover's hideout.

'Who lives there now?'

'Dhananjay's wife and kids. Dhananjay himself comes twice a week to screw her. She's supposed to be an upright woman, who worships her husband.'

Ram Prakash winked at the last statement, slapping Ajit on the back.

Ajit decided to ignore the suggestion.

'Okay, but how am I to get an introduction to the lady?'

'Simple. This upright woman is also screwing some friend of her husband's. I know this through my secret contacts. Spy on her in the night. Catch her red-handed if you please. And then ask her about the address.'

Ajit wanted to tell him that the plan was too crude. He was here as a journalist, not a spy. But then he thought of watching a traditional woman meeting her husband's friend at night—and the possibilities inherent in that excited him.

'Is she fair? This Dhananjay Jha's wife?'

Ram Prakash understood and laughed.

'You haven't changed, you debauch. We all knew about the thing you had for all the fucking *bhabhis* and *chachis* of the world. Of course she's fair; go on, have your fun, you pervert.'

•

Sailani Tola was in the interiors of Narayanpur, a little off the main road. Ajit inspected the spot in the day. Dhananjay's was a ground floor house with a veranda. The main door was slightly ajar when he passed by. From somewhere within the house he heard a woman calling out to a girl, probably her daughter. He was reminded of an older woman he used to fancy in Allahabad. He would imagine her doing household chores through the day and getting laid at night by a servant or some secret lover. For months he had masturbated to this fantasy.

There was no way he could plant himself in the house to witness the proceedings, Ajit thought. There was just the one door he could see in front. It was likely there was an entrance at the back, but he knew from hearsay that when the husband was away, the front entrance was a safer bet. It seemed less suspicious. And if spotted, the paramour could always pretend that he had dropped in on legitimate work.

The house was in an alley within an alley, but there was a deserted spot in front left hurriedly by some contractor who hadn't managed to complete the assigned task. The walls were half constructed and bricks and bits of mortar lay all around. It was a good hiding place.

It was 11.30 p.m. when Ajit returned to the house, and almost immediately felt that he had made it too late. He waited in the shadows for about half an hour behind the half-constructed wall, during which time nothing happened.

Then a torch beamed at the far end of the alley. Ajit ducked behind the wall. He heard footsteps approaching the door of the house and then going past it. From a crack in the wall he saw the receding figure of a watchman. It was well past midnight, and the silence thickened by the minute. Ajit wanted something to happen, at least for the street dogs to start barking and stir things up a bit.

Then he saw something. It was a boy, about six or seven years of age. He was standing before the front door of the house and waving. The door opened slightly to reveal a crack of light and nothing more. The boy waved again. The crack widened. Then the boy walked away, and Ajit watched him disappear into the dark at the far end of the alley. When he returned his gaze to the door it was closing. He glimpsed a man's shoe and trouser, and then it was dark again.

He had just missed a chance to see the paramour. He felt stupid, and anger made him reckless—he walked out of his hiding place, picked up a stone and lobbed it at the door. It made hardly any sound. So he picked up a brick from the rubble at his feet, flung it with all his might and scurried back behind the wall. In the still, dense night the impact rang out like an explosion.

The sound had barely died down when the door was flung open. In the sharp white tube-light Ajit saw a woman clad in a pale blue cotton sari, one hand raised and with a revolver in it. Shouting for the attacker to come forward she fired in the air. Ajit crouched behind the wall and peered through the crack.

Neighbours came out in strength. Two men stood in the doorway, talking to the woman. The men were asking her to go back in, they would keep vigil. The woman told them to go back to sleep—she was the wife of a daredevil, capable of taking care of herself and her three daughters. Her husky voice reminded Ajit of Rukmini, but she had none of Rukmini's city airs. Mrs Jha was defiantly rustic—in her posture, her dramatic manner, her loud bravado. As suddenly as she had opened the door and shouted out her challenge, she banged the door shut. The men stood around talking for about ten minutes and then left. It seemed odd to Ajit that no one had bothered to look around, to try and find the attacker.

Ajit looked at his watch. It was just past 1 a.m. The watchman was still not in sight. And no one had left the house. After waiting for another half hour, he decided to leave the place.

Walking back, he was struck by Mrs Jha's dramatic performance. Her recklessness amazed him, for he had no doubt her lover was still inside when she stood in her doorway, waking up the neighbourhood. And then she would have shut the door and gone back to him, and they would have fucked as if nothing else mattered. The thought excited him, and suddenly he had a vision of himself lying naked on top of her, tongue deep in her ear, tasting the hair and wax, his hands kneading her body. The hand that fired the gun into the night claws his back. He smacks her across the face, and she begs in Bhojpuri to be screwed. The room smells of spice and vegetables and dust and cheap cuticura powder and Ajit presses his body against hers till his bones ache and he is bathed in sweat, and she is begging again. He orders her to take his sweat-drenched cock in her mouth, and when she begins to move, he pins her down again, slams into her and fucks her with violent thrusts. Then he leaves her double bed without once looking back at her.

'So you are from *Times of India*? We used to get a copy in my father's house.'

Mrs Jha was wearing the same blue cotton sari. The voice was still husky. But for that, the contrast with Rukmini could not have been sharper. It was clear that unlike Rukmini she had never stepped inside a beauty parlour. Her eyebrows were thick and unplucked and she had too much lipstick on her dry lips. Her rough skin was stretched tight over her high cheekbones, and her forehead was full of lines. Ajit was reminded again of his fantasy housewife in Allahabad. He could not help staring.

'I am investigating a murder case,' he said.

'And how does that bring you here?' she asked. If the question had unsettled her, Ajit saw no sign of it on her face.

'You must have read in the papers about the death of a girl called Sudha. Your address was found in her drawer.'

Mrs Jha's face hardened. She looked at him stonily and expressed her ignorance about the whole affair. Ajit tried again. Didn't she want to find out how a girl she did not know had her address? Perhaps Jha sahib would know? But Mrs Jha maintained she had no knowledge of or any interest in the case. He was wasting his time. And then she asked him to leave, saying that her husband was well connected politically and would be very displeased if he found out that a young TOI journalist was snooping on his wife.

She sounded firm, but he was reluctant to leave. He was held back by the memory of the casually intimate conversation they'd had before he began asking her about Sudha. With typical Bihari hospitality she had served him sweets and pastries. When she offered him a glass of water, her work-worn hand had touched his, and he had trembled.

There was no one in the small drawing room where they sat. She raised an arm to push back a strand of hair from her face, and he saw the patch of sweat on her blouse, at the armpit. The night's fantasy came back to him, her body bathed in sweat writhing under his own.

'Mrs Jha, I was the one who threw the brick at your door last night. I saw a man enter this house at midnight. I want to know who he was.'

Mrs Jha froze for a few long seconds, then abruptly she slapped him hard on the right cheek. She then tried to get up from the red sofa—but Ajit caught her by the arm and pulled her back. She fell back, stunned by the violence of his grip.

'If you cause trouble, Mrs Jha, I won't go to the police. I will go and link you with Sudha's murder. You can't possibly involve your husband because then he'll find out what you've been doing behind his back.'

'There was no man in here. You are making it all up.'

Ajit twisted her arm and she winced.

'Stop that!' she hissed. 'I have three daughters in the house who'll bring in the neighbourhood if they see you doing this to me.'

'Well, call them in then,' Ajit said, twisting her arm a little more.

'Please don't! Just what is it that you want?'

'Tell me about the man.' Ajit let go of her, and she sank back into the sofa, rubbing her arm.

'You want to see him? Fine. Come back at night. I will let you in through the back door. Hang me from the ceiling fan of my bedroom if you see anyone. But if no one comes, go back to where you belong and never show me your face again. You must promise me that.'

Ajit leaned across to pick a pastry from the plate on the centre table, and considered the odds. He could see that Mrs Jha had something on her mind, but he wasn't sure what. The night was still hours away—she had sufficient time to warn her man. In that case, if Ajit kept his word, he would have to abandon all attempts to find anything here and return to Mumbai. This seemed most likely. But supposing she wanted to have him killed; supposing her man did appear, to catch him by surprise or take him as a hostage?

Ajit saw that by accepting her offer he would be putting himself in mortal danger.

'Done,' he said, and smiled.

Years ago, a girlfriend had accused him of being a coward.

The alley was the same save for the iron rods that had come up near the unfinished wall. Some one was trying to measure the length of the plastered bricks or simply attempting to bring the wall down.

It was midnight again. The watchman was nowhere to be seen. Ajit looked around for signs of a trap. He found none.

The door opened. White light streamed out into the veranda.

Mrs Jha was in a pink sari this time. Her shampooed hair was still wet. Ajit smelled Clinic Plus. The sari was draped in the Bengali fashion, with a straight upper flap. A white blouse hung loosely on the body. It was impossible to say whether she had a bra on.

She took him straight to the bedroom. It had a cot and a big double bed plus a few old wooden almirahs. The dressing table was in a narrow space that led to the bathroom.

'But what am I supposed to do here?'

'Just stay and see if anyone comes tonight. Isn't that what you wanted?'

'But what about the back door?'

Mrs Jha turned away from him and opened the almirah closest to them. From a large tin she pulled out, she offered him a *motichur* laddoo. Ajit took the laddoo without averting his gaze from her face. She smiled.

'You think I made the man escape from the backdoor last night? You're mad.'

Still smiling, she put the tin back in the almirah. Ajit knew he had to say something.

'When a woman smiles like that it means either that she's pleased with herself or that she's hiding an extra-marital affair.'

Mrs Jha laughed.

'You really are mad, *sachchi*. Whom would I have an affair with in this stupid small town?'

'With your husband's friend, who also works with Ashok Singh. This is what the rumours say.'

'Which friend?'

'I don't know; this is what people say.'

'And you believe them?'

'I want to know why Sudha's lover left your address at her aunt's house.'

Mrs Jha pursed her lips and looked at him defiantly. Something in her manner suggested he was close to the answer. He closed his eyes.

When he opened his eyes again, she was still looking straight at him, her face changing colour with the tension.

'Sudha's lover is Ashok Singh's man,' he said slowly. 'This was his hiding place. Then he fell in love with you . . . Ashok Singh—does he knows about it?'

Mrs Jha didn't move an inch. Ajit marvelled at her composure.

'That is a great story,' she said evenly. 'Who is going to believe it?'

'Ashok Singh will; and before him the police.'

'I am not afraid of jail.'

'I know you are not—so is this an admission of the truth? That our mystery man is your lover?'

'Do you like sex?'

Ajit had no time to fathom where the question came from, for the next thing he knew Mrs Jha had turned her back to him abruptly and was tying her hair.

'Did you say something?'

'No. Did you?'

'I think you asked me whether I liked sex.'

Mrs Jha turned around. There was a hint of a smile on her painted lips.

'Do you?'

Ajit's face registered the kind of shock that strikes suddenly, yet insidiously, with a hidden sense of pleasure.

Beads of sweat appeared on his forehead. His cockiness vanished as he struggled to control his feelings.

'What do you mean by that?'

'I mean do you like to do it?'

Mrs Jha moved closer. Ajit averted his gaze from her face.

'Don't worry, I'll keep your secret concealed in my heart. I know you had the hots for me in the morning itself. You had sex written all over your face—you men don't realize how quickly a woman can see that. You agreed to my proposal only because you wanted to be near me—tell me if I am wrong.'

Ajit wanted to regain the upper hand, to dismiss her power over him and say that what he had done was brave and his life was still in danger. But Mrs Jha was quite close now. Her lips were almost brushing his.

'I liked you from the moment I saw you. There is no one in my life apart from my husband. Those rumours are false.'

Her eyes were closed by the time she finished speaking. She stood almost equalling Ajit in height, motionless, her eyes absolutely still behind the thick black eyelashes, expecting—to be kissed?

Ajit was confused. He had come here partially aroused, totally in control, and he had expected to remain so for the rest of the evening, when he could go back and fantasize about her. There was no way he could screw Mrs Jha—she was conservative, and he knew from past encounters that women of her type could get very upset if they got the wrong kind of pass.

But he had always been helpless in the face of his desire to lay a conventional woman. He closed his eyes and thought about one of his many sisters-in-law, a distant cousin's wife. She was in her late twenties, a mother of two kids, when he was in his early teens. She smelt of spices and scented hair oil and rarely went anywhere without her policeman-husband. The most intense fantasies of Ajit's teens were about her. He often thought of his cousin laying his wife, in their dimly-lit bedroom, even the cramped kitchen of their small flat. Mostly, though, he imagined himself ravaging her in seamy hotels, in front of a group of waiters, playing with her huge boobs, telling the waiters he was screwing his sister-in-law. At a family wedding, years ago, when space was short and they had to huddle together on mattresses laid out on the floor, he had found himself beside her one night. He had lain awake in the dark, with his hand rubbing his hard on, till the desire became too much for him and he put his hand between her thighs and began massaging her crotch impatiently through the silk lehnga. She had quietly grabbed his wrist with surprising strength and pushed his hand away. Then she put her little son between them. The following morning she behaved normally and did not mention the incident to anyone. She stopped coming to their house after the wedding, and Ajit's fantasies involving her had got wilder.

He opened his eyes. Mrs Jha was still standing there in the same way. Stepping closer he tapped her lips with his.

Mrs Jha kissed him lightly. Ajit responded by kissing her hard. Shivering slightly she nudged him to open his lips. Ajit instead began exploring her cheeks, going as far as the ears. He put his tongue in her ear, and moved it in deep, making wet circles of saliva.

Mrs Jha began to squirm. Taking her whole ear in his mouth Ajit slurped as fast as he could. She clutched the back of his neck with her left hand, and took her right hand to the crack of his arse. After trying to probe it from over his clothes she suddenly shook her head, dropped to her knees and buried her face in his crotch. Ajit had an underwear on under his tight jeans but his bulge was visible. Mrs Jha closed her teeth on it, making a damp patch of saliva over his jeans.

The upper flap of her sari had dropped, and Ajit could see her full breasts heaving inside the cotton blouse. Yanking her up, he pulled the flap away. She surrendered after a brief struggle. Ripping off her blouse, he went for her breasts like a madman, pressing them, flicking his tongue across her nipples, burying his face between them.

To ease herself, Mrs Jha began using the wall as a backrest. Standing thus, with Ajit slobbering over her boobs she took one hand out of the mess and switched on the fan. Ajit was hit by a wave of cool air. He bit one taut brown nipple. 'Stop, stop, no marks please, don't bite,' he heard her muttering above him. 'No marks—what will my husband—'

Before Mrs Jha could complete the sentence, Ajit was kissing her stomach. Mrs Jha began banging her head against the wall. 'Take off the sari,' she cried, 'don't you want me naked?' Ajit tried yanking at her sari but it did not give. Hastily he began pulling up the lower flaps to press her thighs. Pushing him away she undid the sari and the pettticoat in one single motion. She pulled off her blouse as well, and stood before Ajit with just her panties on. They were wet, freshly washed and blue in colour. Ajit breathed in the smell of surf and cum. He took his hand to the strap, yanked hard and felt her vagina. There was no hair.

His head spun with excitement.

'When did you shave? Was it for me? For that man?'

Mrs Jha looked at him with eyes that could kill.

'Get on with the job you stupid fool. I shave every day.'

Ajit buried his face deep in her pussy. When the the first wave of odour hit him, he wanted to puke. Then he felt a pungent taste on his tongue. He pushed his tongue deeper into her vagina and breathed in the scent of seafood. Mrs Jha moaned, and Ajit had a strange sensation of sitting in some dimly lit restaurant, inhaling the smell of Jumbo prawns.

He pushed deeper and deeper into the pungent river. A few minutes passed before he noticed the sudden silence above him. Mrs Jha had stopped moaning. Then he felt something stale and sticky in his mouth; a taste distinct from the exhilarating pickle-juice of a woman's cum. He took his tongue out and spat on the ground. The spot turned red.

Before he could tilt his face upwards Mrs Jha slumped down without a sound. She stared into his eyes with shock and wonder. There was a bullet hole in her head, right near the vermilion mark.

He had tasted her blood.

Ajit felt like puking again, but was unable to move. He saw Mrs Jha's head slide suddenly to her left. Thinking her neck would break he tried propping it up; then, aghast at his idiocy, he picked up the body and placed the dead, naked woman on her bed.

There was a sound below. Ajit swore he heard footsteps. Running out of the room he saw, in the half-darkness, a tall and muscular man in what appeared to be black trousers and shoes making for the front door. Ajit shouted for him to stop. He waved and vanished.

Mrs Jha's three daughters were now out of their room. They wanted to know where their mother was. Before Ajit could reply, a ponderous, dark man in kurta-pyjama walked in with his cronies—Ajit counted six. The daughters greeted the man with a cry of familiarity.

Ajit understood that Mr Jha had arrived.

•

The room was stuffy and dingy. The ceiling was plastered with cobwebs and there was no cot.

Blood was spattered all over Ajit's shirt. He had been beaten repeatedly for over three hours in every place except the eyes, ears and groin. He had told them how he came to be in Mrs Jha's house. But Mr Jha was not in a mood to take his wife's naked death lightly. He accused Ajit of raping and killing his wife. He would have cut off his genitals and had them displayed in Naryanpur bazaar, but was interested first in understanding the motive.

Ajit looked up, raising his head and wincing at the pain. He waved his hands groggily before his eyes. He had a sickening feeling that he could not see, even though the objects before him were clearly visible. The short, dark man who had disfigured him laughed.

'The bastard thinks he's blind. You know when people who get a beating think they are blind? When the motherfuckers are afraid, when they are peeing in their pants.'

The man finished with a kick to the small of Ajit's back. The men around him laughed louder.

Despite the pain Ajit knew that he hadn't suffered any permanent damage. Even this last kick could have been much more vicious, and aimed at his head. Ajit found that odd. Jha's attack lacked the rage with which a man assaults someone who he believes has raped and killed his wife.

Ajit had earlier told him that probably a silencer-gun shot Mrs Jha while they were making love. He had seen a man in black trousers and shoes going out of the house. Gathering all his strength, Ajit now told Jha what he thought about Sudha's lover's connection with his house. He had barely finished when Jha stepped on his forefinger and ground it into the gritty floor. After the screams died down he kicked again, this time on the face.

'*Betichod, maa ke laude*, you're accusing my wife? We will kill you and hand the body over to the police. What will they find—how a *lund* (prick) was killed?'

As the heavy leather shoe twisted his finger, Ajit thought about the countless victims of police torture, mere names to him before this experience. But it did not help; the pain was too much. In the beginning he had imagined himself being hit by a speeding train—that had minimized the impact of the beatings by belts and shoes. His friend Anil had told him about this technique—'Cook up something unimaginably brutal when you are being tortured. That way you'll be able to lessen the impact of the real thing.' But Anil's theory had worked only upto a point. It became difficult to control his mind once the beatings became regular.

Buckets of cold water rained on him during the let ups when the men relaxed and joked around. Their favourite story was about the cocky police officer who had gone to raid Ashok Singh's premises but found himself surrounded by his own constables in the shoot-out. They were all on the don's payroll. The men laughed hardest when they recounted how, before being shot, the officer had begged to be let in on Ashok Singh's secret.

Jha stepped off his finger and spat on his face, and Ajit had the terrible feeling that he would shit in his pants.

Jha came forward to deliver his next round of kicks, when there was a knock at the door.

The party came to a standstill.

The door opened, and in walked a fair man with an egg-shaped face, slick brown hair and a slight limp. Ajit recognized him instantly as Ashok Singh—his fellow prisoner in jail during the anti-Vishwa Hindu Parishad movement, a student of the painting department of Benaras Hindu

University and a past master at the making and throwing of crude country bombs.

The boy who gave him a bath couldn't have been anything over twelve years of age, but he remained stony-faced through Ajit's gasps and occasional cries of pain. Ajit made the boy rub his back thrice with Lux.

He heard loud voices coming from the room where he was thrashed. Ashok Singh was having an angry conversation with his men.

He took his while coming out of the bathroom. Ashok Singh offered him a hard metal chair; he then pushed a tray of tea and biscuits towards him. Ajit gobbled the biscuits and drank the tea without risking a look at Jha.

'Ajit sahab, what were you doing with this man's wife at night?' Ashok Singh asked, smilingly widely.

Ajit was reminded of a fair boy, lying injured after passing a sodomy test in a Benaras police station, thanking Ajit for fruits and biscuits. 'Ashok *janab*, what are you doing in Bihar as a kingpin of criminals? I witnessed a murder by your men just the day before. You've come a long way.'

Ashok Singh did not laugh; presumably, he too had thought of Benaras.

'I know you are investigating the Sudha murder case. It involves the reputation of Sunil Agnihotri. I work for him.'

Ajit put down his cup of tea. Events were overtaking him again. He had come here to investigate Rukmini's connection with the Darbhanga address. But it was her husband's name that had cropped up. He decided to tell Ashok his reasons for being here, including the truth about the address, and the connection he thought Sudha's lover had with Narayanpur. But he did not mention Rukmini.

When he had finished his report, he asked, 'What has Sunil Agnihotri got to do with Bihar?'

Ashok looked at him and was quiet for a while, his indecision apparent in his eyes. Then he replied, 'It is his recruiting area. You must have always wondered where I vanished after being released from jail. Well, I went to Lucknow, where Sunil Agnihotri, who was then a small-time local leader, picked me up. He groomed me as a goonda. He rose fast, and I rose with him. Before I knew it, he had become active in Maharashtra.'

'What do you mean by recruiting area?'

'Sunil is a big-time operator. He has interests in quite a few major states of west and north India. He lives for the present and doesn't care for the future. Criminals are required for his kind of job. They are recruited from the Avadh-Magadh belt.'

Ajit felt like a schoolboy taking his first lesson in shagging.

'Do you think Sunil could have killed Sudha?' he asked.

'I haven't a clue,' Ajit said dismissively. 'I have no interest in some common murder. Right now I'm preparing for the Aurangabad deal.' Then he turned away from Ajit and called for one of his men. Ajit noticed that Jha was nowhere to be seen.

'What is the Aurangabad deal?'

'Don't ask too many questions, Ajit,' Ashok said calmly, without any irritation in his voice. 'I still don't understand why you were in that woman's house. Normally Jha would have killed you right there, and painfully, even though he knows his wife likes other men a little too much. I'm sure she was killed by one of her lovers. You are here on the Sudha case and she happens to be linked to my paymaster. That's a coincidence and a very strange one at that. I saved you because you were good to me once. There is no other reason. But I don't think as you do that Sudha's lover has anything to do with this place.'

Ashok Singh now asked his men to leave, and followed them. He stopped at the door and turned back.

'Remember that painting I made in the jail? The one with the boy shooting an arrow above Dronacharya's head? Someone told me recently it was displayed in some Delhi exhibition. He read about it in the papers. I had sold it for 100 rupees in Lucknow to buy medicines for my mother.'

Ajit managed to smile weakly.

'You were never a bad guy, Ashok; I always liked you—that officer in Benaras—'

'He's dead. Killed in front of his house, five in the afternoon.'

The casualness was back in Ashok Singh's voice.

Half a minute of silence later, he told Ajit to stop snooping and go back to Mumbai—he might not be around to save him the next time.

'Yes, I am going back; but tell me, what's this Aurangabad deal?'

Ashok stared vacantly at the ceiling.

'I don't see why that should interest you. Anyway, it's a big project. Sunil Agnihotri is constructing a power plant along with Bhigu Parikh, the Gujarati industrialist and politician, somewhere near Aurangabad. They are draining water from nearby lakes and rivers. The region is under severe drought. There is a ban on such activities; besides, the people are up in arms. Criminals from Bihar and UP have been mobilized to bolster the project and to suppress the people.'

Ajit sat still for a long time after Ashok Singh left.

8. Benaras, 26 January 1993

'Bring that motherfucking Bhumihaar here—I'll tear his arse to shreds!'

It was 5 p.m.

Ajit had been hearing the refrain every now and then through the afternoon. He was eating the last of the sweet, ripe guavas supplied by influential relatives in Benaras. The jail compound was neat, circular, with just a bit of dust. It reminded him of a 1950s' Bimal Roy movie.

He had seen the young Bhumihaar boy during the daylong protest at the university. He had a soft, rounded jaw, fair skin and short brown hair. In the crowd of brown-skinned boys trying to prevent a leader of the Vishwa Hindu Parishad from hoisting the national tricolour on the Students Union building, he looked like a foreigner

Suhel had come running in and informed Ajit about the bombs. They were packed in boxes, ready to be thrown at the pro-VHP activists. The boys of the Muslim boarding House had arranged it all, he said. They could not come out openly, but they were still angry about the demolition of the Babri Masjid the previous year and were providing monetary and logistical support.

A small group of brown skins had climbed up the Union

building. They too were carrying the national flag, determined to pre-empt the VHP leader. The police swung into action. They surrounded the boys and went at them with their sticks. Ajit felt a wave of humans pushing him to the ground. He saw the left flank tottering under the Khaki attack, but they held out. The boys on top were now singing the national anthem. A furious inspector pulled out his revolver and was about to shoot when the fair-skinned boy crashed into him. The shot went out into the sky.

Suddenly the University gates flew open and a crowd of saffron-clad VHP boys stormed the site. One of them pulled the fair boy off the inspector and turned him over to the mob.

The retreating students returned and attacked the saffron brigade. Plain Hindus fought pro-Hindus. The boys near the flagstaff atop the building were dancing with joy: they had saved the national flag from the dishonour of being touched by a man accused of demolishing a mosque. Ajit was battling a pro-VHP man when he saw the fair boy being dragged into a police van. Then he took a blow to his head and passed out.

The jail was full of boys from both sides. Most of them were now chatting amongst themselves, and laughing. They stopped when they heard the cries. One of the boys told Ajit it was the fair-skinned boy being sodomized. There was an uncomfortable silence after that, but for the occasional screams from the superintendent's room.

About fifteen minutes later, the superintendent came out with his prey. The boy had been stripped naked and his arse was bleeding.

The officer summoned all the inmates so they could see how effectively he exercised his power over leftists. He kicked the boy before the assembly and ordered him to dance. On cue, a jail constable began a live song in Bhojpuri.

Mori gori kamar balkhaiyan ho Ram
Julmi sajanwa na maane ...

(My fair hips wriggle, O Lord
The heartless beloved doesn't stop ...)

The boy stood still for a few seconds, till the officer kicked him viciously in the butt again. He moved slowly at first, then faster, shaking his hips, looking vacantly at the group before him, till he fainted.

The superintendent spat in his face and walked out.

Ajit had sat by the boy for over an hour after that, till he came around. Swearing to kill the superintendent soon, at exactly 5 p.m., the boy accepted a glass of milk.

9. The Return

The Punjabi taxiwala was following him with irritating perseverance. Ajit turned around and gave him a hard push.

'Fucking Punjabis—won't leave you alone even in Mumbai,' he muttered, then asked the coolie to take him to the side exit of Mumbai Central.

On alighting at the station he had learned that taxis were no longer allowed till the front porch. It was as if he had been away, in another world, for years.

He was in two minds about where to go first. He was surprised at how eager he was to see Rukmini again. Reluctantly, he asked the driver to take him to the *Times of India* office. He had called his office from Darbhanga but the bureau chief had asked him to brief him fully on arrival and not waste his time and the newspaper's money with vague reports delivered long-distance over the phone.

Ajit always liked this about Derek D'Souza, his clipped comments on outlandish assertions made by cub reporters. Though he would hate to admit it to anyone, he was a little in awe of the man.

'Arre Ajitji, here with luggage and all! We don't see such dedication these days!'

The office attendant clearly wasn't pleased to see him. Ajit had tried to be friendly with him in the past, cracking dirty jokes, because that usually worked between men. But the attendant had reacted by warning the staff, especially the women, about the 'young reporter's bad character'.

'You mind your business, tatler—just go and see whether Derek is around.'

The attendant grimaced before replying.

'Derek sir came early today—he's very busy. I think you will have to wait.'

'Your job is to go and tell him that I'm here. It's for him to decide if I should wait.'

The attendant left without a word and soon Ajit stood facing Derek.

'I don't have much time, Ajit. Say what you have to say and—'

'Just wait till you hear this,' Ajit began, taking the chair facing Derek. 'I think I saw the man who may have bumped Sudha off. And guess what—there was talk about an Aurangabad deal in Darbhanga. People from Bihar and UP are being mobilized to suppress opposition to the power plant being set up by Sunil Agnihotri in the district. It will drain water from the canals, leading to drought in the villages. Maybe Sudha knew something about this—that's why she died, maybe—'

'Maybe what, Ajit? Do you have proof?'

Ajit saw that Derek was not impressed. He was surprised—a Westernized city slicker like Derek should have lapped up the criminal-moffusil angle.

'I have a friend in Bihar who works for Sunil—'

'Can you bring him to the *Times* Patna office?'

'No. He is now the kingpin of criminals—and it would be difficult to track him down.'

'See? This is the problem with you bright young guys,' Derek said, throwing up his hands in mock despair. 'All of you have brilliant theories but insufficient proof to back them up.'

'But we can publish the story with my experiences as a Bihar story. That way we can hint at the possible without committing to anything.'

Ajit thought he had said something clever, but Derek snapped at him.

'Are you a Marxist? I'm sure you're a Marxist. But the world is not dialectical, my dear. Tell me whether we can nail Sunil Agnihotri with this report—otherwise fuck the hell out of here.'

Ajit felt an ancient Marxist rage building up inside him—in his early college days any line against dialectics brought him to his feet. But this was a different time and place. It was prudent to fuck off.

'I will be back, Derek, this time with proof right from the horse's mouth which will nail Agnihotri.' Derek laughed and waved towards the door.

Outside the *Times* office Ajit felt like a fool, unkempt, dirty, struggling with his luggage, looking lost and tiny before the imposing Victorian building. He needed to hear Rukmini's husky voice and imagine her naked and doing his bidding in her lawn in broad daylight. But first, he needed a bath.

•

Rukmini's residence was swarming with guests. Ajit had been wrong in thinking Sunil Agnihotri would not be there. The handsome, hefty politician was standing beside his wife, greeting some business tycoon when Ajit walked in.

'Ajit! So good to see you. Come over here, let me introduce you to my husband.'

Ajit was pleasantly surprised by the matter-of-fact warmth with which Rukmini greeted him. Agnihotri shook his hand and thanked him for helping his wife during the shoot-out. He had a fair, pointed nose and high cheekbones; Ajit knew the type—the snooty breed of Brahmin politicians and IAS officers of UP who formed an exclusive class, out of bounds for commoners and even lesser members of their own families.

'My wife tells me you belong to UP?'

'Yes. Unnao district.'

'Great. And you are a Vajpayee, which means you are a Kanyakubja as well.'

Ajit saw this as an opportunity to work his way into Sunil's circle. 'I think we should get together more often. There are so few Kanyakubjas in Mumbai—is there a Kanyakubja association or something?'

But Agnihotri had already lost interest. Cutting him short, he asked Rukmini to take care of him and walked off to greet another guest.

Rukmini laughed. 'You thought you would charm your way into his club with such small talk? He's a politician—he gets bored easily.'

Ajit smiled back, wondering what to say next. 'Why this party?

'Oh this is nothing. We invite people over whenever we feel like.'

'So this is not a political gathering?'

'All gatherings are political.'

Ajit liked her lazy way of dismissing things.

The party was an informal affair—there was no fixed menu. Waiters hired for the occasion were walking around with trays of soft drinks and kaaju. Most of the guests were dressed casually, in rather plain shirts and trousers, kurta-pyjamas or saris. Only one young couple stood out, prancing around self-consciously—the boy in baggy shorts, the girl in a miniskirt. Ajit guessed they were some politician's kids. He watched them harassing the caterers and whistling at passersby. But no one seemed to care. Least of all the hostess. She had her eyes fixed on her husband, mingling effortlessly with the guests and yet curiously aloof.

'Mr Agnihotri is good at this,' Ajit said. Rukmini turned to respond to this and then something made her turn back. A man, clearly an aide, walked up and whispered something in her husband's ear. Sunil Agnihotri stiffened; then he nodded, and the aide went off towards the main gate.

He returned with a short, stocky man in a white kurta pyjama who walked briskly, looking straight ahead, without bothering to acknowledge anyone, with the obvious air of a politician.

The politician reached Sunil and stood before him and lowered his eyes, preparing to say something. He didn't get a chance to speak. Sunil slapped him hard across the face. The sound was loud enough to stop the party. Everyone froze and stared in complete silence. Only the girl in the miniskirt giggled.

Sunil slapped the man again, calling him a third-rate politician who had tried to bad mouth him in public. The man did not raise his eyes or his hands.

Ajit looked at Rukmini, and saw fear in her eyes.

'My husband,' she began in a soft tone, 'he doesn't forgive or forget easily.'

Then she was quiet, like everyone else at the party.

'But who's that man?' Ajit asked.

'He ... used to be a minister in the earlier Congress government. Sunil had got him the assembly ticket. But then he rebelled and joined the Shiv Sena. This time he lost his deposit—he was supposed to come here to offer an apology

... But Sunil has decided to make a public spectacle of the issue, as you can see.'

Suddenly Ajit felt chilly. There was a barely suppressed menace in the air. He felt small and lost. He could sense that at this point Sunil could do anything and get away with it. Even if he shot the man, there would be no witnesses, no one to question him.

Sunil asked the man to squat before him. He then ordered his servant to bring in a large dustbin. Soon the defeated politician was walking among the nervous guests in the lawn, the dustbin on his head and his hands held out before him, telling them he was a *bhikhari*, a beggar, who needed donation. Most people looked away, embarrassed. When he passed the trendy young couple, the girl offered him some marble sweets she had begun chewing, and her boyfriend laughed and kissed her on the cheek.

Sunil scratched his balls and looked in Rukmini's direction. She turned her face away. Sunil waited for the man to return to him, having completed one round of the lawn, then patted him on the cheek and gave him permission to drop the dustbin and go home. He then asked the guests to resume the party.

'So,' Rukmini turned abruptly to face Ajit, 'how was your trip to Bihar?'

'It was okay—didn't find much.'

'You don't look as if you didn't find much—you wouldn't be here otherwise.'

Ajit tried to hide his unease. 'No, seriously. The address found at Sudha's aunt's place turned out to be fake. The high point was my meeting up with a few old friends—'

'My husband—' Rukmini interrupted him, 'he has interests in Bihar.'

She had surprised him again. Did she know about Ashok Singh, he wondered.

'I know about your husband's interests in Bihar. Actually, I was able to find out a lot. Let's go to a safe place.'

'I don't believe your story. A major American multinational company is also interested in the Aurangabad power project. Bhigu Parikh is his friend, yes, but I don't think he also owns shares. Why would he stake so much in the affair?'

'So you deny he knows Ashok Singh?'

'I told you he has criminals on his pay roll in Bihar and UP. But that doesn't prove a thing.'

They had come to the inner lounge where Rukmini had served coffee before Ajit left for Bihar.

'How can you discount the possibility of Sudha's murder being linked to the Aurangabad deal? Maybe she knew something and—'

'And my husband had her bumped off? It sounds silly.'

Rukmini smiled. Ajit found her a bit patronizing.

'Are you hiding something?' she asked.

'No, why?'

'No, I just thought you were.'

Ajit had hidden the Mrs Jha mess up from Derek and Rukmini. He was fairly sure Ashok Singh would have ensured that the matter did not reach the police. He had told Rukmini that he met Ashok Singh by accident. He felt that the Mrs Jha angle would come in handy at a later date—it was a kind of post-dated cheque.

Rukmini walked over to a portrait on the side wall.

Ajit recognized it. For the first time since they had met, he saw evidence of her association with Sameer. 'Beautiful horse,' he said and went up to look at the portrait carefully.

'Isn't he? It was a gift from a friend—a male friend.'

'Oh, so you had male friends as well?' he asked, turning towards her with a schoolboy grin.

'Why, do you think I'm unattractive?'

'Oh no, you must have been very good looking in your younger days.'

'And now?'

'You're still good looking.'

Rukmini slapped him lightly on the cheek. Then she laughed.

'Why do you look so stunned? Never been slapped by a woman before?' She brought her face close to his. 'You're not offended, are you?'

'No. But I thought you were offended.'

'Why?'

'Because I referred to your beauty in the past tense.'

Rukmini turned away and dropped herself on the sofa. She patted the empty space beside her.

'The past is a beautiful place. There was a man in my life before I got married. He was very romantic, a mad, extravagant man, showering me with flowers and gifts. But above all he loved music—he introduced me to thumri and ghazal and dadra—we used to sit for hours listening to light classical on his terrace. We had a tearful parting when I got married. He was honourable enough not to bother me after that.'

Ajit was sitting next to her by the time she finished. The party outside was winding up, and Ajit could see servants running around in the garden, answering Sunil's urgent commands.

'Why didn't you marry him?'

'My parents would not have agreed. Besides, I did not want to marry for love. You see, love and marriage are two very different things.'

Ajit nodded. 'What was his name?'

'Sameer, Sameer Sharma.'

Ajit looked hard at her face for any trace of guilt, or remorse. She stared back at him silently, with only a vague sadness in her eyes. Ajit had to remind himself that she might be lying.

'What is it?'

'Just thinking—why are you telling me all this?'

'I don't know,' she replied blandly. 'Maybe it's something I see in your eyes that makes me trust you. Tell me, have you suffered a lot of pain? I mean, a different kind of pain, more at the spiritual level.'

Ajit was quiet. It was an uncomfortable place she was leading him to.

'I'm very intuitive, you know. Besides, I can sense there's something you want to know about me.'

Ajit felt cornered. He rubbed his forehead, trying to hide his face, and said melodramatically, 'Oh, life has been cruel, and one can't even cry about it. There's so much pressure on men to remain stoic.'

Rukmini patted his head.

'Don't worry, young man, come and talk to me whenever you wish. My husband won't mind.'

•

Ajit walked down Linking Road, eyeing the girls devouring paani-puri at the roadside stalls. He found Mumbai middle-class girls more forthcoming than their North-Indian counterparts, but less good-looking. He was missing Lucknow already, especially the lovely faces that would appear suddenly, as if out of thin air, from a decrepit alley.

Stopping at a small restaurant he ordered tea and began reading a copy of the *Indian Express*. His mind, however, was in Khar, inside Rukmini's house, analysing her actions. He had never imagined that she would utter Sameer's name in front of him. She amazed him, but at least she had given him an opportunity to use the sympathy he had gained and ease information out of her. But he had been unable to link the developments in the Sudha case with Rukmini. The only connection was Sunil's involvement—solid proof about that might further endear him to Rukmini: it was obvious she wasn't exactly in love with the man.

Ajit realized that he had not briefed Rishikesh about the Bihar trip—perhaps something new had came up in Sudha's aunt's case in his absence.

The phone call from a PCO got through in an instant. Rishikesh sounded pleased to hear him.

'So what happened in Bihar? Anything sensational?'

'Lots. Anything new here?'

'*Nahin yaar*—the police is still looking for clues on both the murders.'

Ajit thought it best to let Rishikesh in on some of what he had discovered. 'Listen, there's a new angle—Sunil is involved in some shady deal in Aurangabad. Come over to my place and we'll discuss the details.'

'Why don't you see me at Jaslok hospital? Your friend Rukmini has been rushed there in a critical condition. She was attacked fifteen minutes back by four hoodlums just outside her house when she was seeing off some guests.'

The phone nearly dropped from Ajit's hands.

'Why didn't you tell me about this before, you bastard?' he yelled. 'I was with her just half an hour ago.'

Ajit heard a low laugh at the other end. 'Well, I'm telling you now. Get there quickly—this could be sensational.'

There was a mile-long traffic jam on the road leading to town, and it took Ajit over an hour to reach the hospital. He noticed the row of cars parked in the porch, and inside he saw Sunil Agnihotri, the state home minister, surrounded by petrified policemen and angry bureaucrats, talking to a team of doctors.

Inching his way in, Ajit went straight up to Sunil. After acknowledging him cursorily, Sunil asked his aide to brief him about the incident.

'We were all taken by surprise. Rukminiji was about to step back into the house when four men charged out of a Maruti van and began beating her with rods. Surprisingly, they had no firearms. They vanished before her bodyguards rushed to her rescue.'

The aide's briefing was short and precise. Ajit was struck by the fact that journalists hadn't yet arrived in full strength. He could see two or three Marathi reporters loitering in the compound trying to get information from some stray security officer. Sunil made no effort to contact them—he probably knew of their Shiv Sena affiliation.

'I think it is the Sena's work,' the aide whispered, adjusting his spectacles. 'They are trying to terrorize Sunil sahab.'

Ajit was not convinced. 'But why would the Sena attack his wife in broad daylight?'

'Because they are a bunch of thugs.'

Ajit thought of telling the man he was being foolish, but before he could, Rishikesh came up to him and slapped him on the back. 'So, seen your friend yet?'

Ajit glared at him and led him away from the aide. 'Don't call her my friend here, and not in this way.'

Rishikesh laughed. 'And what exactly do you mean by *this way*?'

Ajit let go of his arm. 'Where is our tribe? And who informed you of the incident?'

'Sixth sense—I called Sunil's home on a hunch hoping to

contact you there. Now the office has put me on the beat.'

Ajit was perplexed. Derek knew that he'd been at the scene when Rukmini was attacked earlier, so why hadn't he put him on the job then? And why choose Rishikesh now?

Rishikesh read his mind. 'Don't worry. You know how things work in the office. I called and I was given the beat. But consider yourself on the job—you can have the byline as well if you want.'

The aide called him over to say that Sunil wanted to speak to him. Ajit strode off immediately, feeling absurdly flattered and glad that Rishikesh was around to witness this. A posse of security guards hid the minister from view, but two of them made way for Ajit as soon as he reached the group.

'Ajit, listen,' Sunil began, taking him aside, 'I want you to handle the journalists. They will be swarming all over the place in a few minutes. Tell them the attack was arbitrary, that there is no political angle involved.'

They were standing man to man in the middle of the hospital corridor. Ajit could see the Emergency Ward bulb flickering in slow motion.

'I can't do that, Agnihotriji,' he replied reluctantly, 'I am a journalist and they will think I have joined your party or something. Besides, there *is* a political angle, isn't there?'

'No. There is none. Do this for Rukmini. I know she likes you. You were there when she was attacked first. I think some friends of the boy who was arrested that day tried to take some stupid revenge.'

Ajit sensed that the minister was suddenly talking at an intimate level. He brought a conspiratorial tone to his own question. 'But tell me off the record, Agnihotriji, why are you not using the attack to club the Sena?'

Sunil looked pleased. 'I'll tell you later. Now please do

as I say. Handle the bugs and bees with care.'

Sunil melted into the security cordon and disappeared from view. The journalists came rushing in a swarm soon after.

Calling Rishikesh over, Ajit whispered something into his ear. His colleague looked surprised but nodded in assent. Going over to the journalists he announced that Ajit would brief them.

'What? Ajit? Why the hell should we listen to him?' The *Hindu* correspondent, a bearded man in his forties, protested.

Ajit came forward. 'Because I was there when it all happened.'

For the next fifteen minutes Ajit talked, smoothly, without faltering, giving the journalists a cooked-up speil about the attack, which he said he alone had witnessed because he was with Rukmini at the time. The credibility accruing from the earlier incident made it easier for him to convince the sceptical tribe of journalists. Though one of them, Shalini, the *Indian Express* scribe whom Ajit hated, grilled him with some uncomfortable questions.

'How can you say the attack wasn't political?' she asked. 'It is very likely that some Sena freaks attacked Ruminiji. Did the attackers wear tags saying "We are not political"?'

Ajit heard the guffaws from the journalists at the rear.

'Come on, Shalini; the Sena isn't nuts—why would it do such a thing—to get more bad publicity?'

He was surprised at the way he toed Sunil's line. It was as if he was part of his inner circle. As a leftist he had always wondered about the other side—how did it feel when you wielded power? Just a few minutes of acting as the home minister's yes-man, and he was already feeling powerful.

But Shalini was persistent. 'Still, how can you be sure?'

'Because I know how the Sena operates. They like to link

things with some communal angle. What benefit would they get from attacking a Brahmin woman?'

'Then why was she attacked?'

'I don't know. Maybe it was a personal act of revenge by some of the boy's friends. Maybe he hired the mafia to avenge his insult—how would I know?'

Shalini wasn't convinced. She had a reputation for being sharp; half the reason why Ajit hated her. 'Yes, how would you know—maybe you're saving something for your own beat.'

Ajit wanted to boo her out but then began answering questions from other journalists. Rishikesh put up his hand, as if to ask a question, and managed to ruffle her hair. When she turned to glare at him, he pretended it was a mistake. She walked out in disgust.

'I fixed the ugly bitch,' Rishikesh told Ajit later, 'thinks too much of herself.'

'You shouldn't talk like that about our mighty tribe. They get angry—and then they fuck you. They're powerful people!'

Rishikesh laughed.

They were now in the hospital garden. Ajit was still pumped up by his short power trip. The journalists had left; Sunil was holed up inside. Ajit had begun to feel uneasy about the lack of information on Rukmini's condition.

'I wonder about your friend—our tribe also did not seem too interested in finding out how she was.'

Ajit felt stupid. He had blown the opportunity to berate his tribe for being callous about the patient's condition.

Then he saw the aide coming out of the hospital entrance. He walked slowly towards them, almost as if he didn't really want to speak to them. He stood silently at the edge of the grass.

Ajit thought something terrible had happened.

Then he spoke. 'Rukminiji is fine, sir. The doctors have said she's out of danger. She has asked for you.'

•

Rukmini had been shifted to a private room. Sunil stood outside, with two politicians in khadi and a tall man whom Sunil was speaking to in an urgent whisper, as if furious but unable to make his anger public. The tall man wore a smart scarf, and rings on all his fingers. Ajit recognized him as the local mafia don Ramendra Tiwari—he'd seen his photograph in the TOI only a couple of days earlier.

Sunil stopped speaking and nodded as Ajit walked past.

Ajit entered the room smiling. He felt strangely high. Rishikesh had winked on hearing the aide's statement.

Rukmini lay under a white sheet. Her hair was tied in a chignon, but there were no bandages on her face.

She smiled. 'The injuries are more internal. The bastards beat me quite badly.'

Ajit was suddenly overcome with sympathy. The woman in white was radiant even after a harrowing experience. Her face was plain and tired but she did not look broken.

She was wearing a white cotton sari—and he saw a white blouse too when Rukmini shifted and the sheet slid down her chest.

'Why don't you come and sit here, next to me on the bed?' she said, and Ajit felt a sudden, sharp stab of nostalgia. The room had a familiar ether smell—the body odour of his mother. In the years before the great break-up with the family, caused by issues more personal and less ideological than he would admit, he loved watching her, walking around in her white coat, being stern with the matrons and patients. It made those other moments so much more special, when she would come home from work with Phantom comics and Cadbury's chocolates for him and his sister.

As he sat on the bed now, he lowered his eyes, unwilling to let Rukmini see that they were moist.

Rukmini shifted away to make more room for him and winced in pain. 'I would have asked you to lie down beside me, but my husband is guarding the door.'

This was said with such matter-of-fact lightness that the notion that it could be a pass did not cross Ajit's mind. In fact it amazed him: it was as if she had read his mind. He had been thinking of the time when as a five-year-old he had gone to see his baby sister in hospital the day she was born. His mother was wrapped in the stiff white sheets of hospitals; she appeared so vulnerable and beautiful that Ajit wanted to lie next to her. She had let him, and he had felt secure and at complete peace, feeling the warmth of her body, enjoying the feel even of the thick plastic sheet that crept out occasionally from under her body.

'Do you have plastic under you?' he asked instinctively.

Rukmini laughed so loudly that an attendant had to peep inside to see if everything was all right.

'No, stupid; am I pregnant?'

Ajit laughed to hide his embarrassment. Then Rukmini put her hand on his cheek.

'Why are you sad? Is it because of me?'

'For you, and for a memory,' he replied.

'That was a great job you did outside. My husband is very pleased. He wants to see you in his office tomorrow. You can go now. I have to rest.'

That was curt, Ajit thought, as he got up. She hadn't even asked him anything more about his sadness. As he turned to leave, he heard her say, 'Wait. Come close.' He went up to the bed and bent forward. 'I need you to do something for me,' she whispered, closing her eyes tight against a wave of pain as she raised her head to speak. 'My husband will be out for a few days. I would like you to come and see me at my house the day after tomorrow.'

Then she turned on her side, turning her back to him.

Ajit did not remember saying anything to Sunil as he came out, save the promise of seeing him the next day. He felt light, like the time when Seema had stood in her balcony and expressed her love for him with a Mumtaz song.

Rishikesh was waiting outside, talking to the aide in a high-pitched voice. Ajit thought they were fighting—but the aide crept away on seeing him.

'What's the matter? Why were you fighting with him?'

'Nothing. I was just trying to tell him how he cannot take women for granted.'

Ajit gave him a puzzled look but did not press the matter.

As he left the hospital, he noticed he had a nice, uncomplicated hard on. It reminded him of his early school days, when he had just discovered masturbation.

10. An Affair to Remember

Sunil had decided to have the meeting not in his office, but at a friend's flat in an upmarket corner of Andheri. The friend had turned out to be Satish Rao Sitamgar, the quirky Marathi leader, better known as a poet, who had left the Shiv Sena because of his love for Urdu poetry. He had a fair, effeminate face, which reminded Ajit of the *nautanki* boys of UP. Ajit had hoped to share some good moments with Sitamgar, talking poetry, before Sunil arrived, but the Marathi's Urdu was poor. He did not respond to Ajit's *shairi*. Their conversation meandered, and at some point they began talking about the Aurangabad deal and globalization.

'I know why you're against the Aurangabad deal,' Sitamgar said after a few minutes of futile debate. 'You journalists are too narrow minded. What happens to your nationalism when the Miss World and Miss India and Miss whatever else contests are organized here? Is that Indian culture? Isn't that foreign influence? But you all love it.'

Ajit ignored the dig and went on to lambast the government's decision to invite multinationals in the private sector.

'Again you go on! I think you are in a particularly bad mood—tell me, do you have women in your life, even one woman? I mean, I have often seen that those who do not have women usually oppose the multinationals and big industry. You should be careful not to do that, I'm telling you, because they will take you to task for doing so, young man, and—'

Ajit would have stood there, struck dumb by Sitamgar's nonsense, had Sunil not barged in with a security guard.

'Oh, you're already here, hope Sitamgar isn't troubling you.'

Ajit found his voice again. 'No sir, he's not—we were just discussing the weather.'

'Ah, the weather—Bombay has no weather. We had weather in UP. Those winter nights!' Sunil rubbed his hands and shivered.

Sitamgar pulled Sunil aside and began whispering something in his ear. Sunil looked apolegetically at Ajit before nodding his head in agreement. Then the Marathi poet pinched the minister's ear lobe and walked out, pointedly ignoring Ajit.

'I'm sorry,' Sunil apologized. 'He should at least have said bye to you. He's not a bad sort, just a little sensitive—these artists, you know how they can be.'

'It's all right. What was it that you wanted to see me about?'

Sunil laughed. 'You don't waste any time, do you? This is what I like about you. Do you like girls?'

Ajit was taken aback by the abrupt private question. Perhaps this was some kind of test, he thought. Refusing the Wills Navy Cut that Sunil offered him, he sat back to answer.

'Girls are okay—but mostly unfaithful.'

It was a simple statement, made deliberately to prove a man-to-man point, but it got Sunil's attention. He took the chair opposite Ajit's.

'You surprise me. I feel that way about women too. You know, my secretary, Sudha—I suspect she was unfaithful too. I think that's why she got killed. But I don't want to soil her name. Why should all women be blamed because a couple of them are bad?'

Ajit grinned. 'Why indeed. But I don't think we should bring ideology into her case.'

Sunil chuckled. 'Well said—and you speak American English, no?'

Ajit smiled but kept quiet. Sunil shifted in his chair.'But things happen that way in India. Too much publicity in the Sudha case is bad for the cause of womankind; it might even affect the revolutionary women's reservation bill issue! You wouldn't want half of humanity to be debarred from occupying their 33% in Parliament, would you?'

Sunil burst out laughing before Ajit did. His entire body heaved and shuddered. When he stopped laughing, he reached out for the glass of water on the table next to him.

'Laughter is great, especially at the expense of women.'

He laughed again. So did Ajit, pleased that they'd made a connection. He found the minister funny and accessible.

Then Sunil became serious. 'I have asked you here because I want you to give a different angle to the Sudha case. I know what happened in Bihar through Ashok Singh. I think we share a connection through him. Whoever played the part of Sudha's lover is best forgotten, and I want you to help me ensure this.'

Ajit flinched on learning that Ashok had talked. He wanted to give his own version of the events, but thought it discreet to remain silent.

Sunil leaned forward, holding his glass of water like a glass of whisky.

'You look like a loyal sort, and I know you are fond of

my wife. This whole business is giving her a lot of heartache as well.'

Sunil's voice was impassive, almost cold. Ajit felt uncertain about its import.

'I respect Rukminiji a lot. But we don't close cases like the police in investigative journalism.'

Sunil looked at his trimmed nails. 'Well, I did tell you about Ashok Singh—the TOI editor and the police would find it very strange that you were found making love to a dead woman in a remote Darbhanga qasbah.'

Ajit froze, unable to respond. His instinctive reaction would have been to dare the man, to get on the offensive, but he had sensed that Sunil was far tougher than anyone he had met before. A memory rescued him. He remembered a room, well lit and neat, with wooden *takhats* covered with expensive sheets. Ajit switches on his dictaphone; the Allahabadi BJP leader starts talking about cultural nationalism. Ajit listens wide-eyed to fantastic stories about India's great past. Then the leader gets enthused—he begins telling him about how everything emanated from India—flying machines, missiles, the Aryans, even the Palestinians. The Palestinians? Yes, them as well—they were Indian traders who migrated in one of the BCs. Ajit interrupts—But surely this is taking things a bit too far—the Palestinians as Indians? Do you have proof?

'Throw this man out!' the leader thunders. 'He is a fake. I have been trying to prove something sincerely and he is asking for proof. He is a plant with a political agenda.'

Later, some opposition leaders were to use the leader's outburst as proof of the BJP's fascism and Ajit had felt self-important for a while. But he knew he had goofed—had he kept quiet, the leader would have come up with more fantastic things. He could have had a scoop had he really warmed up to the man, let him reveal more about the party's sense of history.

'This is the problem with Indian leftism,' a colleague had told him, 'it never allows you to get smart enough.'

Sunil waited out the silence patiently. When Ajit finally spoke, he did so carefully; he had rehearsed the words in his mind. 'You are taking all this too seriously, sir—of course I understand it is a delicate situation. And I appreciate your taking me into confidence, sir.'

Sunil softened his tone again. Perhaps he liked being addressed as sir, Ajit thought. 'There's nothing to worry about, just write what I say. Write that Sudha was of a loose character and had embezzled money from me so she could live the fast life. She committed suicide when I found out the truth. There is no need to mention her aunt—in fact, what you should do is create such hype around Sudha, with the right amount of sleaze, that people won't even notice that we are omitting the aunt.'

Ajit sensed he was close to something big.

'That's fine, sir, but other journalists may take some other line. I need to know the facts of the case if I have to rebut their arguments.'

Sunil looked amused. 'You're a tough one. I will let you in on the facts if I am convinced about your sincerity. Okay, if the sleaze bit's too much, take any angle you like—link the whole thing with some American plot.'

Ajit didn't get the link. 'The Americans, sir?'

'Don't you know that the government is allowing the FBI to open an office in India? I met some of these chaps—pretty arrogant. Think nothing of Indian intelligence. For them the CIA and the Mossad are the last word in espionage. Even the MI6 is rubbished.'

'That is pretty extraordinary,' Ajit blurted out after a short laugh.

Sunil laughed too. 'It would be fun to say that Sudha got the boot after being dumped by an American boyfriend who happened to be part of some covert FBI operation in India. We can then really nail the bastards—I mean, even the press has stopped talking about the FBI thing. There is something really fishy going on at the Central Government level. They are giving the Americans a secret foothold even while they talk Swadeshi.'

Ajit was genuinely amazed. 'That is a great line, sir. We can really pursue this angle and—'

'Don't be a fool, I was only joking. Handle TOI the way you see fit. Leave the rest to me.'

The minister waved his hand, which brought his moustached bodyguard running to the room.

'Now I'll leave. I have to go out of town for a couple of days. I want to see what you have done after I get back.'

The bodyguard was standing in rapt attention.

'Are you a Brahmin from Pratapgarh?' Ajit asked impulsively.

Sunil smiled. The guard looked pleased.

'How did you guess?'

'I'm from Allahabad. People sporting your kind of huge moustaches are found manning petrol stations all the way from Allahabad to Delhi.'

'Yes, we all belong to a mafia—Sunil Bhai's mafia.'

Sunil laughed and abused the guard fondly. '*Abe saale chutiye*,' he said in one breath. Ajit felt relaxed. To him North Indian abuse always signalled the return of male camaraderie. And that gave him the courage to ask, 'One other thing, sir. Are you involved in some Aurangabad deal?'

Sunil stopped at the door. 'I don't remember all the deals I'm involved in.'

'Well, then how come you know Ramendra Tiwari, the mafia don?'

For a second Ajit thought he saw blind fury in the minister's eyes. But then he mellowed: 'Ramendra is a *chhota bhai*—all of us politicians have mafia connections. At least I'm open about it.' Then he smiled and patted Ajit's shoulder, 'You are a pucca Brahmin,' he said and walked out.

•

Rishikesh bit deep into his chicken roll before replying.

'The police are no longer pursuing Sudha's case. They've given up.'

'What I don't understand is the silence of the opposition. Surely they would like to embarrass the minister.'

They were sitting at the same spot opposite the Danai bookshop, where they had had a minor fight before Ajit left for Bihar. The bookshop was flanked by rows of long tables covered with clean white sheets, where a blood donation agency had pitched camp. A small crowd had gathered there—the buzz was that some top actress was expected to inaugurate a donation show.

Rishikesh shook his head. 'You don't understand the funda. Maybe someone from the Sena is also involved in the Aurangabad deal. I heard Derek talking to Delhi on the phone about this. Things are not what they seem out here.'

Ajit was exasperated. 'Well, why doesn't the TOI do something about this? I mean, I have a good line to Sunil. It can be used to launch a covert operation like the Tehelka one on the match fixing. We can really pull the rug from under their feet.'

Rishikesh put his chicken roll down and sat back, looking Ajit straight in the eye. 'Look, don't get so excited about this story,' he began calmly. 'The TOI people are not buccaneers like the Tehelka guys. They are staid. Go to them with some covert operation nonsense and they'll laugh it off. Bring a political angle which interests them and they'll listen.'

'But I have a political angle—'

'That one's useless. Who do you think will be interested in reading some hypothesis about Sudha getting bumped off because of some power project? This kind of thing happens all the time—besides, this is the era of globalization, such murky deals aren't as interesting to people as they would have been in the past. Look around you, who cares about these things?'

Ajit contorted his face in disgust but did not say anything.

The Khar road ahead was full of scooter-rickshaws and smaller vehicles jostling for space. A girl got out of a rickshaw and began screaming at someone inside. Seconds later a boy got out, clutching his head, as if in pain. The two then began fighting in the street. The boy grabbed her by the hair and began slapping her hard repeatedly on the cheeks.

By the time they were separated by a cop, the girl was bleeding from the mouth. The cop led the two away.

Ajit turned his attention back to Rishikesh. He had returned to his chicken roll but was eating it distractedly, eyeing the poster of the actress Saumya. Ajit remembered their earlier meeting at the restaurant, before he'd left for Bihar, and said, 'Forget her, she's a heroine.'

Rishikesh didn't respond. He chewed silently for a while, then said, 'You know what you should do? Bring some sleaze and violence into the story. Why don't you bring Rukmini into it? Paint her as a sex maniac who got Sudha killed because she would not satisfy her desire for a threesome.'

Ajit laughed.

'Just a suggestion,' Rishikesh smiled.

Ajit watched him wash the last of the chicken roll down with Fanta. He had come to like the Jhadav. But he did not want to get too pally—friendships, like love, had a way of petering out after the initial euphoria.

A sleek, black Mercedez Benz drew up in front of the bookshop.

'This city's rich,' Ajit said. 'Take a look at that.'

Rishikesh turned to look. A crowd had gathered instantly around the car. People began waving and shouting as the actress Saumya stepped out and walked up to the white tables. She wore a green sari with golden lapels and looked quiet and reflective.

'Ah, your favourite. Let's go and hear what the bleeding heart cinema queen says. Might be fun.'

Rishikesh turned to look at Ajit—his face had hardened.

'You go—I'll hang around here.'

'Why? What's the matter?'

'Nothing.'

Saumya had finished the autograph signing round by the time Ajit posted himself at a nearby general store. She was being polite to the autograph hunters, asking them their names and urging them to donate liberally for the camp. Ajit found her in charge of the situation—she looked like an upper-class schoolgirl keen to be sincere to the masses.

Then someone put a mike in front of her.

'Friends,' she began in rehearsed English. 'You all know that blood is thicker then water. It has no religion. In our films we always donate blood without asking about a man's religion. You should do the same in real life. Spread the message of peace and harmony—there is no need to shed blood. Remember, moral values should be upheld at any cost—the youth of today must uphold morality, and help their fellow countrymen ... '

It was a short, jumbled speech, typical of film actresses and models, but Ajit liked the way Saumya rendered it, in a snappy but dignified manner, taking care not to overstep her limitations. He had visions of her going home and making *shrikhand* for her family like a normal middle-class Maharashtrian girl.

Her speech over, Saumya waved at the crowd and turned to go. She seemed in a hurry to get back to the car and tripped over a large stone lying on the pavement. The Benz's back door opened and Ramendra Tiwari stepped out to help her. His famous scarf and rings were in place, as always. The crowd fell silent. The don led Saumya back to the car.

They had barely reached the open door when two Armada jeeps drove up, and in a flash Ramendra had pushed Saumya to the ground behind the Benz. People began running for their lives even before the first bullets were fired.

The general store owner pulled Ajit into the shop. As the bullets rained outside the man talked excitedly about how this was Chhota Rajan's revenge against Ramendra Tiwari for defecting to Dawood. Ajit barely listened. He noticed a group of young girls and boys huddled inside the music shop for safety. Rishikesh had moved in too, but he didn't seem interested in the commotion. He had his back to the road, checking the music titles on display.

The Armada shooters hadn't stepped out of the jeep for a better aim. The place was now full of smoke. When the wail of sirens announced the approaching police jeeps, the Armadas sped away. There was the sound of gunfire at the far end of the lane, and the screeching of tyres.

Rishikesh was back at their table in the snack shop, on to another Fanta, when Ajit returned. Ajit told him about what the store-owner had said, that these were Chhota Rajan's men, and that the attack was more of a warning than a murder attempt. Rishikesh didn't seem interested.

'How can you be so cool about the whole thing?' Ajit said. 'That's your favourite heroine. Don't you wonder what she's doing with a don?'

'These things happen all the time in Bombay,' Rishikesh snapped. 'Concentrate on your meeting with Rukmini.'

•

'Didi is out, she has asked you to wait.' The female servant was curt.

Ajit had arrived at Rukmini's bungalow at seven sharp, after taking a long detour through Shastrinagar and Juhu, asking the autorickshaw driver about Mumbai's locality brothels. Situated in the middle of respectable colonies, they had a good reputation—clients were not robbed and were serviced in the filmi way, with painted women paraded in a room full of mirrors and loud sofas. After the encounter with the eunuchs, Ajit was a little wary of venturing into the realm of adventurous sex. But the thought of fucking a hooker in front of a mirror caused a familiar stirring in his groin. Then he thought of Rukmini, and nervousness replaced desire—the hard-on subsided.

The nervousness had grown by the time Rukmini arrived. At one point Ajit wanted to give everything up and run away.

'Arre, Ajit? What are you doing here?' Rukmini said flatly when she walked in. The maid took the shopping bags from her and walked out. A little surprised by her reaction, Ajit attempted a smile. She did not respond. He got up. 'I thought you'd wanted to meet me. Maybe I got the time wrong. I'll come back later.'

'Arre, sit na—now I remember. Actually I got busy and forgot all about you.'

Ajit saw a faint love mark at the base of the plump neck. The minister's wife quickly pulled up her sari pallu to cover the spot.

'So what should we do?'

Ajit had begun to feel uncomfortable. He had pinned too much hope on the meeting.

The woman before him looked hassled—she had either forgotten or was trying to remember something.

'A thin line of difference,' Ajit heard himself mutter.

'What?'

'Whether you forget something or you try to remember something—not much difference.'

The minister's wife frowned for a second and then laughed. 'Look, I really did forget that I had called you here. I'm sorry.'

'Wish I had forgotten I had to come here.'

Rukmini put her hand on his arm. 'Come, let me show you my library. I've collected some nice books over the years.'

Ajit allowed himself to be led to an inner room, which had plastered walls and a rust-coloured carpet on the floor. He was amazed by the number of bookshelves—the room was full of them, they covered three walls and half of the fourth, the one with the door. Books were jammed into every available space—it was difficult to differentiate one title from the other.

'James Joyce and Jaishankar Prasad pressed against each other?' Ajit said, pulling out two titles from the shelf closest to him.

'Yes, isn't that interesting?'

'Have you read either of them?'

Rukmini smiled. She was wearing small silver earrings, which swayed and trembled as she moved her head.

'Are you looking at my earrings?'

'Yes. They're very pretty.'

The rings were out and in Ajit's hands in an instant. He began examining their irregular surface.

'Almost as interesting as your books. When did you buy them?'

'The earrings?'

'No, no, the books, many of them are quite old.'

'In Delhi and Allahabad. Most of them were gifts from the man in my life I told you about.'

There was a sudden tremor in Rukmini's voice. Ajit looked up at her. She stood near him, a shelf crammed with musty books behind her, looking resplendent and vulnerable in a pink sari.

Ajit felt a hot wave pass through him, and suddenly he felt bold, like a man with two stiff whiskies down.

He returned the earrings.

'Sameer?' he asked, taking a step towards the shelf.

'Yes. Did you know him?'

Ajit was reaching for a book on Mughal and Renaissance painting. He stopped midway.

'Why did you ask that?'

'Just—something in your tone suggested that you knew him. You're from Allahabad too, aren't you?'

'Yes, I am from Allahabad. And I did know someone by that name. In fact, he told me all about you.'

A two-feet space separated Rukmini from Ajit. She pulled out the book closest to her and flung it at him. The missile hit him on the chest.

'Don't even joke about this. I don't like it,' she said.

Ajit picked up the missile. It was a copy of Engels' *Anti-Duhring*.

'He gave you—Engels?' The laughter that accompanied

the question was not intended but there was no stopping when it came. When he did stop laughing he was surprised to see Rukmini looking amused rather than offended.

'Of course. How could someone like me have what it takes to understand Engels.'

'Well, *do* you know anything about Marx and Engels? I mean, why the hell was he trying to give *you* this stuff?'

'Why? Because he was a romantic. In fact, at the time I thought he was the last of the romantics. You know what that means? Romanticism began in India with Urdu poetry; it ended with political activism. Sameer was a Marxist and a nationalist. Sometimes we used to talk throughout the night. He would read out passages from R.P. Dutt's *India Today*, especially the portion dealing with the Gandhi-Irwin pact which showed how Bhagat Singh was betrayed by Mahatma Gandhi.'

Ajit tried to hide his stupefaction. Was she trying to put up a show? How was it that she was so good with history?

'This was his idea of romance?' her sniggered.

'Yes, and it was great. He was a saccharine idealist. Perhaps not the best of men, but sometimes he reminded me of Dr Zhivago. And you know, you remind me so much of him. Are you sure you've never met him?'

Ajit looked away. It was as if she was casting a spell on him.

'Have you read Pasternak?'

'No. Only saw the film.'

'But did he gift you a copy?'

Rukmini hesitated for a moment before saying no. Ajit thought she was going to say yes.

'Didn't your husband question you about these books, or your past life, when you got married?'

'He did. And I told him everything.'

Ajit looked at her, to try and make out if she was lying. But he couldn't make anything of the slightly amused look that she still wore. She reached out and put a hand on his shoulder, and he was startled by the shiver of pleasure that ran through him.

Rukmini went past him and sat on the lone cane chair near the entrance.

'This man Sameer—what else did he do to love you?'

Ajit had followed her to the chair and stood beside her now, his left hand dangling near her face.

'We used to live in a large house. My parents slept early, but we had to be careful. I would leave the back gate open at night. He used to enter my alley, stand there till it became completely deserted and then steal in at around midnight. We spent what remained of the night lying in each other's arms. He loved me in my green satin night suit. He left before anyone woke up. We also met in his house sometimes.'

Ajit felt his hand touching her skin. He closed his eyes.

'Did you make love?'

There was no answer.

'Did you make love?'

'Yes we did.'

Dropping to his knees Ajit let his hands fall on her thighs. She did not resist. He looked into her eyes. They were quiet but inquiring. He then saw the plump neck. The love mark was still there. He took his face forward, bringing his tongue close to the flesh.

This time Rukmini closed her eyes.

The first thought that came to Ajit was of Sameer standing in an Allahabad alley, alone, expectant, waiting for the road to clear of people ...

Inside, a younger, slimmer Rukmini glances at her watch—her parents are having dinner. They ask her why she is dressed in a satin night gown ...

The tongue was now moving towards the cheeks. Ajit hadn't felt soft, round cheeks before. Seema had high cheekbones, and her skin wasn't as smooth.

The road is deserted—Sameer moves towards the iron gate; closing it gently he steps into the veranda. He sees the door to her room open slowly. A foot wrapped in green robes comes forward.

Ajit moved his toungue from her cheeks to her closed eyes and back. She did not stir or open her eyes.

Sameer is now kissing his beloved. His hands cup her breasts. He realizes she isn't wearing a bra. He goes wild with desire. He tries to lift her off the ground but she resists.

Ajit rubbed his hard on with his free hand—he had a partial erection. That surprised him—her taste inebriated him, his pants ought to be bulging out.

Then he began kissing her—on the nose, the forehead, beneath the eyes, the ears, the brow, and then the cheeks again. He applied his teeth gently to her cheek and waited for some human response. There was none, so he ate into the flesh. There was a sharp cry but no protest.

Sameer is pressing her breasts wildly; he has her pinned against a wall. He grinds her into the brick and plaster and lime. She is crying for him to stop but he won't—he tugs at the portion of her gown covering her breasts. It doesn't give way. He tugs again, with much greater force, and the cloth begins to tear. Rukmini asks him to stop. He rips the nightie apart; her breasts dangle freely. Cupping them in each hand, he begins to lick. Rukmini moans as he strips her naked and rubs his rough hands fiercely on her thighs, her stomach, her buttocks. He carries her to the bed and slams her down. He takes his cock out and rubs it all over her face. He asks her to massage her thighs and watches her slim fingers move on her smooth flesh, hears the faint rustle when they slide over her jet black pubic hair. He puts his finger in her cunt—then his cock in her mouth.

Ajit bit her lower lip, softly at first, then harder.

Sameer wants to tit fuck her—he pulls out of her mouth, takes his jeans off and puts his wet cock between her tits. She turns her face to a side, raises her butt and gasps with pleasure. He presses his cock on her tummy, parts her thighs. At the first thrust she screams and wraps her thighs around him.

Ajit began urging her with his tongue to open her mouth. She obeyed. She sucked his toungue into a wet, warm abyss, and just when he had surrendered all of himself to her passion she caught him by the hair and pulled him away from her mouth.

'What are you thinking about?'

'How great your skin smells without perfume.'

'I use a powder with no smell. It is white and pure. What else?'

'About Sameer and you. How he must have humped you in an old Allahabadi room.'

Rukmini smiled. 'What does the room smell of?'

'There's the smell of lime, of dust—and your sweat and his sperm.'

Rukmini yanked his hair.

'And the books, you idiot—you forgot the musty books.'

'Yes the books.'

Letting go of his hair, Rukmini went for his pants, unzipping his jeans with in one movement.

'Stand up and remove your underwear—I want to see what you look like.'

Ajit felt like a schoolboy in front of his teacher as he

complied. As a child he had a maid who loved unzipping him—she would sit there and laugh, enjoying the authority that came with the act. At first Ajit had felt humiliated—then he started enjoying it.

The minister's wife had taken charge. She had him naked from the waist down, and put her mouth to his cock. Ajit tried thinking of Sameer but Rukmini's vigorous sucking blocked the fantasy. She was working like a jackhammer. Ajit looked down at her, fully clothed—he hadn't even seen her breasts yet. The thought made him angry—he reached down and began to squeeze her breasts. Rukmini released his cock and sat back. She asked him to stop, but he went on, managing ultimately to slide one hand inside her cleavage.

It was warm there. He pushed his hand in further.

'You don't wear a bra?'

'What?'

'You're not wearing a bra,' he said, sitting down before her. 'Isn't this what you did for Sameer too?

Rukmini looked at him in confusion and anger. He thought she would slap him across the face.

'How do you know that? Are you his fucking agent?'

'Just guessed—you and I, we have a connection.'

He tugged at her blouse—the buttons were tight and the cloth did not give way. He waited for a few seconds and then yanked hard, tearing the blouse down the middle. Rukmini groaned and closed her eyes. Putting his arms around her shoulders he pulled her down and buried his face between her breasts.

He licked the thin film of sweat off her skin, slid his hands down to her ankles and pulled her sari up to her knees. He squeezed her thighs and she threw her head back against the chair. Ajit pulled away from her tits and began licking her knees, which shone as if they had been polished.

He felt her fingers in his hair, and moved up, bringing the sari and the taffeta petticoat up till it covered her naked breasts and neck. He rubbed her bushy cunt. She had trimmed the hair to produce an imperfect triangle.

He did not ask where her panties were. Burying his face deep in the bush he thought about Mrs Jha and the smell of Jumbo prawns. As his tongue licked her clit she shuddered.

'Was Sameer good at this?'

Rukmini pushed his head down against her cunt.

'This was what he was good at—shut up and get on with the job.'

Ajit opened his mouth, wanting to cover all of her cunt with his lips. Rukmini wrapped her thighs around his face. He felt crushed, but dug his tongue in deeper. When she asked him to stop being impatient and do his job with care, he sat back abruptly.

'My business is to screw you hard. I want to tear your sari off your body and then wrap it around you again after I've fucked you.'

He was at the job before Rukmini could protest. The petticoat string was undone and the pink taffeta pulled down and off her legs. While she slipped her blouse off, he pulled at the knot of her sari. It gave way after a brief struggle.

The sari lay like a lazy, sinuous thing over her and the cane chair.

'Not here,' Ajit said, 'let's do it on the floor.'

Rukmini let him pull her to the floor. The chiffon sari came with her, rustling quietly. He ran a hand over her body, down from the neck, careful not to disturb the chiffon that lay casually over parts of it. He liked the image, as if from a painting.

Rukmini lifted a leg but Ajit brought it down. He then

began wiping her cunt with the sari. He smelled the cunt juice on chiffon, then rubbed it on his cock. Rukmini was looking at her watch when Ajit lowered himself onto her.

'Stop,' Rukmini said. 'Let me do it; I'll place it myself.'

Before he could reply, she had taken his cock in her hands and placed it at the cunt line. Ajit pushed in with all his might.

Rukmini cried out aloud. Ajit looked down at her with surprise; he had encountered a smooth, wet passage—how could she feign such pain? He wanted to stop and ask her about it but then his cock began swelling. It was beyond him to withdraw. He gave a second push, more violent than the one before. Rukmini cried again, but made no effort to stop him. Ajit kept pumping into her—enjoying the cries, which melted into less expert moans.

He lost all sense of time. A portion of the sari slung lazily across her breasts and the sight fascinated him. As did his own heaving, panting shadow in the brightly lit room. Her body was darker in his shadow. Her nipples appeared darker still; Ajit tweaked them whenever he got a chance. He thought of a 19th-century painting he had seen in Lucknow's Avadh museum, which revealed a lady's nipples through multiple layers of fine muslin. As Rukmini's body arched up with each thrust, Ajit imagined himself as an Avadhi nawab, screwing his begum and a whore by turns through the night.

Ajit did not feel like asking whether he should withdraw before coming. He had wanted at first to come on her stomach, spilling his white semen all over her fair skin. But as his veins contracted and his cock throbbed, he remained inside.

'Did you come?' He asked after what seemed like a long time.

'Yes,' she replied without making an effort to get up. 'Thrice.'

He was in her bedroom, pressing his cock under his zip, trying to come to terms with the ache. His request for an encore had been turned down. 'You're too much for me—how many times will you come before tiring out? But I have work to do.' Then she had quickly put on her sari and cleaned the place. For an instant Ajit had felt abandoned; it was as if the task he was there for was over. But then Rukmini had kissed him lightly on the cheeks before asking him into her bedroom.

'Why didn't you stop me if it was hurting?' he had asked.

'It didn't hurt—was I crying out aloud?' she had replied.

He was still wondering at that when she disappeared into the kitchen to make coffee.

Ajit watched the curtains in the bedroom window swaying gently. He did not know whether it was the sea breeze which caused the movement. He had stopped trying to figure out the way the wind blew in Bombay. The city sometimes reminded him of Benaras, with the difference that there were three or four main roads here instead of one, and the sea was grander than the Ganga.

Rukmini's room had modest furniture—the bed wasn't too large and her dressing table wasn't stacked with cosmetic implements. Ajit found himself staring into the dressing-table mirror. He examined his profile—fairly tall, reasonably good looking, slim—and yet not entirely handsome. So what had worked? Was it the look or the attitude?

The encounter with Rukmini had come as a surprise—he had not expected to lay her so soon. But he thought of the sudden power he could exercise at certain decisive moments.

During the student movement days, he would often overpower much stronger colleagues who found him too lethargic and laid back to qualify as a winner. Sometimes he would even shock his mother by his aggression.

Jutting his jaw forward, Ajit smirked at himself. He then leaned to a side and narrowed his eyes for the tough guy look.

Growing up in Allahabad he had admired the American films that were available in the video libraries. The city was stocked better than Delhi or Lucknow in the '80s and Ajit identified himself completely with the westerns and their heroic code. Once in a Marxist class he had described the object of Indian revolution as a grand design aimed at replicating the world of Wyatt Earp and Doc Holliday in India.

But then he felt his heart droop—that he had managed to have sex with Rukmini so soon may have nothing to do with his looks or his attitude. Maybe she just liked sex, and any partner would do—or maybe she was playing a game.

Then he thought of Baby Johnson.

Taking his eyes off his reflection, he began rummaging around in the dressing table. It seemed an absurd thing to do—even if it was possible that Rukmini would have an old powder bottle tucked away somewhere. And yet, he felt it was important for him to procure a specimen.

The two top drawers were locked. He looked in the third. He was cooking up an excuse already—if caught in the act he would give her some story about a compulsive desire since childhood to rummage through women's personal belongings. Or some other inanity. In spite of torrid sex in a musty room full of books Rukmini knew nothing about him—their relationship was still at a stage where they had no option but to make do with what the other revealed.

There was nothing in the drawer save a few medicines, and a key. He took the key out and applied it to the tiny lock on the second drawer. It opened with a faint click. There were many slips of paper and visiting cards and a couple of passports. He closed the second drawer and moved to the first. The little aluminium key worked again, and this one too contained only loose papers.

He was about to turn away, disappointed, when he saw what looked like an old letter filled with slightly smudged lines written in red ink. The red looked like dried blood. And he saw Sameer's name in the jumble of words.

Ajit grabbed the letter. He heard someone coming towards the room. In a flash he had sprung across to the toilet and shut the door behind him. He collided with the sink. He had forgotten to switch the light on, but had assumed an empty space at the entrance. He steadied himself and fumbled for the switch. A fan came on first, and then a tube light flickered on.

In the dull white light the ink looked more like old blood than before. But for some reason he found himself unwilling to accept that. It's not blood, he whispered to himself, as he smelled the paper. The letter was in long hand and it wasn't addressed to anyone. The opening line was abrupt, and as he read it, he realized it wasn't a letter but a page from some diary. But there was no date written at the top or at the bottom of the page.

Don't be stupid, I told Sameer—what a nice name, reminds me of a smart Muslim living in the city's posh area—my brother-in-law actually abused me, I said. I was 12. He was in the habit of getting himself massaged every afternoon before he took a nap. I went to their house often to be with my sister. That afternoon the maid said she was teaching late at her school but sahab was in. He heard me and called me in. He was lying wrapped in a blanket. When I went up to his bed he removed the blanket. He was stark naked. His body glistened with oil. He grabbed me and pulled me onto the bed. I resisted. He lifted my frock and removed my chaddhi. *I protested again. He pressed me down—take it, take it, it's a nice toy, hold it, he laughed, bringing my hands down to his penis. He put his hand on mine and made me masturbate him. I don't know how I wriggled out of his grip. I ran, leaving my chaddhi behind. I heard the maid laughing . . .*

But Sameer wouldn't believe me. He accused me of making up the story. He is very forthright and doesn't believe anything I say now. Just because I told him once before about my brother-in-law and then retracted. You'd lied then, he says, you're lying again. I'd retracted earlier because I saw he was hurt and I did not want that. Why do men get hurt so easily? He can't take the truth, so it's my fault. But I don't want to loose Sameer.

But he suspects me all the time. He suspects that I have affairs. He suspected me of lying about my last Lucknow visit when I returned with expensive new clothes. After sulking for a few days he accused me of selling my body for money. I was devastated. But I love him. I told him that. He wouldn't listen. He was crying. He said he saw something in my eyes—what did he say?—yes, the look of guilt. The guilt of someone who had betrayed her love, betrayed a principle, betrayed something pure. I tried to reason but he wouldn't listen. He gets so hyper, thinks only he is right. I think his politics has harmed him. He is too much of an idealist. Blind to his own faults and to everyone else's virtues. Doesn't realize that life is not simple and straight. A naughty look in my eyes doesn't mean a guilty look. I was happy when I came back. Wanted to go and sing a song for him on the Jamuna. I remember the last time we were there. It was evening and the wind blew hot and slow. He asked me to sing the Girija Devi dadra. I began slowly, conscious of the boatman. It wasn't my favourite song but he loved it. He found Benaras thumris too mellifluous for his taste. He wanted something less sweet but more sophisticated. Girija Devi is perfect, he used to say—Deewana Kiye Shaam . . . I began. The evening called out to me from far away, from the other side of the Jamuna. The temples stood resplendent in the hazy dusk. I wanted to swim in the river, to swim across, but I don't know how to swim. Neither does he.

Ajit flipped the page—there was something scribbled in Hindi.

Kya jaadu daara
Deewana kiye shaam
Kya jaadu daara
Is galiyan mein aana na jaana
Aur karna bahana
Kya jaadu daara

There was a knock on the bathroom door.

'How long are you going to take in there? The coffee will get cold.'

Rukmini's voice was merry. Folding the paper neatly he put it in his pocket.

Rukmini was standing near the dressing table, next to the open drawers.

'Did you open these?'

'Yes. I was looking for a weapon.'

'What kind of weapon?'

'I was looking for condoms. I want to use them the next time we make love. This time I came inside you. It's not safe.'

A nervous note had crept into Rukmini's voice when she began questioning him. But his answer relaxed her.

'Forget condoms. Nothing will happen.'

She was smiling as she closed the drawers.

She poured milk into his coffee.

'Sugar?'

'Two.'

Rukmini had changed into a blue sari. The fabric was some cheaper material, not chiffon, but still looked gorgeous in the bedroom light. She handed him his cup and sat on the bed with hers.

'Why are you so quiet—suddenly you don't seem to be the person who did all that back there.'

Ajit decided that the time to play a good boy was over. 'I could have done a lot more. How about laying you right here in your husband's bed.'

Rukmini exclaimed something inaudible in disgust; her face contorted for a second and he thought she was angry.

But then she reclined on the bed and gave him a very sweet smile. 'You must appreciate the fact that I don't sleep with other men in my husband's bed. I am faithful as a wife. What I did with you concerns my other self.'

Ajit put his cup of coffee back on the bedside table and went and sat on the bed.

'I'm not like other men, am I?' he said, tickling her feet.

Rukmini closed her eyes. He made her laugh for a long time. He began kneading her thighs, but she sat up, looked at her watch and said it was time to go.

•

Rukmini asked Ajit to roll down the car window. 'I love the breeze from the sea at this time of the evening.'

They were approaching Haji Ali. Ajit saw the a huge board announcing Haji Ali Juice Corner, but he was interested in the shrine, situated, he liked to imagine, in the middle of the sea. A long corridor led from the seashore to the saint's *mazaar*, and it was not uncommon for some unfortunate pilgrims to get washed away during high tides. Ajit was reminded of a couplet he had once read:

Kisi dardmand ke kaam aa
Kisi doobte ko uchhaal de
Voh nigahmast ki mastiyan
Kisi badnaseeb pe daal de

(Service the one who is in pain
Lift the one who is drowning
The good fortune of the eyes drunk with joy—
Direct them to the one who is unfortunate)

He began humming the lines as Rukmini stopped the Zen by the juice corner.

'You're a terrible singer. But the lines are good. Who are they by?'

'Haji Ali himself.'

'You're joking.'

'I'm serious. I once read an article on him in *EPW*. The author had quoted these lines. We used to sing this song in one of our street plays.'

'Did you say *EPW*? Sameer used to write in that magazine.'

Ajit turned to look at her. 'Under what name?'

'Sameer, of course.'

'Never heard of anyone by that name writing in the magazine,' he said dismissively. 'I used to contribute too.'

The juice arrived in a big glass.

'This is not juice, it's pulp.'

'Yes, but isn't it great?'

'It is. We should come here more often.'

'We will,' Rukmini said and turned towards the sea to catch the breeze on her face.

'Tell me, what kind of a character was this Sameer? Did he really screw you while reading Marx and Engels?'

Rukmini tried to look offended but burst out laughing.

'You're a nice young man—so charmingly irreverent. I wish he was a bit like you.'

'Oh I'm very different. Not a Sameer-type at all—those 70s' and 80s' Marxists. The standard joke during our days was about their girlfriends. How the Marxists used to take their girls to their hostels and talk a lot about peasants. They'd show them a poor man—"Look, there goes a peasant," they'd say, and lay the poor girls while they thought about poverty.'

Ajit laughed loudly at his own joke. Rukmini remained quiet.

'There is a lot of sex in idealism.'

Ajit laughed again. When he had stopped laughing, she said, 'That was a good one,' and started the car.

'Where's the bowling alley?' Ajit asked as they entered the Phoenix Industrial Area. The guard at the gate mumbled something unintelligible, but Rukmini pointed ahead, indicating that she knew her way around.

Ajit snorted at the listless, colourless setting of the estate which was supposed to house Fire and Ice, the city's most happening disco. It had been his idea that they should go to a nightclub, and Rukmini had suggested Fire and Ice.

'Don't judge so quickly. Get inside; it's a different world.'

'Why didn't you wear a salwaar-kameez?' Ajit asked as they ambled along on a road lined with impersonal office-type structures.

'Why? Does the sari embarrass you?'

'No, but—'

'No buts—I would have looked fat in a salwaar. Coming here was your idea anyway.'

Ajit smiled at her, but he couldn't help feeling foolish going to a disco with a plump woman in her late thirties dressed in a sari. All around them seriously trendy guys with gelled hair were walking past with their dates in miniskirts, talking with an acquired slang. He couldn't remember the last time he took a girl out to a nightclub. Allahabad had no nightclubs. Even had there been any, Seema couldn't dance, and the one time they'd happened to be in Delhi together, she had refused to go out in a skirt.

Rukmini was walking proudly, eyeing the young couples with unconcealed curiosity. Watching her in this mood, Ajit felt light. What the hell, he thought, how did it matter whether his date was modern or traditional—at least he was taking a woman out.

The road turned right, bringing the first stylish signboards into view. Painted in blue, white and black, the wooden signs bore funky names atop bare, tiled walls. Through the glass panes of bars and restaurants with Mexican and French names Ajit saw the smart decor looking more sophisticated or hip in the dim lights. He thought about his city and the restaurants of the 70s, which had neon lights and neat boat-shaped ashtrays and a sensual décor full of mirrors.

'Given a chance Allahabad might have evolved like this.'

Rukmini looked at him with suspicion. 'I don't think so—why are you so obsessed with Allahabad? This is the new world.'

Ajit wanted to tell her that he used to watch *Easy Rider* and *Citizen Kane* sitting in Allahabad when his Bombay friends could not find anything beyond *Rocky* and *Terminator* in their video stores. But he kept quiet.

They had now entered the main segment, which housed the bowling alley on the right and the nightclub on the left. A couple of boys sauntering down the alley stairs started a jig in front of two girls standing near the counter. The man at the counter cheered them on and clapped. The girls laughed. They were in faded shorts and T shirts; one of them lit a cigarette and abused a boy in playful Marathi. The boy cackled and took his mouth close to her face but didn't kiss her. The girl shoved him away with her hips.

'Come on, let's hit the floor—*yeh hai Bambai meri jaan*,' Rukmini whispered.

Ajit liked the sense of abandon in her voice. He looked at her closely—she was dressed in a brown sari of light crepe and a sleeveless brown blouse that contrasted nicely with her fair, slightly plump arms. She had a silver amulet on one arm, and understated silver jewellery in her ears and round her neck. And suddenly he felt proud, not embarrassed to be her date. In the crowd of trendy young things she looked exotic and supremely confident.

'What if people recognize you here?'

He was walking close, so that his fingers brushed hers.

'They will not. And if they do, well, I'm with a friend.'

'*Aap toh badi forward hain*,' Ajit said teasingly.

'*Aur aap bade chaalu hain*,' she replied and laughed.

They had now reached the door and could see celebrities, small-time actors and models mainly, talking into their cellphones, twisting their necks around as they cooed and cackled, to check if they were being seen.

All of a sudden Ajit felt like doing something nasty; Rukmini seemed impossibly self-possessed and superior. 'Listen, you look familiar—why don't you try a little harder and you'll really look like Moon Moon Sen's daughter.'

Riya Sen shot him a murderous look. The group of cigarette-smoking girls and guys laughed their hearts out. Rukmini turned the tables on him and joined in their laughter. 'Next time, I promise,' she said, taking his arm and stepping inside a space-ship type enclosure.

The club spread sideways from the door, along huge walls lined with railings. The bar at the ground floor was dark and full of perfumed silhouettes drinking and gossiping. Rukmini had purchased coupons worth Rs 1200 at the counter and was intent on using up all the paper money.

'Let's drink ourselves silly tonight—I'm very happy.'

She put her arms forward towards him as she said this. Ajit remembered having seen something similar before—Waheeda Rehman in *Guide*, atop a Rajasthani monument, stretching her arms out towards Dev Anand as she sang: *Aaj phir jeene ki tamanna hai* . . .

Rukmini ordered a large vodka, and was about to ask the barman for a whisky as well, when a young boy with a baseball cap standing next to her commented loudly on the *sariwali amma* in the bar. Rukmini turned to him casually and poured the vodka on his cap. The startled boy called out to his friends, who gathered around Rukmini and began arguing with her. Ajit grabbed her arm to pull her away, but the boys stopped him, a couple of them shouting out loud that there was also a boyfriend with the *sariwali amma*.

Ajit sensed the situation turning ugly; Rukmini had already called the boy she was arguing with a bastard and shoved him against the bar.

'Why're you acting like this? What's wrong with you?' he hissed.

'There's nothing wrong. I'm having a nice time.'

Ajit shrugged and resumed the task of confronting one of the boys. Rukmini was having fun all right, but he knew that if things worsened he would be the one expected to handle the mess. She'd said something again while his back was turned; he heard the boy yell at her. He made his way to the door to talk to the bouncers.

Rukmini looked disappointed as the bouncers intervened and carried the boy with the cap away. The other boys objected and got into a scuffle with the bouncers. Rukmini egged on the muscled men to take on the boys. Soon a minor war had broken out at the bar. Drawing Ajit away from the tumult Rukmini took him to the dance floor, where some couples were dancing, oblivious to the fight.

'See what I did? And you were afraid. Trust a woman to start a fight.'

'So this is your idea of fun?'

'At least for tonight it is. Come, let's go up. I don't like the scene here.'

Ajit didn't either. And he didn't like the music. The DJ was playing some unfamiliar rap tunes which he found harsh and linear. They did not have the thin line of raucous melody that distinguished good rap from bad.

The top floor was worse. It had a bar table, which was not dimly lit. There was no dance floor; couples were dancing in the narrow space in front of the bar, throwing around bits of the eatables they were carrying. A girl in a yellow miniskirt was dancing with her sozzled boyfriend, smacking her hips with each movement. Another girl, in loose grey pants and yellow shirt, danced facing the wall. Her escort, a hunk with a slight hunchback, stood motionless, watching her without any expression whatsoever on his face.

'That must be some junior artist who's come out with a stuntman,' Ajit commented as they settled at a free table.

Rukmini was not looking that way. Her eyes were fixed on a white couple dancing on the floor below. The man was blonde, and his pointed jaw had a thick stubble. He was talking earnestly, clearly trying to soothe his girl who appeared agitated about something.

Ajit watched Rukmini's expression change briefly from

reckless exuberance to one of something close to sadness.

'Do you know these people?'

'No.' She looked up. 'Why do you ask?'

Ajit shook his head and looked back at the floor. The white man was trying to ward off a Sikh pressing on his date. He was well built, with a clean, upper-class look and appeared distinctly uncomfortable at having to brush someone off impolitely.

'What do you think—is he American or European?'

'American,' Rukmini replied instantly. Then she hesitated. 'No, European, actually. Yes, positively European.'

The girl in the yellow miniskirt began a wild movement as the DJ switched from rap to bhangra pop. Ajit cursed. The white man left the dance floor. Ajit watched him steer his date gently through the small group of dancers. At the edge of the dance floor, directly below where they were sitting, the man looked up and caught Rukmini and Ajit looking at him. Then he disappeared from view.

'Why don't we drink something; I'm getting bored here.'

'What? Bored when I'm around? Okay, what do you want? I have a whole lot of coupons here.' She flashed the paper money. Ajit got up to order the drinks.

They were walking down the Marine Lines road—infamous for being spooked. Coming here was Rukmini's idea.

'You know the story, don't you?'

'No. Tell me.'

'When this building you see on your right was being constructed the builders demolished a couple of graves. Since then a woman in a flowing white sari appears on some special nights and waves down a lone car or taxi. The driver invariably bangs his car and dies.'

The road was deserted, and strangely quiet for Bombay.

Ajit felt a chill in his back, but no fear.

'I have an aversion to horror stories,' he said impatiently. 'They're—so stupid!'

The night breeze was gentle and relaxing. The mood was in sharp contrast to the scene back at the club before they'd left. After sipping their customary drinks, Ajit had invited Rukmini for a dance. She still looked preoccupied, and was staring at the exit door.

'Did you lose something?'

'No.'

'Then?'

'Oh! I was looking for celebs. Shahrukh is supposed to frequent this place.'

'I don't like Shahrukh. He's a wimp.'

He started dancing before her, to a regular disco number. Though he had heard the song several times over he wasn't familiar with the band's name.

Rukmini rose and began to move to the music.

'Shahrukh is a good entertainer. And aren't all Indian heroes wimps?'

She moved her hips slowly. Ajit was impressed by her sense of beat. 'Yes, but Dilip and Amitabh cried with dignity.'

To this she said nothing, only smiled, and again he felt as if she was patronizing him. He put an arm around her waist and pulled her roughly to him.

'How about letting me screw you on this dance floor?' he whispered nastily in her face. She laughed and pushed him away. She began moving her hands faster, mixing some old Asha Parekh movements with an occasional jig in the MTV tradition.

Ajit was losing the rhythm. 'I think wimpishness is politics—the Indian aristocratic code was forced to go soft to please women. It also suited the Bania-inspired state power.' He wished he could have said that less confusingly.

Bringing her hands together over his head, Rukmini clapped in glee. 'Great words. Only they're way off the mark. I wish you could have met Sameer—you two are *so* alike. You like Hollywood, don't you?"

'How did you guess?'

'Sameer did too. What do you like about Hollywood?'

'Westerns—Wyatt Earp, Doc Holliday, Jimmy Ringo—these characters showed that ultimately you make your own destiny—and there is no one, friend, beloved or parents when you face the man you hate at High Noon.'

'Really? I never understand American cinema,' Rukmini said and closed her eyes, as if finally lost in the dance.

The floor was getting packed. Some boys were climbing onto the platform in front in order to demonstrate their skills. They were being cheered by a group of loud girls in miniskirts standing in a row. They went down at the knees and came up in unison, shaking their tits and pushing their arms out before them.

Ajit tried the movement too. He urged Rukmini to do the same; and as he'd hoped, her boobs bounced like footballs.

'You're trying to make me look like a fool and have some fun at my expense,' she complained, but didn't sound genuinely cross.

The boys who had fought with her had also joined the floor. They were trying to get close to where she was dancing—one of them laughed about the bouncing boobs.

Ajit told him to shut up. 'The music is lousy and you guys are making things worse. This is a shitty place—who recommended it anyway?'

The boys began whispering amongst themselves. The couples around shot him inhospitable looks; some of them even protested at his statement, saying they liked the music.

Ajit turned to Rukmini. 'I'm so pissed off with this place.

Let's pick a fight. Why don't you hit out like Rani of Jhansi or something.'

Ajit had intended this as a joke but Rukmini took it seriously and nudged the man beside her roughly for extra space. A heated argument was raging in no time at all. The boys gathered around. Ajit crept up to the DJ. 'You play crappy music,' he yelled. 'Only morons can dance to it. It is horse shit.'

The DJ balked, and panicked when Ajit picked up a couple of CDs and made as if to throw them to the floor. He pleaded with Ajit to stop. The top-floor crowd had gathered at the railing; some of them were throwing chips and kababs and peanuts at the people below.

'See? The crowd's going wild. They want real music, not this crap. Put on that Rekha number from *Gora aur Kala*—have you heard of a fucking film called *Gora aur Kala*?'

The DJ shook his head. Turning to the crowd Ajit began shouting that the idiot DJ hadn't heard of *Gora aur Kala*.

'What the fuck is that? A new album by Lucky Ali?' someone shouted back.

'This guy's crazy. Is he from the Shiv Sena?' a girl screamed.

'No, no he must be from the Congress. They're all equally crazy these days.'

Ajit walked back into the crowd. He noticed that the boys around Rukmini had started to retreat in the face of a severe dressing down. She was yelling at them, and had one of them by the collar.

'I am a minister's wife, you understand! That boy there is my nephew. I will have your balls ripped off in no time!'

The boys did not believe her but then she pulled out her husband's I-card from her blouse and waved it at them. After a few anxious glances they melted into the crowd.

Ajit elbowed his way up to her. 'What was that speil you were giving them?'

She smiled like a mischievous child, watching the boys debate their next move. Most of the couples had left the dance floor and were eyeing the commotion distrustfully. The bouncers were nowhere to be seen.

Ajit said something in Rukmini's ear. She blushed, then snapped her fingers and said, 'Okay, let's do it.' Ajit went up to the DJ's podium. 'You guys must have seen Latino, Australian and other dancers from godforsaken countries shaking their arses. Now watch a *desi devi* showing off to a raunchy Indian number.'

The crowd was silent. 'Stop the music, you ass,' Ajit commanded. The DJ complied. Then he saw Rukmini sway and snap her fingers. The girls in the crowd clapped and asked for more. Rukmini began tapping her feet.

She sang the first line in her husky, heavy voice, then stopped dramatically and looked around. Ajit stared at her in wonder—'Oh my god,' he thought, 'she really is singing.' The girls cheered again, and Rukmini resumed her song.

She put one hand on her heart, swayed her hips, bit her lip and held her pallu up to cover her face.

Ek to mera deewana shabaab
Us pe pilayi hai toone sharaab

It was apparent she did not know the complete song. She moved her feet like a kathak dancer, and every now and then tapped her foot sharply like a Spanish bullfighter. But the audience couldn't have cared a damn. They were enjoying the show. Ajit suddenly had a vision of Rukmini and him opening a nightclub in Bombay, which would specialize in organizing performances to very special film and *mujra* numbers. Dancers would be selected from all over the country on the basis of their sex and sensual appeal. Prostitution would not be allowed, but the exclusive girls, those with enough meat on their boobs and buttocks, would be reserved for Ajit, the master. But by then he would have changed his name—to Amir Khusro or Sharang Dev, someone closely linked with music. Rukmini of course would be divorced and having her bit of fun as well, which he would get to watch.

'Start tapping the board, the lady needs some back up,' Ajit shouted at the DJ, who responded by filtering out some tunes on his system.

'They don't want your fucking music! They want something raw. Beat it with your hands, man.'

The DJ now saw in Ajit a man from his own clan. He responded to the manly challenge, and beat out a rhythm with his bare hands, mixing the *keherva* with an improvised beat of eight. Rukmini kept repeating the first two lines, improvising on the tune, alternating the soft and high emotions that she put into her voice.

'She's using the film song like a thumri—you fools, none of you would know this.'

Ajit laughed a superior laugh. Rukmini stopped soon after, asking the audience the resume their stupid routine.

'*Rekha zindabaad!*' Ajit shouted as he led Rukmini away. The boys with whom they had faught came forward to congratulate them. They told Ajit he and his woman could come to them in times of distress.

'Why would we need anything? Didn't she show you her I-card?' Ajit said triumphantly as he led her out.

It was drizzling when they retraced their steps to the estate gate.

The drizzle had stopped by the time they reached the Muslim

graveyard. It was an enclosed space on a large ground near the estate. The large estate building had encroached on the space around the graveyard, almost up to its walls, like an offending and arrogant neighbour.

'See how we're destroying our past? Muslims have a great history. It is evident from the way we have destroyed it in every part of the country.'

Rukmini sat on a stone bench in the compound. 'So you are pro-Muslim? I can't stand them.'

'Why?'

'I don't know. Why are you standing?'

Ajit sat on the bench. The road where the ghost in the white sari supposedly caused the fatal accidents was just in front, deserted but for a few stray dogs.

The compound was long, with arched pillars on three sides. The fourth side was broken in the middle, showing unmistakable signs of a demolition.

'Why did you make me dance like that?' Rukmini asked in mock anger.

'Why did you dance like that?' Ajit replied, nudging her with his shoulder.

'I don't know what got into me. I'm not that wild, you know.'

'Just a simple housewife. I know.'

Rukmini giggled and hit him playfully on the head.

'You are nuts. I can't get over the way you made me dance at Fire and Ice. And the way you enjoyed watching me swing!'

'Yes I did enjoy that. You see, I'm a voyeur.'

'What's that?'

'A man who loves watching others do it.'

'What, sex?'

'Yes—that as well.'

'Can you watch me do it with someone else?'

'I don't know, perhaps—is that shocking?'

Rukmini looked more bemused than shocked, as if such revelations belonged to a realm beyond her comprehension.

Ajit broke the silence that followed.

'Why is this place so deserted? I bet no one would come here even if we had wild and screaming sex.'

Rukmini got up abruptly. 'You're mad, and a sex maniac too. Let's go home.'

'But why did you bring me here?'

'I don't know, maybe I thought it would be a change after Fire and Ice.'

Ajit pulled her back. 'Okay, forget it. Tell me, what's all this about you getting abused by your brother-in-law in your childhood.'

Her hand was resting on his thigh. She pinched him hard.

'How do you know? Did you rummage through my drawer?'

'Yes. Was it a crime?'

'No. Men have always used me—from the brother-in-law to Sameer to my husband. Perhaps you'll do the same. But you have to understand that I co-operated too. I had no choice.'

Ajit looked at her without emotion.

'Your husband—I understand him.'

'How?'

'He has an evil streak but he's sharp—and patronizing—very much like the UP elite. He called me a tough Brahmin during our meeting at his friend's house. No one has ever comented on this side of my personality.'

Rukmini looked flustered.

'But forget all that,' he said, taking her hand. 'Do you think I've used you too?'

'No. That's why I want to talk. The minute I saw the condition of the drawers I knew you had found the letter. Why were you searching my table? I don't know. Why have you suddenly revealed the fact that you stole the letter? I don't know that either. And I don't want you to explain. The fact is that I want to share some things with you, things that I have never shared with anyone before. And I don't know why I want to tell you all that.'

Ajit felt unsettled by the seriousness of her tone. 'I will listen only if you promise you won't hate Muslims,' he joked.

Rukmini sounded genuinely surprised. 'I never said I hated them—you don't listen. It was pro-Muslims I was talking about, not Muslims.'

'Okay, okay, go on.'

'Whatever you read in the letter is true. The past came to haunt me during my relationship with Sameer as well. The brother-in-law wanted to sleep with me, to revive the practice of abusing me. He threatened to divorce my sister if I did not comply. My mother in fact was trying to persuade me tacitly; the bastard had even promised to marry me if I said yes. I mean, the whole situation was so bizarre—my family agreeing to my violation at the hands of a man I detested, all to save my sister's marriage. He wanted to rape me again, every day if he could.'

Ajit felt his cock rise. He imagined a traditional UP home, with the family preparing a daughter for sleaze. But then he felt revolted, and he held on to that sudden feeling of revulsion. He wanted to enter that setting and smash everyone to pieces; especially the old woman who would have calmly prepared tea as her daughter got fucked in a room with a low ceiling.

'I refused to comply. There were big scenes and I told Sameer about it. He refused to believe me. Then I told him about how I used to get fits as a child. How I was under psychiatric treatment. He sympathized at first but then became suspicious. He wanted to meet my doctor—but that would have meant exposing our relationship to my parents. Then one day he started accusing me of sleeping with other men. He also said I was actually sleeping with my *jeeja*, when the truth was I had turned my whole family against me by refusing to give in. He would beat my sister day and night. Yet I did not agree. But Sameer would not believe me. He said if it was true he would confront my *jeeja* and beat him up, but I stopped him from doing so and he found that strange and called me a lying slut.'

'Did Sameer make love while making you talk about what happened at home?'

'Yes. How did you guess?'

'Go on.'

'Well, this went on for quite some time. Then Sameer wanted me to meet a friend of his, a psychiatrist from Lucknow. I think he wanted to confirm whether I was really ill. The friend was supposed to come to Allahabad. He died before he could make the journey.'

The bait had worked. Ajit tried to mask his excitement, and asked calmly, 'What was this friend like? Did you ever see him?'

'No. I told you, he died before I met him.'

Ajit looked at her face for any signs of regret or guilt. She appeared forlorn and distant, as if reminiscing about an old acquaintance.

'But how did he die? I bet Sameer must have told you something about him.'

Rukmini was quiet for a moment. 'Well, Sameer—,' she began but couldn't go on. She lowered her eyes.

Ajit saw the tears. He had imagined the scene when

Rukmini might cry before him. He had expected a more restrained show, slow, silent sobs. But she was crying unashamedly, her body trembling violently.

He wanted to reach out to her, but he was so close to finally trapping her. It was time to remain tough.

'Well, Sameer what?'

Rukmini's voice quivered. Ajit was surprised to find it less shaky than he had expected.

'The friend was killed in a road accident. But some witnesses suggested that he was chased and stabbed by goons. The police found no evidence to suggest this.'

'Then?'

Rukmini looked at him as if she was pleading for support.

'Sameer accused me of murdering his friend. He said I had him killed to prevent him from finding out about my lies. Why would I do a thing like that? I loved him.'

With this she burst out crying again. Ajit had to place his hand over her shoulder. He suddenly felt compassionate towards this woman—was she really a victim of Sameer's delusion?

'But what were his reasons?'

'What reasons?'

'Why did he think you had his friend killed? I mean, what did he say could be your motive?'

'I don't know. He said I was so obsessed with him that I wouldn't let go—that I had invented the mental illness story to chain him down. Well, he was good looking and it's true that I was afraid of losing him. But that was actually the reason why I did not want to hide anything from him. But he never understood.'

Ajit was now genuinely perplexed.

'But the motive—what did he say was your motive?'

'He said that I was involved with the mafia and was evil.

That I had some fear about being found out and had asked one of my friends who got me into the call girl business to do the job.'

'What call girl business?'

'Sameer also suspected me of screwing clients in UP's three-star hotels. He thought I was a slut.'

They sat like that on the bench, talking sometimes, but mostly, him holding her, till morning. A coffee-and-cigarette vendor found them half-asleep—he advised them to scoot lest the police came and discovered them in that condition.

'There is a law—nowadays you can't do what you like in Bambai.'

He looked quite pleased to have said this. Ajit gave him a ten-rupee note before leaving.

11. Surprise

'Damn the phone—why won't she pick it up!' Ajit yelled as he banged the receiver down. He had tried calling Rukmini several times, but each time some servant had answered the phone, to say that Madam was out.

What had happened? Had her husband returned?

After his last meeting with Rukmini, Ajit had felt confused—a state he hated. He tried piecing together the puzzle that stared him in the face. He was amazed at the ease with which he had been able to get near his target. But he also felt unsettled by the turn of events. Having sex with Rukmini was great for his confidence. It was also the kind of experience he had dreamed of when he had started on the mission. But he knew he was nowhere close to finding out the truth about the shrink's murder. His brief was to nail Rukmini—but what if she was innocent?

He did not doubt Sameer's version of events. And yet, what was Rukmini's motive? Just to keep Sameer hooked? Were woman really so naively evil?

He phoned again—he had to get inside that house and conduct another search. And it could only be done now, when her husband was away. Rukmini had told him that Sunil Agnihotri would be back only the day after, probably later, and that they should meet today. But where was she?

More than eight hours had elapsed since they had parted on the way back from the graveyard. Ajit had slept for barely three hours before he was awakened by the cleaning woman. The paying guest arrangement at Colaba was turning out to be a pain. Sameer had paid for everything well in advance, but the Parsee landlord was a stickler for time and maintenance.

He dialled her number again and got the maid this time, who gave him the same response. The only option left was to pay Rukmini a visit. She had asked him specifically not to arrive unannounced.

It was time to violate certain norms.

•

'Memsaab is not here,' the guard said politely.

'You remember me? I was here yesterday. She had asked me to meet her today. When did she leave?'

'I don't know, sir. The other guard was on duty when she left. I was told to say that she's not in.'

Ajit felt something amiss. 'You were told? Who told you?'

The guard fumbled for a reply. Ajit deposited a hundred-rupee note in his pocket.

Darting a quick look at the house, the guard told Ajit to come after some time. Ajit spent the next half hour loitering around the area, eyeing a girl who was running a cyber café near the main road. She was wearing a lemon yellow shirt, and a blue scarf and skirt. From her plain features but attractive demeanour, Ajit guessed she was of Goan origin. He thought he'd go in and check his mail, when he saw a car, a blue Alto with tinted glasses, drive up to Rukmini's house and speed past it after slowing down. Then, instead of speeding away, it swerved from the middle of the road and reversed swiftly.

The guard saluted the occupant and waved at the gateman. The Alto was inside almost as soon as the gate opened; by the time Ajit reached the gate it had closed again.

The guard wasn't pleased to see him.

'I told you, sir, I will do what I can. Memsaab is not at home right now.'

'Well, why did the car go inside if there is no one in?'

'You ask too many questions; it is not my job to see why someone goes inside.'

'You could have stopped the car and asked a few questions before allowing it in. But you saluted, which means you knew who was inside. Now out with it—who was it?'

The guard pulled out the hundred-rupee note from his shirt pocket. 'Take the money, sir, I don't want it. Now please go away or I'll raise an alarm. I don't know you, I've never seen you here. Come back when the other guard is on duty.'

Ajit could see that the man was ready for a fight.

'You're from UP, aren't you?'

'Yes. What difference does that make?'

'I'm from UP too. Allahabad—no, originally from Lucknow.'

'I'm from Jaunpur,' the guard said flatly and was silent. The conversation wasn't going anywhere.

Rukmini's was a big house—there had to be a second entrance somewhere, he thought. The house was on a corner plot, and from the manner in which the compound curved back from the road, it appeared the house had a long back portion. There would probably be an entrance at the back.

'You're good at your job. I suppose I'll just have to come

back later,' Ajit said and walked off. At the corner, he turned right. He circled the house, and found an alley tucked away beyond Khar road.

Ajit remembered the alley he had entered in Darbhanga and what that had led to. He paused to survey the setting—it could well have been Narayanpur—Indian alleys, after all, are the same everywhere—but this one was broader and cleaner. There was a door at the far end—a dilapidated wooden structure—and it wasn't locked. Ajit found this strange, because back doors were usually secured first. This one was badly maintained as well. Ajit went up to the door and pushed it slightly; it did not give way. He then looked at the place where the knob should have been. Someone had tied a rope there to fasten the door.

Ajit untied the knot and the door sprang open.

He was filled with a sudden feeling of dread. He knew Rukmini was inside, and he had a strange feeling that she was in danger.

She stood there, her back to him, in the inner veranda, talking to someone. A pillar blocked Ajit's vision but he assumed that her co-conversationist was a man. He had thought he would encounter a back garden on entry, but the veranda came immediately into view, indicating that the door was part of an inner chamber that must have been demolished some time ago. Sunil Agnihotri had built his Bombay bungalow like an UP house.

The strip of land before the veranda was stacked with huge boxes bearing 'safe cargo' labels, as if freshly unloaded from a flight. Ajit hid behind them.

The man moved to Rukmini's left and Ajit saw his fingers brush the outer border of her sari. He saw the fair skin and the ring on the index finger. Veering to the left, from where he could see beyond the pillar, he froze.

The man moved his hand up her arm, to her shoulder, and then her neck. He was blonde, and had a stubble: the white man from Fire and Ice.

Ajit sank to his knees, as if he had been struck. His left leg shook involuntarily and he had to hold it to steady himself. He felt betrayed—she could have introduced him at the nightclub if he was just a friend. Why did she have to lie to him? Okay, they weren't lovers, but they had made love—and Rukmini had revealed her past to him. How could she entertain another man the morning after they had been together all night?

But it was no use getting personal. What had he expected, anyway? Ajit shook his head and reminded himself that he was here on a job. What was this meeting all about?

Moving forward he saw a room to his right where he could hide. If only he could get to it—then Rukmini turned and went inside the small corridor facing them. Assuming that this was his chance, Ajit stole into the room inches away from the white man's back.

Rukmini returned soon after. Ajit strained his ears to eavesdrop.

'Here's your water; you shouldn't have come here, you know.'

'Just wanted to see you when your husband was away. That's not such a big deal, is it?'

His accent was American; Ajit had initially thought him to be English or Irish.

The American spoke again.

'The thing about the Aurangabad deal—I have a few men working on it. I'm in close touch with the CBI and the blokes have given me a lot against your husband. Seems he's gay or something?'

Rukmini was quiet for a few seconds. When she answered, she sounded fierce.

'He is also cruel. His being gay wouldn't have been such a problem, but less than a week after our marriage I discovered someone else, a man, sleeping in my bed. He had a paunch and a strange name—Sitamgar. From that day Sitamgar was part of our life. I had to watch my husband having sex with the man several times. Later he brought over a woman, a famous South Indian actress—I had to watch as she made love to Sitamgar. I was beaten when I refused. Sunil enjoyed that as much as sex.'

The man put his hand on Rukmini's head. Ajit thought of the way she had cried the night before about the cruelty of another man.

'Don't cry, love,' the American said. 'I'll take care of you. I have a lot against your husband; I mean, we know he's opposed to us opening a FBI office in Bombay—thank god his party's not in power at the centre.'

'But he's a clever man,' Rukmini interrupted, 'and—'

'Don't worry about that. I'm still an old-fashioned American and I keep my word. I have information about your husband's involvement in the Aurangabad affair. He has propped up a leading Gujrati industrialist and minister as his front man, but the deal stinks. It involves draining water and impoverishing the countryside. It also means that the men involved will make a killing. Under the terms of the agreement the Maharashtra Government will have to buy electricity from Sunil and Bhigu Parikh at twice the normal price.'

Rukmini wiped the sweat that had appeared on her brow.

'If only he could be displaced from the show—that would teach him a lesson.'

'That's the way to go about it! We're interested in scuttling this deal too. One of our multinationals will do a cleaner job than these guys.'

Rukmini shook her head impatiently. 'I'm not interested in politics. I'm only interested in harming him. I've seen too many third-rate men justify what they do in the name of ideology. Ideology means nothing to me.'

The American laughed and ruffled her hair. 'Our interests coincide; remember how we met at a diplomat's party where I caught your husband's hand before he could slap you? He has been dying to find out about me since that day but has failed to get beyond my cover.'

'Well, he took it out on me. I suspect he was behind the attack the other day.'

The American stepped close to her; his nose brushed Rukmini's cheek.

'I am a spy. Your spy—we'll displace your husband together.'

He struck his forehead lightly against hers.

'I love this—*saar se saar thaakrana*,' he said in broken, American-accented Hindi. Rukmini brushed her lips against his. He dipped his head and nuzzled her neck. She pushed him away gently.

'I will not allow you to kiss my neck. You gave me a love mark the last time. I'm another man's wife, after all, and my husband is due tomorrow.'

'What about a light peck, eh?'

'Okay. But be quick.'

From barely two feet away Ajit saw the American kiss his previous night's beloved. But there was no time to feel angry.

The American left after the kiss and Rukmini went inside to order her servants around. Ajit could hear her husky voice berating them for not doing their job properly. He collided into a young boy as he came out of hiding.

'Who is this? Memsaab—there is someone hiding here!'

Slapping him hard across the face, Ajit ran for the door, tripping on the pile of boxes. They came down with a thud, attracting the attention of the household. The boy had caught his leg and was being dragged along. Ajit kicked him on the face with his free leg; the boy shrieked and let go. Ajit was reaching for the door when Rukmini came running, shouting for help. He was out into the alley and onto the main road as he saw a swarm of servants and guards emerging from the alley in hot pursuit.

In all likelihood she had not seen him. But it was a big risk he had taken. This kind of rashness was dangerous. But then he thought of the American and it filled him with rage. For one mad moment he felt a strong urge to turn back, barge into Rukmini's house, call her an ungrateful bitch and slap her in full view of the servants who had given chase. Then the rage passed, and he thought about what she had said about Sunil Agnihotri. Was he really such a rascal? Did he really beat her for sex?

It was likely, and yet, at the moment he couldn't think of her as a victim. She had never spoken to him about her involvement in the Aurangabad affair. And the American hadn't asked her about him, though he had seen her with him in Fire and Ice.

Ajit was now walking on the main Linking road, his hands behind his back, lost in thought. He did not notice the car stopping next to him. He walked on. The car was now behind him. He heard the loud slamming of car doors and turned around to find two men running in his direction. He thought they were pursuing a target beyond him; he turned back to see who they were chasing, when one of them pushed him to the ground.

The impact threw him against an auto rickshaw parked at the side. Both the men were hefty, moustached creatures and they charged at him. Soon Ajit was on the ground, being kicked mercilessly in the stomach. He shouted at them to stop, saying that they probably had the wrong guy. But they laughed and started abusing him. Ajit waited for the beating to stop so that he could reason with them—he got up and began to run when it did not.

He was too new to Bombay to know the directions, but took the next available side road, shouting all the while for help. The traffic was thin and Ajit realized he ought to have taken the main road—there was a better chance of his being saved there. Then he went for the nearest house, pleading with a man surveying his garden to let him in. The man looked at the hefty men behind and refused. Asking him to phone the police Ajit resumed his run. He reached the end of the road, saw the men closing in, and decided to tackle them head on.

'*Hat saale madarchod! H-a-a-t!*' he shouted as he brought one down with his charge. The other man however was quick to recover from the impact. Catching Ajit's free hand he pulled him towards him and banged him hard against a nearby pole. Ajit was stunned for a second; he began gasping for breath and saw the fallen man getting up, readying himself for the attack.

But now there was space for some talk.

'Who are you? Who has sent you? I have no quarrel with you. Why are you beating me?'

Ajit sounded strange to himself.

The men grinned and kept coming at him. Ajit picked up a brick lying near the road. His aim was faulty and missed one of the attackers by inches. Finding no other option, Ajit again slammed straight into the men.

But they were prepared for the manoeuvre and caught him before he could do any harm. Then one of them twisted his hand and pushed him to his knees while the other planted a kick in his face. They then smashed his face onto the road. He saw blood and was so overcome with fear that he began shouting at passersby to come to his aid.

His head was down again for the second smash when he felt the attackers relaxing their grip. He saw a pair of black shoes next to him and heard someone shouting at the men to get back. He looked up and saw a man in a blue suit waving a pistol.

12. A Way Too Long

The Honda was cruising past a slum area when Ajit spoke.
'Where did you get this suit made?'
'Ramson's Allahabad. I still trust the place.'
'Go back to Allahabad then. Get out of the city and your obsession with Rukmini. The woman is bad news.'

Sameer smiled and patted his knee. After saving Ajit from the goons he had hustled him into his car. They had driven fast in silence, past crowded traffic and seedy-looking localities before slowing down in front of the Mahim slums.

Ajit wanted to stop for a cold drink. Sameer asked him to hold his horses—they were close to NSCI, where Sameer said he was putting up for the present.

Haji Ali's mazaar again loomed into view. Ajit muttered the lines he had hummed before Rukmini.

Sameer's room was a variation of the rooms in old Nehruvian hotels, with separate beds, square tiles, an air-conditioner and a cupboard stacked with the menu and other information. Sameer bandaged Ajit's broken nose and told him not to ask any questions. He should be grateful that help had arrived in time.

'Have you been following me?'

'Yes and no. I've seen that no harm comes your way.'

'I was with Rukmini for quite some time yesterday. Did you see that as well?'

'No. What did you do?'

Ajit changed the topic. 'I have done what you asked me to do. Well, almost. Rukmini acknowledged her affair with you. But she says she didn't kill your friend. According to her it was an accident.'

Sameer was sitting on a wooden chair next to the bed on which Ajit sat. Ajit saw him clench his fists, then relax almost immediately. He got up.

'Will you eat something?'

'No,' Ajit answered nervously.

The call button was pressed and the waiter appeared almost immediately. Sameer ordered two plates of omelette and sandwiches. Ajit did not protest.

Sameer went back to his chair. He kept looking at a briefcase kept on the other bed.

After a while he looked straight at Ajit and said, 'You haven't asked why I'm staying in this fucking place.'

'Well, why are you?'

'I don't know. I've been in and out of Bombay. I'm into the film scene, actually. I've written a script which has the backing of some NRI producers.'

'Is the script based on Rukmini?'

Sameer did not like that. He got up again and began to shuffle around impatiently.

'Is it?'

Sameer ignored the question and asked instead, 'So you think Rukmini is innocent?'

'I never said that. But she's unwilling to admit she committed the murder.'

'What is your gut feeling?'

'I don't know, I—'

'You're lying. Something has happened between you and that bitch. I can see it in your eyes. She's entrapped you.'

Ajit felt slighted. 'No one's entrapped me. I've managed to get close to her—enough for her to confess quite a few things. I even found a letter in her drawer.'

Sameer grabbed his collar.

'Which letter? The one with the red ink?'

'Yes.'

'That one's a fake. The bitch made it up. She was trying to get back at me. I know her very well. She can put on any appearance at any point.'

Ajit nodded. 'Maybe you're right. She's also seeing an American.'

Sameer let go of his collar.

'I don't know whether you are aware of all that has happened here,' Ajit said. 'I began investigating a murder case, which took me to Bihar. There I got to know something about an Aurangabad deal. There's something sinister going on—some plot involving Sunil Agnihotri and Rukmini. I think she wants to get rid of him.'

'What?'

'I think Rukmini wants to get rid of her husband. She's friends with a white FBI agent. He's working secretly to further American interests in the Aurangabad power deal.'

Backing off from where he was standing Sameer lit a cigarette. Then remembering something he took out a joint from his pocket.

'Remember this? The thing that united us in the beginning.'

Ajit was grateful. 'I'd forgotten completely about the joint family in Bombay.'

'Why, you didn't dope?'

'No. Somehow I didn't get around to buying some. Besides, I haven't found the right company for it here.'

Sameer laughed and lit the joint. Ajit inhaled, feeling light and easy after a long time.

'This stuff is great. Got it in Bombay?'

Sameer didn't answer his question.

'So tell me more. What do you know about this FBI agent? I'm sure she's screwing him. And I can tell she's planning another murder.'

Ajit felt chilly. The air-conditioner was directed full blast at where they were sitting.

'Can we tone the AC down? It's really cold.'

Sameer fiddled with the AC board before turning to Ajit.

'So I was right after all. The woman is not only a murderess, she is big time into conspiracy as well.'

'But why would a FBI agent do things for an American company?'

Sameer waved his hand impatiently. 'Don't you know the Americans? Their secret service goes in the name of nation-to-nation cooperation and ends up helping American business interests. But to think that the Allahabadi bitch would hook a *firang*!'

Ajit inhaled again, enjoying the lightness it filled him with. 'Maybe the firang hooked her.'

'No, it was her job. I can smell her actions from afar, like I can smell the baby powder without a scent that she uses.'

Recalling his encounter with the Baby Johnson skin, Ajit smiled. Sameer was watching him, and he asked, 'You did it with her, didn't you?'

'Yes. I don't think I can lie to you.'

Turning his face away for a second, Sameer began fiddling again with the AC.

'How was it?'

'What?'

'The bang, damn you. How was the big bang?'

'It wasn't a big bang. A series of small potshots, actually, spread over a length of time.'

Sameer looked back at him. He was angry.

'So it was good,' he said quietly despite his anger.

'If I hadn't known about her, I would have married her. She has that kind of appeal.' Ajit spoke almost wistfully. He expected Sameer to explode at this but he slumped on the bed like a defeated man.

'She destroyed me. But I will destroy her yet. You know, women like her succeed by sowing discord between men like us. Never allow that to happen.'

He stood up and patted Ajit on the shoulder.

'I think the time for pursuing an old murder case is over. We should think about what is coming up. You should publish a story on all that you've found out about Rukmini. That would be sensational. No, wait—actually you should just lay off for a while. Let me handle things—I'll summon you when I need you.'

At first Ajit did not understand the implications of his statement. 'What do you mean? You want me off the job or something?'

'No. I mean just lie low for a while. There will be plenty of action later on.'

'But you've got to take me into confidence. I mean, I'm too far gone in this racket. The attack today might have been Rukmini's doing.'

Sameer winked. 'Yes boy, you're deep in it too. But don't worry, I'll get you out of the mess. Just keep looking over your shoulder. Who knows when she might strike next.'

Sameer came down the NSCI stairs to see Ajit off.

'Can I have your phone number?' Ajit asked. 'How will I contact you?'

'Don't worry—I'll contact you soon. Don't call here. You won't find me.'

The cab arrived, Sameer slapped him on the back and told him again to be careful, and then Ajit was off to Colaba.

This time the cab driver was a middle-aged, pot-bellied Sardarji who kept glancing furtively at the sea, as if it were something to be feared.

Ajit found a copy of *The Week* lying next to him on the back seat.

'Do you read this magazine?' Ajit asked as he leafed through the pages.

'What do I have to do with *Angrezi* magazines? Some customer must have left it there.'

Ajit went straight to the astrology column. The prediction for his zodiac sign said something about dangers emerging from unknown sources—and the failure of an old enterprise.

'Bloody astrologers—always prejudiced against water signs,' Ajit mumbled and flung the magazine away.

The cab was speeding past the Haji Ali juice corner when the Sardarji slowed down his vehicle. A motorcycle horn was disturbing him. A little while later Ajit saw a mobike draw level with the rear window to his left. The driver, wearing a black helmet, tried peeping into the cab; he had a pillion, also with his face concealed behind a black helmet.

Drawing in front of the cab, the mobike stopped, forcing the Sardarji to swerve sharply to the right. He got out of his car cursing furiously as only a Punjabi can. The mobike driver had taken his helmet off.

'Arre don't be angry, Sardar. I forgot my magazine in your taxi.'

The voice was familiar. Ajit stepped out to greet Ashok Singh.

The magazine lay between them as the Sardarji drove them sullenly through heavy traffic. Ashok Singh had given the mobike keys to the pillion rider and asked him to ride on.

'Surprising you like this was too much of a temptation, I saw you in the taxi and couldn't be bothered with propriety.'

Ajit grinned. The Bhumihaar was leaner and meaner—he was sporting a thin line of moustache and his hair was drawn back in style.

'Where should I go now?' Sardarji asked wearily.

'Take us to the Irani restaurant in Colaba. The one that serves those great biryanis.'

'Biryani?' Ashok Singh spoke in a sceptical tone, 'I eat biryani at Nooranis.'

'Oh you will forget Noorani-voorani after you've eaten at this place.'

Ajit was pleased to have bumped into Ashok Singh. He was reassured by his presence—he had started feeling uneasy after the discussion with Sameer.

He knew that in one of the deep pockets of his smart pants, Ashok Singh carried a weapon.

The cab stopped on a Colaba road, and the Sardarji appeared glad to see the occupants get out.

'There's no mutton biyrani here, sir,' intoned the man in the Muslim skull-cap. 'We serve it only after six o'clock.'

Ajit looked at his watch. It was only five.

'Can't you prepare it an hour before?' he asked exasperatedly.

'We can try, sir—what would you like to have in the meantime?'

'Chicken biryani will do.' After the man had left, Ajit

turned to Ashok. 'So what brings you to Bombay?'

'Maybe I am here to catch you in the Jha case.'

Ajit laughed nervously. Ashok did not press the issue.

'Actually I'm here on a mission. I will tell you if you promise not to talk.'

Ajit promised not to talk.

'And that's not all. After I tell you this you will have to remain in touch with me throughout the time I'm here.'

Ajit had no objection to that.

'Well, remember the Auranagabad affair? There is big trouble on that front. Rukmini Agnihotri is laying the foundation stone of the project next week in a place called Dhursal, just outside the city. The news has been kept from the press because Sunil wanted to confirm something. I suspect it concerns his wife.'

Ajit found his pulse racing.

'What does he suspect?' he asked as casually as he could.

'I don't know, but I heard Sunil talking to this film actress he knows who has been after him for a share in the deal. She knows you—I think she's your friend's sister. Anyway, he told this actress that you know something about his wife.'

'This is too fantastic—which actress is this?'

'Saumya—she's Rishikesh Jhadav's sister.'

Ajit almost fell off his chair.

'Sunil wanted me to fix this woman. So I went to her house. She was having an argument with her brother—he was accusing her of compromising her dignity in the profession, and she was screaming back and crying. Sunil's aide was also there. I beat her up before warning her to stay out of Sunil's life.'

Ashok was eating as he spoke. Ajit had lost his appetite.

'What did you do to her?'

'Nothing. Gave her two slaps before plunging a figure in her pussy. It tasted good.' Ashok was licking his fingers covered with the curry shorba served along with the chicken biryani. 'These heroines think too much of themselves. English-speaking touch-me-nots. They all fall for power and money—never mind if it speaks English or not.'

By now the mutton biryani had arrived. Ashok Singh was praising Ajit to the skies for having brought him to the place. Ajit was preoccupied, thinking of Rukmini telling the American about the actress she was forced to watch her husband having sex with . . . and Rishikesh eyeing the Saumya poster and telling Sunil's aide that he should learn to respect women . . .

Ashok Singh had taken out his pistol and was showing it to the Muslim, who was staring back at him with pride and meloncholy in his working-class eyes.

'And another thing,' Ashok spoke suddenly. The Muslim had left.

'I want to tell you who killed Mrs Jha. It was not one of her lovers from Bihar. It was a man Sunil had sent from Bombay to stay with me in Darbhanga. A nice man—though a bit cracked in the head. Some Sameer Sharma from Allahabad.'

13. You Trusted Me

Ajit hoped he had recovered swiftly and easily enough for Ashok not to have noticed anything.

'Why did he kill her?' he asked.

The Bhumihaar laughed. 'He was obsessed. Maybe the bullet was meant for you. I don't know.'

'He killed her just like that? Just because he was obsessed?'

'No, stupid. I think he got scared or something. You see, he was the one who killed Sudha and her aunt.'

Ajit looked at him—did he know he was there? Almost without thinking he said, 'I was with her when she died. Sudha's aunt, I mean.' Ashok looked up at him and smiled but said nothing. He went back to his biryani.

The place was now filling up with men of working-class origin. Most of them seemed to belong to UP and Bihar. Ashok Singh appeared pleased by this fact.

'People of our area,' he said, looking around in a patronising manner, 'they are everywhere in Bombay. We own the city.'

Ajit wasn't amused. 'Yes, but we don't have our own mafia.'

Ashok stopped and looked at him.

'What do you mean? Most of Dawood Bhai's men are from Azamgarh.'

'Yes. But there's no big don from UP operating here.'

'You forget Sunil Agnihotri. He's a minister in the Maharashtra governement and has his hands deep in a project in which God knows what international politics is at play.'

Ajit had not touched his mutton biryani. 'Is Sameer connected with Sunil Agnihotri?' he asked.

Ashok Singh was then in the middle of tearing off meat from a fat bone with his teeth.

'Of course,' he mumbled. 'And I think he was involved with Sudha.'

'How do you know this?'

'I'm sure of it. I think Sunil and Sameer had a fall-out over Sudha's murder. That is why he was packed off to Bihar. I was supposed to keep a close watch on him, but the bastard gave me the slip and got involved with one of my men's wife. And then he killed her, as I told you.'

Ajit felt his head reeling. He closed his eyes and rubbed his forehead.

'Are you okay? Do you know this Sameer fellow?' Ashok Singh asked, eyeing him keenly.

'No. Does he work for Sunil or does he just know him?'

'I don't know. Never heard of him before he landed up in Bihar. But he has a way with women. The sluts just can't keep themselves away from him.'

Then Ajit felt like eating. He ordered two more plates after finishing the first, beating the Bhumihaar in the competition.

'You can't beat a Brahmin when it comes to eating,' he said and the Bhumihaar laughed.

But Ajit's head was too full of thoughts.

'Okay, so goodbye then—till we meet again. I have your address, I'll be in touch.'

Ajit suggested they go back to his room for some post-biryani booze, but Ashok excused himself, saying he had an urgent meeting at Sunil's house.

'I bet Sameer is going to be there too. Do you want to meet him?' There was mischief on the Bhumihaar's face as he spoke.

'No. I know what you're thinking—how it would be meeting the man who had screwed the same woman you were screwing. Well, believe me there would be nothing new in the experience. I have done it all before, maybe with the same man.'

Ashok Singh looked puzzled. 'What? Well, it doesn't matter—you and your riddles. You could have been something if you were not so fucked up in the head.'

The Muslim was now at the door of the café with the cab Ashok had ordered. He was mighty pleased with his guests who had waited for more then an hour for his mutton biryani and then devoured six plates of it.

'Come again. Try our custard the next time.'

•

The road Ajit was walking on was under construction and he had to cover his nose with his hand because of the fumes and the dust. He had not taken a taxi after Ashok's departure; he just wanted to drift for a while before taking a decision.

The obvious question concerned Sameer—was he really the mysterious man responsible for the death of the three women? How exactly was he connected with Sunil?

And why was everyone, including Sameer, interested in the American angle?

The streets were being bored with merciless precision.

The heavy machine sound tore into his ears as he passed a test point. Everywhere people were on to some job or the other, in the unquestioning, active Bombay style.

The same guard stood outside the house, looking nervously up and down the road. He was wearing a plain shirt instead of the customary uniform of his agency.

'These bloody security agencies—they will replace the police one day,' Ajit muttered as he ducked behind an autorickshaw to avoid the guard's gaze. He had made the journey from Colaba to Khar in a taxi, getting off at Linking road and walking the rest of the distance. The point was to move undetected towards the back of the house, to the rickety door.

He now knew what he wanted—see Sameer and Sunil together; find out what they were up to. Following Ashok Singh's revelations, Ajit had begun to feel small and stupid, as if he had been used, and was now being edged out from a big drama. It was not a nice feeling—he felt offended and challenged.

Operation hoodwink was successful; the guard did not see him enter the lane. Walking past the garbage dumps and drains, he reached the back entrance. They still hadn't bothered to secure the door. This time there wasn't even the rope holding it shut.

Inside, the boxes were still there, but there was no one hiding behind the pillar this time. The room where he had hidden was also empty.

From his previous encounter Ajit knew that the kitchen was close to that room. That meant servants, and the possibility of being spotted. He was familiar with the part of the house that had the study. The study led to Rukmini's bedroom, and then to the drawing room.

Ajit was thinking up a post-discovery excuse—just in case—when he saw a female servant emerge from the kitchen with an ice-box. He immediately slipped into the room ahead. She was about to go inside when she was stopped by a male counterpart.

'You're only carrying ice? Sahib has also asked for *moong falees* and *pyaaz*.'

The maid appeared hesitant. 'I don't like going in there when these men are around. The one with the brown hair looks at me with strange eyes.'

The man laughed.

So Ashok Singh was in there.

Ajit glued his ear to the door. The maid was now almost whispering to the male.

'That woman is also here. You know what happens when she appears. Memsaab goes out.'

Rukmini was out—who was this woman they were talking about?

'But that man, what's his name, the one with the square jaws—he's nice. He always says thank you.'

Square jaws? Sameer?

'Now let me go. Sunil Sahib will get angry if I'm late. He doesn't drink his whisky without ice.'

Ajit heard the male chuckle.

Ajit waited a while before peering out. They had both left. The coast was clear. He had to find the study.

Just ouside the room he found a narrow passageway. Rukmini had brought him to the study from the front; calculating the distance from the opposite end, he guessed that the room almost at the end of the passage would be the study.

The door was open. He went inside and took the risk of feeling around for a switch. The bulb came on and he saw the books lined exactly as he had left them.

Anti-Duhring was still on the floor.

There were voices coming from the adjoining room. Ajit was right, it was the bedroom. He moved towards the door.

Ultimately he found what he was looking for. The interconnecting door was closed but he had noticed a crack, the last time he was in this room, all along the side of the door where it met the wall. He put his eye to it. It seemed as if the crack had been deliberately designed: through it, much of what went on in the centre of the other room could be seen clearly.

A woman in a green miniskirt stood facing the bed, supporting her weight with her buttocks against the edge of a partially visible table. Sunil was standing a couple of feet away, near Rukmini's drawer, dressed in a white sports jacket, arms folded across his chest. Ashok Singh sat on a stool, a pistol in hand, looking satisfied, like someone who has just had a hearty meal. And to his side, looking nonchalant and well-groomed, stood Sameer, sporting the same blue, fake Ramson suit that Ajit had seen him in earlier in the day.

There were two whisky bottles and some glasses on the part of the table that was visible. But no one appeared tipsy.

Sameer took a step forward and put his hands in his trouser pocket.

'Turn around,' he commanded, 'I want to see your arse.'

The woman turned. Ajit saw her face: it was Saumya.

Sameer went up to her and patted her arse, then lifted her skirt up and put a finger in her underwear.

'Never had a woman from behind. Will you allow me to do it with her?' he asked.

'Be gentle,' Sunil drawled, then added with a chuckle, 'she's a nice girl.'

Sameer looked at Sunil, as if to make sure it was okay, before pulling her towards him. 'She may be nice on screen, sporting saris and playing a Sati Savitri, but she's one horny woman.'

Suddenly he softened his tone.

'Now tell them how you acted when I found you here in this very bedroom by accident. Remember that time? Come on, let them hear it.'

Ashok Singh leaned forward to listen, and put his pistol on the ground, between his feet. Sunil too shifted slightly in anticipation.

'You will never believe this, Sunil,' Saumya began. 'This was the time after I had given a statement that I had no contacts with the mafia. But I was seeing Dawood Bhai through Ramendra Tiwari—this was before the Bombay blasts, when you too were quite close to him, and he had instructed me to pass on a message to you. So I came visiting—aware that Rukmini wasn't in—and walked into this bedroom, and here I find not you but this handsome man,' she said, putting a hand on Sameer's chest. Sameer smirked. 'And he was staring at me. I wondered who he was and what he was doing here? He told me he was Azeem bhai, Dawood's close associate, and was here to talk to you. He came on strong, saying that he wanted to screw me—Dawood bhai would be angry if I refused. I sensed the absurdity but there was something in his tone which made me play along. I was a slave to his instructions—he started off with the usual, remove your top, take off your jeans kind of thing—I was wearing new Levis jeans, by the way. Before I knew it I was naked. He then wanted to tie me up. I had to attend a shooting where I was supposed to cry over my husband's death, dressed in white and looking chaste and devastated ... but I don't know what came over me; I agreed. He tied me to the bed post and started giving more intsructions—"Wriggle your arse, bite your lips, roll your tongue, think that you are a slut, beg me to take you." I was so horny by then that I actually wanted to be his slave. He slapped my arse cheeks. I asked for more, I had not done it in the arse but I could have taken anything at that point. And you know what he does? He unties my hands and orders me to leave. I was so exhausted that I did not even call him a bastard.'

Her hands were on Sameer's cheeks.

'You want to take me as your slave now?'

This is the stuff I have dreamed of, Ajit thought. A helpless woman forced into sex by powerful men—and she enjoys it.

Sameer bent his face over Saumya's.

'In front of these men? You won't say no?'

'No, I won't.'

Sameer was about to speak when Sunil intervened.

'Be patient, Sameer. We have to talk first. Remember this is supposed to be our reconciliation.'

Sameer's eyes were burning like those of a distracted man and his voice was hoarse when he answered. 'Let's reconcile by putting our cocks in the same woman—you take her pussy and I'll take the arse. Ashok can join in later if he likes. She's my slave tonight.'

Sunil looked at Saumya and shrugged. Ashok picked up the pistol from the ground and put it on his cock.

Separating her legs gently, Sameer asked Ashok Singh to feel her up. He agreed, stopping in between to ask her in chaste Hindi if it felt all right.

Sunil laughed. 'She won't understand your politeness. This is sex, not Lucknavi etiquette, you fool.'

Saumya giggled—Ashok's hands were touching her pussy.

'Put it in, Ashok, make her scream.'

Yes do it, Ajit whispered behind the door. Even as he said it, he felt he shouldn't be here, this was not what he had come here for, but he knew he wouldn't leave now; there was no use trying.

Ashok followed Sameer's instructions, but Saumya did not scream. Without moving from his place, Sameer ordered Ashok to tie her face down between two chairs.

Grabbing her by the hair Ashok took her to the middle of the room.

'Where should I place her?'

'Between the chairs—wrench her arms behind her and tie her fucking hands to the chairs! What's wrong with you, didn't you hear me?'

'I did, but it will be difficult to sustain it like this for long. What if she falls forward with the impact?'

'She won't fall. She's hardy.'

'But what if she does—we'll be interrupted if that happens.'

'Shut your stupid mouth—okay, if that's a problem one of us will put a cock in her mouth.'

'Will the two of you stop talking and take her clothes off? I haven't seen her body for ages. She has slimmed down. I saw her do the *Dil dhak dhak kare* song and thought—my god, the next time I lay the bitch I'm going to really make her slap her thighs around my face.'

Sameer stopped and looked at Sunil. 'You like getting your face slapped with thighs too? Your wife's good at it, you know.'

Ashok shot them both an alarmed look. Sunil had taken out a small pen-knife.

'Don't you dare talk about my wife like that,' Sunil barked, pointing the toy at Sameer's neck.

'What is this, why're you putting up a fucking show? You know she was a slut.'

'No, I *don't* know. It was *your* job to furnish proof. That is why I hunted you down from obscurity. I only knew about her obsession with a man called Sameer. You were a drug addict, a gone case when I found you running errands for the mafia in the Gonda-Ghazipur belt.'

Sameer pushed the knife away. 'Your wife brought me to this. I loved her. She lied to me. She was unfaithful. Then she killed my friend.'

Sunil looked at him without a trace of emotion. 'So you keep telling me. Actually at first I didn't even care what she was. I brought her here thinking she would co-operate like a traditional housewife. But she started objecting to my mafia links. I mean, this was before the blasts—Dawood Bhai was king. Then she refused to participate in my sex life. I didn't really want to expose her to my sordid side, but she caught me with Sitamgar one day, and you know how he is—like a child. He began insisting on seeing her pussy—I told him, she's your bhabhi, you are not supposed to do things with her. But he wouldn't listen. So I said okay. I had to beat her into doing it—not much, just knocked her around a few times. After the first couple of times she began complying, but then started resisting me in other matters. And then one day I brought Saumya over and fucked her in her bed. She made a scene, so I made it a point to make her watch, till she offered that I could do what I liked but she should be told in advance so she could leave the house. I was bored with her anyway, and I don't really like violence, so I said okay.'

Behind the door Ajit had already given up trying to get a hang of the situation. The constant to and fro of bodies and all the disjointed talk had had an exasperating effect. He had a raging hard on in anticipation of something perversely unique—but now he felt the reality would not measure up to any fantasy.

He found himself thinking of Sitamgar drooling over Rukmini's pussy.

Sunil was still speaking.

'But she was harbouring resentments all along, even when I let her do as she pleased. I should have guessed, but I thought she was weak and would give in. But I forgot she was a Brahminee—they are hard nuts to crack. She was scheming against me all along. I really panicked when I found out about her American connection. She was getting into the big game now.'

He turned towards Sameer. Ashok Singh had relaxed his grip on Saumya.

'Then I found you. You told me about her sordid past. I didn't believe it first but then I thought, what the hell—I needed to somehow scare her into submission, do something about this American connection. Then you came up with the idea of using this man Ajit—how did you find him?'

'Simple. I knew a friend, Shekhar Tiwari, in college. He used to tell me about this nephew of his who was a Marxist with a sexually disturbed past. He seemed so much like me. So I hunted him down and persuaded him to trail Rukmini. We could have laid a perfect trap but—'

Sunil slapped Sameer hard, sending him sprawling to the bed.

'But before Ajit arrived you went and had a fucking affair with Sudha! Why couldn't you just keep your dick in your pants for once? We could have nailed Rukmini—you could have had your revenge and that stupid portrait of yours and the mouth organ back. What was this fucking thing about the mouth organ anyway?'

Ajit racked his brains. Yes, what was it—what was it? Had Rukmini told him about it?

'That fucking thing contains my talent. I used to play the organ. She asked for it one day. I wanted it back after my friend's death. She then produced a new organ, an exact replica. She still has the real one. I want it back after I am through with her. I could have been a musician, you know!'

Ajit could see that Sameer was crying.

Sunil hugged him. 'I don't know what to do with you. I wouldn't have minded your affair with Sudha, but then you got emotional. And then you killed her.'

'I didn't,' Sameer shouted. Sunil gestured him to stop doing that.

The two men were facing each other squarely.

'I did not kill her. Yes we were arguing in the garage that night. And I did slap her once or twice. But that's all. I went outside to pee and the next thing I find when I return is that she's dead. Either she killed herself or someone did her in.'

Ashok was playing with Saumya's boobs; he stopped and looked at Sameer with some curiosity.

Sunil was livid. 'Who did her in? Why didn't you tell me about this before?'

'I tried but you wouldn't listen. I was too distraught. Sudha was my second love.'

'Don't act. You even got involved with Jha's wife in Darbhanga.'

'So what? I needed some diversion. I know what you think, but I did not kill her. I was perturbed to find Ajit there that night but the bullet wasn't fired by me. I swear to God it wasn't fired by me.'

Sunil looked at Ashok Singh.

'I think he's right,' Ashok said. 'My men tell me there was a third man there that night.'

A third man? Ajit could not believe his ears.

'What third man?' Sunil was almost beside himself with apprehension. 'What the fuck is happening?'

He turned to Sameer. 'And Sudha's aunt?'

'I didn't kill her. I think I was boarding the train to Darbhanga at that time.'

Sunil's hands were on his forehead as he sat on the bed.

'Ashok Singh, what the *fuck* is this? Why didn't you tell me about this third-man angle?'

'I was going to; just needed time.' Ashok Singh was now caressing Saumya's hair.

'So I'm in a real soup now. I'm sure it's that bitch who's behind all this. The wife who is going to lay the foundation stone of my dream project is working behind my back to do me in. We have to do something about it.'

'I'm sure we can still do something,' Ashok Singh said absent-mindedly and kissed Saumya on the cheeks.

Suddenly Sameer pushed Ashok away, grabbed Saumya by the hand and led her towards the chairs. From his trouser pocket he pulled out a rope—Ajit recognized it as the rope he had found on the back door the previous day.

Saumya winced when he pushed her down, pulled her arms back and tied them to the chairs.

'Don't mind the inconvenience, baby. We know you'll enjoy this.'

When he'd finished tying her up, he ordered her to part her legs. She did, and he yanked her panties down.

Ajit noticed that she wasn't wearing shoes.

Sameer pulled her skirt over her buttocks. He then asked Ashok Singh to strip. The Bhumihaar obeyed and Ajit saw his bare arse for the second time in his life.

Sunil had already stripped. He had refused to take off his vest, saying that he was too embarrassed about his paunch.

Ashok stood facing Saumya, trying to work his short, thick cock into her mouth. Sunil went behind her and began to caress the back of her thighs.

'Don't waste time, ' Sameer said impatiently, 'give it to her. Put it in her pussy from behind.'

Sunil tried thrusting in. He failed in the first attempt. Sameer went up and held her by the hips for him.

'Try again,' he said, 'here.'

The minister did his bidding like a schoolboy. He began the motions even before he was properly in. Sameer had to tell him to raise himself on his toes. Finally the minister got it right.

He grunted as he began to clobber her pussy. Ashok Singh had his hands on the back of her neck and kept telling her this was the first time a film actress was sucking him off.

This went on for about half an hour. Both Sunil and Ashok came and then exchanged positions. The second time they were fiercer, even violent, but Saumya did not protest. Ajit wondered if she was enjoying it. Or was she merely feeling numb?

Someone had told him, long ago, that for a woman having sex with men she did not like was not a big deal. How could women be so impersonal about sex, he had thought.

After Sunil and Ashok were through with her, Saumya only complained about being kept in a painful position for so long, though she was quite a sight, and could barely stand straight.

'The fun is over,' she said, adjusting her skirt.

'No it isn't,' Sameer said evenly. 'There's more.'

She looked at him, alarmed, and made a dash for the door. Sameer lunged forward and caught her in mid flight. He pulled her to the table and ordered her to bend over.

'Now her arse will be auctioned. Come on, make your bids.'

Either because of exhaustion, or as part of some compromise, Saumya did not protest. Ashok and Sunil took the bid upto ten thousand bucks and then Sunil stopped.

'You take her,' he said to Sameer. 'We've enjoyed enough.'

Sameer unzipped his trousers.

'Scream for me, baby,' he hollered and went at her.

This is it, Ajit said to himself—the best part. He felt a rush of blood rise to his head.

Saumya shouted at Sameer to let her go. But Sameer wouldn't listen.

Saumya was now crying and pleading with him to stop.

Almost despite himself, Ajit began to feel sorry for her. And then he heard the main door of the room open and saw Rishikesh walk in, followed by two servants.

The servants froze at the sight of their master naked. Rishikesh pushed Sameer away from his sister. He then began helping her to her feet. Pulling down her dress he slapped her hard on the face.

'How could you do this? I have been following you all around, you—'

Ashok Singh was over him before he could finish. The naked Bhumihaar threw him on the bed; soon Sunil was on him, punching his face and abusing profusely.

'You motherfucker—how did you get inside? Love your sister, *gaandu*? I will fuck her in front of you!' He smashed his fist maniacally into Rishikesh's face.

Saumya, who had been silent till now, saw the blood pour out of her brother's mouth and pulled Sunil away.

'You shouldn't have come here, Rishikesh. Now get up and go back. This is not your scene, you won't understand.'

Ajit felt like breaking down the door and hitting her for

that, before saving his friend.

Sunil pushed her away.

'You go back to Sameer. I'll teach this brat a lesson he won't forget.'

Rishikesh spat in his face. 'You'll teach me a lesson, you pimp? Your activities will be all over the papers tomorrow. Then let's see who wins.'

Sunil sniggered, and a chill went down Ajit's spine at the pure cruelty in his voice. 'You will expose your sister as a whore? Well, I gather you can do that. But I will leave you in a state where you won't be able to show your face to anyone, let alone publish something against me. Come on, Ashok let's fuck this bastard.'

Ashok was standing beside the bed. He planted two blows straight on Rishikesh's face till he blacked out. Saumya remained quiet as he pulled the jeans off Rishikesh and turned him on his stomach.

'Lift his arse up, how am I going to put it in?' Sunil snapped.

Ashok was propping Rishikesh up when Saumya spoke.

'That's enough. You can leave him alone. He must have got information about my being here from my mother. Forgive him; he's only a brother, he means no harm, he couldn't understand it, that's all. Let him go!'

But Sunil was already pushing his dick in.

'The bastard is strong. He's resisting.'

Ashok landed another blow on Rishikesh's head. Sunil paused briefly before giving a violent thrust.

Her brother's screams made Saumya lunge towards Sunil. She took Ashok's fist full in the face.

'This slut need's to be taught a lesson too. Hold her Sameer, she hasn't had enough of a Bhumihaar's dick.'

Pulling her away from Sunil, Sameer pushed her head to

the ground. Ashok was behind her in no time to repeat what Sameer had done, only more violently.

Saumya screamed again, drowning Rishikesh's desperate pleas to be spared. Sunil and Ashok looked at each other, and Ajit thought he saw them wink. Through it all, Sameer stood back and watched, playing with his balls.

In the end Saumya and Rishikesh were curled up in bed, their arms around each other. There was blood on the sheets.

Ajit faught down a wave of nausea. He felt paralyzed, unable to move from his spot behind the door. He hadn't been able to save his friend.

He watched the three men get dressed. Ashok Singh casually cracked a joke about Sardars and sex. Sunil and Sameer guffawed.

As he zipped up, Sameer told Saumya to clean up the mess before she left.

Ajit felt a knot of fear tighten in his stomach: he would end up like Sameer some day.

Sunil turned to Sameer.

'Kill Rukmini in Dhursal. My men and Bhiku's men will be around. Some motherfucking drama!'

Ajit looked at Ashok. He was smiling.

14. The Minister's Wife

Derek listened to Ajit with impatience while chewing his cigar.

Ajit repeated his story. Derek gestured as if he understood.

'It sounds fantastic. I tell you, the whole idea is tremendous. A multinational fighting for a project, a minister's wife caught in the middle, sex, murder—everything. But you see, we don't deal with all this anymore. We are a conservative newspaper—bring us something on religion, something quirky on conventional politics, you understand?'

Ajit was exasperated. 'Don't joke, Derek. You know this is sensational. Why are you behaving like this?'

Placing the cigar on the table Derek took out some old TOI issues.

'I have work to do, man. Now, if you can get me a witness—Rukmini Devi herself—then I might listen. Why should I waste my time with you, anyway? I don't even know how you were appointed.'

Ajit stared at the bearded Goan. He knew the end of this conversation was at hand.

'Men with beards are suspect,' he muttered under his breath.

'What? What did you say?'

'Nothing. You are probably right. I'll try and make someone talk.'

'By the way, I haven't seen Rishikesh around. Sound him off if you see him. He has to do some work for me.'

'I haven't seen him either,' Ajit replied and walked out.

•

The VT station was teeming, as usual, outside the *Times* office. It's big, black passageways reminded Ajit of the pontoon bridges that were laid out during the Kumbh and Magh Melas in Allahabad.

He had gone straight to Colaba after stealing out of Rukmini's house. His mind had cleared after two glasses of rum and coke.

He was finding it difficult to take sides in the Rukmini-Sunil war. Then he thought of doing something for Rishikesh.

He had told Derek everything save the Saumya angle.

He was standing on the Victoria crossing, not knowing where to go, when a Honda stopped at the non-U-turn crossing just ahead. The traffic inspector saw the violation but said nothing.

The American stepped out of the car and summoned Ajit. He went ahead, as if drawn by an unseen force.

'Hi.'

'Hi. I was thinking about you.'

'You are lying. Get inside. The effect of an expensive car is only going to last a few seconds on the traffic cop.'

Rukmini was in the back seat, dressed in a blue chiffon sari. For the first time since they'd met, she greeted Ajit with a 'Hi'. The American got into the front seat, beside the Indian chauffer.

Ajit noticed that Rukmini was also wearing black goggles.

She took them off and smiled.

'A gift from my friend. You had a pretty rough yesterday, I gather.'

Ajit was sizing up the woman he had made love to.

'Where were you? I called and there was no answer. That's not fair.'

Rukmini smiled. 'You came to my house and saw us talking. I also know what happened next. You see, I have my own ways of getting information about what's happening in the house.'

'So you know about Sameer and me?'

'I had a vague idea. But I'm still not entirely sure. He put you on to me, is that it?'

'Yes. But there's more.'

'What?'

'It was Sunil who actually asked Sameer to put me on to you. He wants to kill you. A man called Ashok Singh will do the job in Dhursal.'

The American had turned around briefly. Rukmini put her goggles back on.

'I know Ashok Singh. He's my husband's man.'

Ajit remained quiet. He did not know why he had blurted out the things he knew. Nor why he had told her that Ashok Singh would kill her, though he'd clearly heard Sunil charge Sameer with the job.

'So how was it last night? Fun?'

'It wasn't as casual as you think. It was brutal.'

'So now you think my husband is a brute? And that Sameer is mad?'

Bombay's slums were whizzing past, the squalor one endless blur.

'Did you really kill his friend? Come on, you can tell me now.'

Rukmini looked at him. She had never seemed more mysterious.

'I did not. This is all a figment of Sameer's imagination. He was very talented. But wrong choices did him in. He then began expending his energies in make-believe. And then he turned on me.'

'Why should I believe you?'

Rukmini removed her goggles. Her eyes were full of tears.

'Because a woman may lie, but her tears speak the truth. I have paid dearly for trusting men. Sameer and Sunil, the two men in my life, both betrayed me.'

'What are you going to do now?'

'Do you trust me?'

'I'm not sure.'

Rukmini began playing with her goggles.

'You know where I met Singleton? At a diplomatic function where I had gone with my husband; he seemed so different from the men I knew. He did not come on strong, the way Sameer did, and yet made it known that he was interested in me. He was very good at showering the usual kind of affection and yet he never imposed conditions.'

'Did you have an affair with him?'

'Yes. Are you jealous?'

'A little.'

Rukmini patted Ajit on the thigh.

'Don't worry. You have helped me and you will get your reward. But I think you ought to go back to Lucknow. Come back when this business is over.'

'What do you mean go back?' Ajit protested. 'We are talking murder here. I have already spelled out the details to Derek at TOI. He's waiting for a witness. If you talk to him the whole thing will be out in the press. Those men won't move against you then.'

The American asked the chauffer to stop the car near a clean middle-class locality. Saying that he would see Rukmini later in the evening, he thanked Ajit for helping his friend and disappeared. His demeanour was brazen but not offensive; he was without the cautious, mildly disdainful, extra-courteous air normally associated with Anglo-Saxon guests in India.

Rukmini watched him walk into an alley just ahead, then asked the driver to drive to Tardeo. 'A friend of mine has a flat nearby, in Tardeo. Let's go there. I think we need to talk.'

Two of the rooms in the flat were locked. The drawing room was full of dusty furniture. There were also a few unused computers lying around.

'What does this person do? Software dealing?'

'No, he's a consultant. Brokers deals between politicians and industrialists.'

Ajit picked up an old copy of *India Today*, showcasing the findings of the controversial JB Commission on a senior central minister's assassination.

Rukmini had gone to the kitchen to boil water. She saw him looking at the cover when she returned.

'Old news, but it has an interesting angle.'

'What?'

'This report you're looking at. The flat's owner, my friend, knew JB.'

'And?'

'And one day he went over to his place. You see, JB was in the thick of the controversy then. But my friend, an industrialist who flirts with politics, had helped him through rough times. So you know what JB did?'

Ajit waited for her to go on.

'He opened the report before him. He told him he

wanted to return his favour. He asked him to suggest anything—it would be included in the report.'

'You are joking.'

'No I'm not. This was much before the report was leaked and the hue and cry that followed.'

'But why would he do a thing like that?'

'I don't know.' Rukmini went back into the kitchen and returned a while later with two cups of tea.

'You mean he would jeopardize national security just to oblige some friend?' Ajit asked.

'You don't understand. This sort of thing has nothing to do with big issues and integrity or national security and all the other big words you keep coming up with. There is a world—the political world—which appears in the press, and that is what most people know. Then there is a world which operates on the side, a seamier, darker world where big shots do things for trivial reasons, nothing is sacred. Power, money and just about any kind of twisted diversion—that is all that matters.'

Ajit felt uncomfortable with the tone of her voice. He gulped his tea down.

'Isn't there an unlocked bedroom here?' he asked.

'There is. We are going in there.'

Ajit sat on the rust coloured bedding.

'This guy—why is his flat so sparse? You use it for your liaisons, don't you?'

Rukmini laughed. 'What do you think I am, some kind of a whore?'

Ajit shrugged. 'Well, Sameer thought you to be so. Can't say I blame him entirely. You have something in your eyes, which communicates a very alluring yet unsettling feeling. It is as if you are being used.'

'And?'

'And you want to be used. And then manipulate that to your advantage.'

'Well, if I do, can't say I blame myself for doing that.'

Rukmini sat beside him. He kissed her on her forehead and then her cheeks, and pushed her down on the bed as he did so. He spread her arms out and pinioned her, holding her palms down with his.

'I don't want this moment to end. Don't go to Dhursal. They will kill you.'

'And run away with you?'

'Yes, that will be great. But where to?'

'That's what I'm saying. Don't worry about me. I'll be okay. I know my husband. He was just bragging. Killing me won't suit his interest at this point. I think he'll just wear me down, use you to print a few stories against me.'

Ajit stopped her from speaking further by shutting her mouth with his hand.

'I'm not going to publish anything against you. I love you.'

His hair had fallen over his face. Rukmini brushed it away.

'I love you too. I know nothing about your past, but you are someone special. You have a lot of pain hidden there,' she said, pointing to his heart.

The tears were welling for some unknown reason but they came in fits and starts, not as a sudden release.

'That's how I cry,' he said, still looking down at her.

Rukmini touched his smiling, crying face.

'Come, let me soothe my baby.'

Ajit knocked his head with his knuckles. 'The pain is in here. When you don't sleep it is because of the demons hammering away inside your head.'

Rukmini kissed his forehead. Ajit wanted her to drink his tears but she avoided them, preferring instead to kiss his neck.

'You like that, don't you?' she asked.

'Yes, but kiss my nipples.'

Without asking him again Rukmini opened his shirt. She put her mouth on his dark nipples, sucking them vigorously.

'A man's breast—not enough meat.'

'Why, have you done this with a woman?'

'Maybe I have.'

Ajit laughed.

'We have ways of doing things you can't imagine.'

Ajit urged her to bite him hard there. She literally tore into him. His hard on was instantaneous, but he did not go for his zipper. Pulling her head back, he lay it on the bed.

'I will disrobe you, slowly. But I won't make love. I want to see your beauty.'

He pulled her pallu down, and undid her blouse and bra. Rukmini raised her hands back, above her head.

'How does this look?'

'Great. A romantic painter would have loved to paint you like this. He would have draped your shoulders with velvet and strewn pearls around you. Imagine the sight: velvet, pearls, chiffon, bedspread, wall, breasts and thighs ... Tell me, was the American as romantic as me?'

Rukmini stopped smiling and looked into his eyes, a shadow of sadness clouding her own eyes.

'*You* are the painter, Ajit. There's an artist inside you. Go back to Lucknow. This is not your scene.'

Ajit suddenly became rigid.

'Tell me about the American.'

'No, he isn't romantic. He's more interested in sex.'

'You are using him, aren't you?'

She seemed reluctant to answer.

'Aren't you?'

'We all use each other.'

'But why don't you allow me to help you in this case? I'm ready to switch sides. Damn Sameer.'

Rukmini laughed. 'But this is the battle of the two underworlds, Ajit. There would be something indecent about it appearing in the press. It would be like the real news of JFK's murder or Sanjay Gandhi's death coming out with a byline.'

'But why not? Journalism is for truth.'

'You are naïve. That is why I say go back to Lucknow.'

'Will you remain in touch if I do?'

'Yes. I can sneak into UP to hear my lover speak about velvet and romanticism.'

After that she closed her eyes and he put his head on her stomach. He rubbed the smooth warm flesh and put his lips to it. He ran a finger along the dry gash of a stretchmark below the navel.

'You never talk about your children.'

'It's better they stay out of this mess.'

'You're a very sensitive woman.'

'I used to be—far too sensitive.'

The parting was without much emotion, with Ajit asking a question.

'When did you stop using *sindoor*?'

'I don't remember. All that was ages ago.'

•

Ajit later regretted not asking her about the attack on him: was it done on her orders?

Though he had called his travel agent and booked tickets for Lucknow, he was in two minds. He knew he had a great story, but as Rukmini had said it was more a part of the secret world. And as Derek had pointed out, it was cold meat without a witness.

The phone rang. It was Rishikesh on the line. 'Can I see you?'

'Yes of course; where have you been?'

His voice sounded hoarse.

'I'm in trouble. I need your help.'

They were at their favourite eating joint again, just outside the bookshop that neither had ever entered.

'What will you have? The usual?'

'No. I don't feel like eating.'

Ajit nevertheless ordered his favourite snack. Rishikesh was about to say something when Ajit spoke.

'First I have to tell you something. I was there in Sunil Agnihotri's house. I saw what they did to you and your sister.'

Rishikesh was silent for a while. He did not even look at the girls filing out of the music shop. Then abruptly he slapped Ajit hard on the left cheek.

'I think you will understand why.'

Ajit was quiet. The waiter looked at them and then decided to leave the friends in peace.

'What should I do, Ajit? I had this stupid idea that I should save Saumya. So I went there and got humiliated myself.'

'I understand. Your sister is part of that secret world. This is how things work there. It is not our scene.'

Rishikesh frowned at him. 'Where did you get that one from?'

'From Rukmini.'

The snack was still lying untouched when Ajit finished talking.

'So you want to run away?'

'What else? What is there in it for me now?'

'I think you were used by both Sameer and Rukmini.'

'More by Sameer and Sunil. They wanted information about Rukmini's American connection.'

'Don't be a fool. They would have known about it anyhow. You were there ... I don't know—as some kind of a diversion, perhaps, to distract Rukmini's attention while they went on with their schemes.'

'And Rukmini? Do you think she's genuinely fond of me?'

'I don't know. Isn't she part of the same—secret world, as you call it? But why don't you find it out?'

'How?'

'Let's go to Dhursal. Let's see what happens there. I guess we'll see a lot of action. They are not expecting you—maybe your presence will trigger off something interesting.'

Ajit began eating his friend's chicken roll.

'What time does the train leave?'

'I don't know; but I will take my revenge too.'

'How?'

'I'll nail the bastards. I don't know how but I will nail the bastards.'

15. Dhursal

The train was late by three hours. The two friends had gone off to sleep in their compartment shortly after boarding, till they were woken up rudely at the local stations near Aurangabad. Hundreds of plain-looking men and women, shouting slogans, filtered in, forcing the reserved passengers to vacate their seats.

Rishikesh was aghast. 'I thought these things only happened in UP and Bihar.'

Ajit had laughed. 'There is nothing unique about UP and Bihar.'

Most of the rallyists were dressed in drab dhotis; whatever glamour there was came from the women, some of whom sported frilled *chunris* over their lehnga-blouse. After a while Ajit had started talking to the rallyists. He didn't understand all of what they said, but he was able to piece together the fact that the village folks were also going to Dhursal.

A minister's wife was coming there to inaugurate a power project, they said. It would help electrify the rural areas of Marathwada in Maharashtra. The government had extended all help but there was apprehension that a canal flowing in the area would be drained of water. This would affect the lives of the thousands of peasants living in the region.

'So you're going there to protest?'

'We don't know,' replied an old man with a broken nose and a scarred face. 'We will see which way the wind blows. If the project really benefits us farmers then we will support it. Otherwise we will oppose.'

Ajit chatted with him for a long time, reviving old memories of his interactions with peasants during his Marxist days.

'Things have changed,' he told Rishikesh. 'During the days I was active, peasants were more clear about what they wanted.'

Rishikesh nodded absent-mindedly. He had not eaten much, preferring to while away his time reading a Robert Ludlum thriller.

'*The Bourne Identity*, read it a long time ago,' Ajit said.

Rishikesh did not take offence. They had fought mildly the previous night over Ajit's objection to a couple of bawling kids.

Ajit interrupted him with a nudge. 'Hey, we have the perfect cover to enter Dhursal without rousing any suspicion. Let's mingle with the rallyists.'

Aurangabad station was like any other Maharashtra station—Ajit was quite disappointed.

'You are a character. Always looking for something unique and historical,' Rishikesh laughed. They were now following the crowd towards the bus station.

'Why're they not shouting? We would all have been shouting *Inquilab Zindabad* by now.'

Rishikesh ignored his observation. 'Have you thought about what we'll do once we get there?'

'I don't know. This was your idea. Anyway, let's first get there.'

The bus ride was without any charm whatsoever. The rickety bus rattled on bad roads through dull country. And some kids had started bawling again. Ajit had expected much more from Maharashtra tourism.

The canal was on the far side, to the left of a series of tents where workers could be seen hurrying around, acting to the orders of their foreman. They had obviously been constructing the large bust of Gandhi Ajit saw in the distance, which showed the Mahatma flashing a patronizing smile near the podium. A fairly big crowd had gathered in front of this hastily fabricated structure, which stood a little distance away from another grey-coloured statue, an older one, of Chattrapati Shivaji—the Maratha warrior and the political icon of the Shiv Sena.

It was obvious that Gandhi was being used to undercut Shivaji.

Sections of the crowd could be seen trading charges and accusations and the police were having a tough time controlling them.

'The scene's pretty hot here. Let's join in.'

Rishikesh restrained his excited friend. 'Don't be in such a hurry. Look around for the cast. Can you see anyone?'

'I can't see anyone. Let's ask the police.'

A harried officer told them that yes, Mrs Rukmini Agnihotri, Sunil Agnihotri and Bhigu Parikh were expected but had not arrived. In all probability, the administration had detained them on the road.

'You see, this foundation stone business is a big problem. Suddenly there are protests and rallies being organized by some NGOs.'

Ajit showed the policeman his I card. 'Look, we are journalists. And we believe that the project is for the good of the people. Now tell me, where are the representatives of the government? I don't see any.'

The officer eased up. 'Well, a huge convoy is accompanying Sunilji and Parikhji.'

Ajit leaned over and whispered in his ear. 'I have heard that there's some opposition to the project by some rivals?'

The officer grew apprehensive. 'What rivals? An American company was bidding for the project but they are out of the reckoning now.' Then he laughed and added, 'We are still a socialist state, you know.'

'You two look like journalists, so I will let you in on a secret,' the cop continued. 'We are expecting violence. You know what all these anti-project groups are like—hell bent on creating trouble. They may launch violent attacks any time.'

Rishikesh couldn't control his sneer. He told Ajit to let the officer go and do his duty.

'The *chutiya* talks as if we have eco-terrorism here.'

'But I'm a bit suspicious,' Ajit said. 'Why would he say such a thing? Do you think they'll engineer some sort of clash?'

Further questions were drowned in the roar that came from the field. The *sarkari* entourage had arrived: twenty cars, ranging from ambassadors to Toyotas. The occupants hurried towards the statues to pay obeisance to the old man and the warrior. Ajit could see Marathi journalists eyeing Rukmini with awe.

She wore a plain white sari and had her head covered with the pallu. Her husband was dressed in a black safari suit.

'I can't see Sameer around.'

'Don't be stupid. Why would Sunil have him tag along if he intends to have him bump Rukmini off?'

'So what's the gameplan?'

'Let's get closer to the podium. But we must keep our distance, okay? We shouldn't reveal ourselves. We'll spring into action once the fireworks start.'

Ajit stopped Rishikesh. 'Shouldn't we tell the police?'

'Don't be foolish. The police will never believe our story. Besides, there is something gripping about what you told me in Bombay—we'll spoil all the fun if we disclose the plot.'

Rishikesh grinned wickedly. Ajit felt excited and alarmed. The crowd was growing wild; a fistfight had broken out between two groups. The police were in the thick of it all, ready for a lathi charge when Ajit saw Rukmini take control of the situation.

Flanked by security guards and a few sheepish politicians in white, she looked unusually painted—stylish in a ferocious way. Her lips were a brutal red and her brows had been freshly plucked, giving her the appearance of a varnished eagle-woman.

'Get back from the podium, she'll recognize you!' Rishikesh pushed him back towards the rear. Just then Rukmini turned her head in his direction. He ducked and squatted behind a row of men, avoiding detection by a whisker.

'We will listen to all your grievances. We will not let anyone down. You all know Parikhji. He is a trustworthy man.'

People began quietening down to hear a lady speak. Parikh whispered something to an aide. He in turn began talking to Sunil Agnihotri.

A couple of hot-headed women in cotton saris were trying to rouse the crowd against Rukmini.

'Look, we are in Shivaji's country,' Rukmini said firmly. 'Let's not try to undo each other. Especially if we are women.'

It is cotton against chiffon, Ajit thought.

The women quietened down after a few more shouts. Rukmini's charisma was working on the crowd.

Her pallu was now fluttering in the wind, which had begun blowing out of nowhere. Still squatting at the rear, Ajit saluted the banner.

And then he froze as he felt a revolver's nozzle on his back.

'So, this is where you're hiding. Thought you would do something foolish. Don't make a sound. Come with me.'

He was taken behind a clump of trees in the adjoining field. He looked back; even from that distance he could see a scuffle had broken out again in the crowd.

'Why are you here?' Sameer demanded, even as he pushed him against a tree.

'You look handsome—white suit and all. What tree is this?' Ajit asked feeling its bark.

'Don't play games with me. Why the fuck are you here?'

'Where's Rishikesh? I know what you really want to know—why am I here with Rishikesh, isn't that it?'

Ajit glanced again at the scene near the Mahatma's statue. The space from there to the trees was empty. There was no sign of his friend.

'He's safe.'

'I don't believe you. I saw what you, Sunil and Ashok Singh did to him and his sister in Sunil's house. I also heard that you plan to kill Rukmini today.'

Sameer brought down the nozzle. He then threw the gun to the ground.

'See, I have thrown the gun down. I have no quarrel with you. I didn't want to involve you in all this. But now that you're here I'm asking you to join our side.'

'Why?'

'Because of Rukmini! Why can't you see the woman's evil? Look how she two-timed you with the American. You know what's happening here, don't you? She has sold out to the Americans. That fucking giant multinational was angling for the project and now they have this FBI agent behind them who's trying to subvert our project.'

Ajit leaned against the bark. It was rough and hot.

'First tell me what you've done with Rishikesh.'

Sameer looked at the fallen gun before replying. 'He's all right, in one of those tents. We frisked him away when you were eyeing Rukmini. Ashok Singh is with him.'

Ajit felt easy but not relaxed. 'Is he okay?'

'Oh yes. Don't worry—what we did to him that day was simply to teach him a lesson. Fucking his sister was a different issue. Don't confuse—'

Ajit shot forward and stood with his face inches away from Sameer's. 'I don't know if there is really anything against the Americans here. Both you and Sunil have an axe to grind with Rukmini. You want to get rid of her because she stood up to you both.'

Moving quietly, Sameer caught Ajit by the collar. The grip was loose.

'She stood up to us? What else?'

'Well, I did not like what you did to Saumya and Rishikesh. It was brutal.'

Still holding his collar, Sameer pointed towards the field. Rukmini was speaking to the silent crowd.

'What do you see there? See the way she has plucked her eyebrows? See the way she has applied the lipstick? Isn't that brutal too? She's the fucking villain, why can't you see that!' he hissed fiercely and hit his own head with his free hand. Ajit felt a shock of recognition and stared at the older man.

What were the demons in his head?

Sameer released his collar. 'As for what we did to Saumya, you're being too simple minded about it. What do you think happens in Bombay?'

Sameer picked up his gun. Pointing it at an empty space away from Rukmini, he smiled sardonically.

The bullet hit him in the back. He fell forward; but his grip tightened on his revolver.

'Get back,' he shouted to Ajit. 'The fighting has begun.'

Ajit lunged forward to attend to him.

'Watch your fucking back!'

Ajit looked at his face. The handsomeness was contorted in pain. Suddenly he felt that his life may be in danger as well. Drawing back from the wounded man, he began looking around frantically, trying to determine the origin of the shot. The field stretched before him, almost desolate but for the crowd at the other end. The trees too were lonely and morose.

'Who the fuck is out there?' he shouted. 'Why are you shooting?'

Sameer was gone when he turned around. He saw him staggering in the crowd's direction, waving his revolver.

Ajit turned towards the tents—the workers had seen Sameer and were flapping their hands at the police stationed near the podium.

He began running in their direction—he knew something had happened to Rishikesh.

He was halfway through when he saw Sameer dodging the policemen.

Sameer moved to the side tackling the inspector in front with his left foot. He then began trotting towards the Gandhi statue.

Ajit forgot to run for the tent. He stood mesmerized as

Sameer slumped against the statue and blood began to flow over the Mahatma.

Rukmini had seen him; turning to Parikh she began shouting frantically.

'Look! That man's coming to kill me. I think the people protesting against the project have sent him here. Stop him!'

Parikh looked at Sunil. The minister was looking desperately in Sameer's direction, ashen-faced.

'We've been tricked Sunil bhai! The bitch knows about our plans!' Sameer yelled in a hoarse voice.

Parikh shook his head; Sunil did not move.

Rukmini was hounding Parikh. 'What are you looking at? Why are you not moving? This man is here to kill me! Get your bodyguards to do something!'

Acting as if on cue, the crowd siding with Rukmini began bashing up the protesters. The women in cotton were being thrown around—the men had already bolted or were at the point of making a run for it.

Parikh ordered his aide to ask the police to act. Rukmini heaved sideways as a bullet fired from the Mahatma's bust missed her by inches.

'Why are you not acting?' She was almost hysterical now. 'What are your compulsions?'

Parikh stopped shaking his head. Just then a jeep full of armed men stopped near the podium. They sprang out one by one—Ashok Singh was in the lead.

Without waiting to think, Ajit rushed towards him. Ashok was asking his men to fan out and encircle the place when Ajit caught him by the neck.

'Where's Rishikesh? What have you done to him?'

Ashok opened his mouth to reply but fell on his knees; Ajit saw the inspector levelling his nozzle. He too fell to the ground to avoid the shot.

The second shot got the Bhumihaar in the chest. His men began firing wildly, directing a few panicky shots at the crowd as well.

Ashok Singh beckoned him to his side. Ajit hesitated; Ashok threw a stone at his face, which hit him on the chin.

'Come here, you bastard. I am dying.'

Ashok pointed towards his socks as Ajit approached.

'There's a pistol strapped there. Take it out. I have to settle scores with the bitch.'

Ajit came up with the gun.

'I will give it you but you must first tell me where my friend is.'

'There, in the tent ... the blue one. I didn't even touch him. Now give me the fucking gun.'

Handing him the weapon, Ajit sprinted towards the tent. He entered to find Rishikesh tied to a chair.

'What the hell is happening? I am all right.'

Ajit began speaking while untying the knots. 'I don't know. But the tide seems to have turned. Sameer was shot and so was Ashok. Sunil looks paralyzed. What the hell is happening?'

Rishikesh was now up on his feet. 'I have something to tell you. Ashok Singh was bragging just before he went out to address the commotion. He was the one who killed Sudha, her aunt and Mrs Jha.'

'What?'

'On Rukmini's instructions. She had won him over, with sex and money. At the time, Ashok had not met Sameer, and she thought by getting Sudha killed she would create a rift between Sameer and Sunil. But Sunil found out about Sameer and Sudha before that. He decided to pack him off to Bihar in anger. Sameer scribbled the address you saw at the aunt's house. He wanted Sudha to know where he would be staying.

'By the time you reached Sudha's aunt's house, Rukmini had instructed Ashok to finish off Sameer as well. He saw you and thought you were Sameer. The bullet that got the aunt was not meant for her.

'Then Sameer landed in Bihar. She then asked Ashok to try again. Again the bullet was meant for the man when Mrs Jha died. Ashok thought it was Sameer who was making love to her. You're lucky Ashok is a bad shot.'

Suddenly Ajit felt calm. It was as if a huge weight had been lifted from his shoulders.

'Then?'

'Sameer and Ashok became friends in Bihar. Ashok said he was playing a practical joke when he told you that Sameer committed all the murders. On learning of Rukmini's American connection, he had a big showdown with her. He went back and joined Sunil again. As you know they had planned to kill Rukmini. But it seems she's got wind of their plan. I wonder who told her.'

Ajit lowered his head. 'It was me.'

Rishikesh came forward. His eyes were burning. 'Serves the bastards right. This was the only way of getting rid of them.'

Ajit shook his head. 'I don't think so. I think Rukmini duped us all. These men may have been bad. But in this case they were battling the Americans.'

'Open your bloody eyes, Ajit,' Rishikesh said, shaking Ajit by the shoulders. 'There are no good guys in this mess. How does it matter who wins? They are all the same.'

'Yes and no. Rukmini says this is a secret world and I should stay out. Sameer meant the same—but it was they who drew me into this ruling-class madness; Sameer even called it my tour of paradise. I like it here—and I don't like liking it here. This dilemma makes me angry, I hate dilemmas—and I act when I get angry. What makes me angrier still is the way Rukmini and Sameer have wasted their energies fighting each other. They should have been together, but they want to kill each other. Sunil and Ashok too are two distorted, talented bastards; but Sunil, Ashok and Sameer are at least open about their kind of thing—Rukmini is the sly one. I sit here seeing the Americans take advantage of their obsessions—and I can't sit like this.'

Rishikesh shook his head. 'Don't glorify men like Sameer. If he and the others were women, they wouldn't have been any less sly than Rukmini, they wouldn't have had a choice. Do you think they are men of honour? And forget this American nonsense, it's foolish in these times.'

'Call it foolishness, the call of my generation, or the call of the old North-Indian aristocratic code. You know, we grew up in the '80s, which were presumed to be boring—maybe they were, but then we fought old concepts and the kind of life our parents led. No one helped us and there were big failures—but we tried breaking new ground. We were also political—almost by default. Then the '90s came and we were asked not to take sides. In fact it was difficult to take sides—the anti-reservation movement, the mandir agitation, then globalization, men losing their honour, women going berserk—all this moral relativism! That's the dangerous thing, Rishikesh, this moral relativism.'

Rishikesh looked at him in silence.

'We Indians, Rishikesh, we are known in the world for not taking a stand, for not sticking up for each other. I want to prove that theory wrong—even if it means choosing Sunil over the American.'

Rishikesh looked dismayed as he finished. 'This is not going to endear you to anyone, Ajit. And I don't think this is any position at all.'

'I don't care.'

Ajit did not look back to see if his friend was following him as he came out of the tent.

A bleeding Ashok Singh had taken position behind the jeep and was firing desperately at the police posse closing in on him. Sameer was near the Mahatma's statue, bleeding. The podium was empty. Sunil was moving with Rukmini towards his car. Parikh too had his security cordon around him; his guards were waving at the driver to bring his car.

Ajit saw that Sameer had two more shots lodged in his chest and leg.

He was now very close to him. Sameer saw him and smiled.

'Where were you? Did you find your friend?'

'Yes. He's okay.'

'See, I am dying. But I still have my gun with me.'

He struggled to his feet and staggered towards Rukmini and Sunil. A shot fired from a police rifle hit him on the thigh but he kept on moving. Another shot missed him by inches. He finally fired, grazing Rukmini's left ear. Then he fell as another bullet shattered his right shoulder.

Ajit saw Ashok Singh's men running for their lives, being chased by the police. Near the jeep the Bhumihaar had both his hands up in the air.

Sunil made an attempt to put his hand on Rukmini's shoulder. She brushed it away. A Tata sumo emerged from the trees and drove up to the jeep. The injured inspector saluted the occupant. Ram Prakash Yadav got out from the Sumo; Singleton followed him.

Climbing back into the Sumo after talking to the inspector, they began making their way to Rukmini. Ram Prakash stopped the jeep as it neared Ajit. He got out, waving at the American to go on.

'What the hell are you doing here?'

Ajit laughed a bitter laugh. 'Don't tell me you're involved in this mess too.'

The Yadav adjusted his goggles and gamchha—he looked resolute, prepared for any eventuality. 'I wasn't till I was recruited by Singleton to work for him.'

'You helped the American? Are you working for the FBI?'

'What FBI? What do I stand to lose? The guy paid well. I took him to Ashok Singh's men. Most of them have sold out. Sameer and Sunil lost the battle before it had begun.'

'Do you know the details?'

'Yes. See the American mind—he shot Sameer, and Sameer ran towards Rukmini, waving his gun, triggering off a chain of reactions that upset Sunil's plans completely. Sunil couldn't do a thing. He had Parikh on his side, but even he couldn't order his police escorts to open fire on Rukmini with an armed man charging at her. Besides, the police officer in charge was on our side. The American had paid him well in advance—Agnihotri may be a minister, but the officer knows he's finished. Singleton has connections at the very top.'

The American was helping Rukmini up. He was about to haul her into his car when Sunil stopped him.

'You can't take her like this. She is my wife.'

'Try and stop me.'

Sunil punched him hard on the nose and shouted to Parikh, 'Ask your police escort to arrest the American. He shot the man lying near the statue.'

Parikh was soft and unassuming as he spoke. 'I can't do that, Sunilji. It would look odd. That man came charging at Rukminiji. Besides, I may be a minister but this is not my home state—it is yours, and this is your police. Mr Singleton is a state guest, he has come via the embassy at the government's special request. You know you can't touch him—and you really shouldn't expect me to do your dirty work for you.'

Stepping forward, Sunil grabbed Singleton by the collar and smacked his face. Rukmini screamed.

Leaning on the Sumo for support Singleton tried driving a fist into Sunil's chest. The Minister dodged the blow and kicked him in the stomach. He then took out his gun.

'I will finish this damned business! *Bahut Lallo chappo hua.*'

He pointed the gun directly at Rukmini, then collapsed to the ground.

Parikh pushed the man who had fired. 'Why the hell did you press the trigger?'

The man barked back. 'He was going to kill her, sir.'

'So what? Did I tell you to fire?'

Parikh was kicking the man in a blind rage. A few of the journalists who had started clicking began putting away their cameras. Parikh left the man and walked towards Sunil.

Ram Prakash Yadav had walked over to Ajit. He looked grim but impassive.

Sunil was trying to stand straight. It was a struggle. When he succeeded, he lurched forward and spat at Rukmini. The saliva was still trickling down her face when he fell again.

'The bullet was fatal, Parikh. I'm going to die!'

Parikh turned back without giving him a second look. He began summoning the journalists and talking hurriedly to the people he knew. After a while the journos were following him to his car.

Ram Prakash sniggered. 'There goes the tribe. I'm sure

they'll toe the line. Parikh's going to come out of this clean.'

Ajit had moved back to where Sameer was lying in a pool of blood.

He was still alive. He called Ajit to his side.

'I will not ask you to kill anyone, but keep my revolver. I could not live like a warrior . . . but at least I'm dying like one. They—they've installed Gandhi and Shivaji here—they forgot Aurangabad is Aurangzeb's country. Hey Rukmini—can you hear me!'

Ajit looked up. Rukmini was staring unblinkingly at her ex-lover.

'Why did you have to kill my friend? All right, you kept the portrait. But why didn't you return my mouth organ?'

When Ajit looked back, Sameer was lying still. 'Why did you have to lose it the way you did?' he mumbled before picking up the revolver and putting it in his pocket.

Sameer closed his eyes. Ajit watched him die. Ram Prakash turned his face away.

Ajit heard another shot being fired and turned around. Ashok Singh went down on his knees. A bullet was lodged in his forehead, even as his hands were still held up in the act of surrender. The police officer who had shot him removed his cap before ordering his men to clear the area of bodies.

Ram Prakash came over and slapped Ajit on the back.

'What a scene! The American's got everything exactly the way he wanted!'

Ajit got up and kicked him in the stomach.

'What was that for, you bastard?'

'For being a Marxist and a Hindu revivalist and an American agent. For changing trains too often, you bastard.'

Singleton was arguing hotly with Rukmini when Ajit drew near. She kept on touching her ear, asking the American to do something about it. The police had cleared the crowd and the vast field was nearly empty, save Parikh and the journos.

'I told you to keep out of this. Why didn't you go to Lucknow?' Rukmini said as Ajit went up to her.

'Why didn't you return his mouth organ?'

'What?'

Ajit stayed quiet.

Rukmini pointed to her wound. 'I wasn't supposed to survive either. Or have you forgotten? Look, Ajit, I know you helped me and I thank you for that. You know that Sameer was a psychotic and—'

'No.' Ajit was so loud that the officer turned around to see whether everything was all right.

'No. I don't know anything. Maybe you killed his friend. Maybe the things he said were true.'

Rukmini's plucked eyebrows twitched. 'Of course you'll believe him.'

Singleton crept up from behind and tapped Ajit on his shoulder.

'I think you ought to go home, young man. You—'

Swirling around, Ajit punched him on the nose. The American was so taken aback that he did not budge an inch. Ajit felt an immense sense of satisfaction surging in his veins. He drew back and kicked Singleton in the groin.

'That was for shooting from behind. Why couldn't you act like a man?'

'Fucking madcap,' Singleton abused, clutching his balls and moaning.

Rukmini was standing apart, near her car, looking defeated. She did not stir as he approached.

'You won't touch me. Not after what we've been through.'

Ajit planted his fist on her left cheek.

'Yes. Some of it was fun. Why did you have me beaten up?'

The police and the journalists were talking amongst themselves as he left. They had not bothered to intervene.

Epilogue

Newspapers lay on his bed in a heap. He had bought all the major issues to read their version of the story.

Contrary to his expectations, most of them had reported the happenings faithfully. They had dwelt on the Rukmini-Sunil conflict, hinting at its darker aspects. But there was no mention of Sameer—or of Singleton. Only Parikh had been quoted.

There was also no mention of the power project. In fact, in all the reports the location of the event was only mentioned in passing in the first few lines. It was possible for a layman to read the stories without even wondering what had led to the violence and killings.

Ajit had finished packing his bags when the phone rang. It was Rishikesh.

'Rukmini wants to see you.'

'Why didn't she phone me?'

'I don't know. She called me up.'

'I don't think I can see her.'

Rishikesh was quiet for a while.

'Then?'

'Then? Well, I'm not leaving Mumbai.'

'But?'

'But I'm packing my bags.'

'So what are your plans?'

'I don't know. Right now I want to fall in love with a beautiful woman.'

'UP or elsewhere?'

'Elsewhere.'

Rishikesh laughed.

1/3

SMALL FRY

PLAY
Inspiration for creative play with kids

SUSIE CAMERON & KATRINA CROOK
Written by SUE CANT

ABC Books

Contents

FOREWORD	5
PREFACE	6
INTRODUCTION	8
KIDS AND PLAY	10
Encouraging play	12
Playing it safe	14
Development	18
Limits	28
Toys	32
Child's eye view	38
WHERE THE SIDEWALK ENDS	44
Pretend	46
Experiment	50
Let's communicate	64
Create	70
Music	82
Let's move	88
Nature	94
TECHNOLOGY	100
Tuning in	102
Tuning out	106
PLAYING AWAY	110
Outdoors	112
My community	116
Play dates	118
Holidays	124
FAMILY	130
We are family	132
Playing together	134
IN THE END	138
REFERENCES	140
ACKNOWLEDGEMENTS	142
INDEX	144

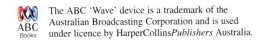 The ABC 'Wave' device is a trademark of the Australian Broadcasting Corporation and is used under licence by HarperCollins*Publishers* Australia.

First published in Australia in 2009
By HarperCollins*Publishers* Australia Pty Limited
ABN 36 009 913 517
www.harpercollins.com.au

Text copyright © Susie Cameron, Katrina Crook and Sue Cant 2009
Photography copyright © photography Katrina Crook 2009

The rights of Susie Cameron, Katrina Crook and Sue Cant to be identified as the authors of this work has been asserted by them in accordance with the *Copyright Amendment (Moral Rights) Act 2000*.

This work is copyright. Apart from any use as permitted under the *Copyright Act 1968*, no part may be reproduced, copied, scanned, stored in a retrieval system, recorded, or transmitted, in any form or by any means, without the prior written permission of the publisher.

HarperCollins*Publishers*
25 Ryde Road, Pymble, Sydney, NSW 2073, Australia
31 View Road, Glenfield, Auckland 0627, New Zealand
1–A Hamilton House, Connaught Place, New Delhi – 110 001, India
77–85 Fulham Palace Road, London W6 8JB, United Kingdom
2 Bloor Street East, 20th floor, Toronto, Ontario M4W 1A8, Canada
10 East 53rd Street, New York NY 10022, USA

National Library of Australia
Cataloguing-in-Publication data:
Small fry: play/Susie Cameron, Katrina Crook, Sue Cant
ISBN: 978 0 7333 2337 9 (pbk)
Includes index. Bibliography.
Play. Games.
790.1922

Designed by Seymour Designs
Typeset by Seymour Designs
Printed in China by Phoenix Offset on 157gsm matt art

DISCLAIMER
The publisher makes all reasonable attempts to credit copyright material. If a copyright holder has not been acknowledged, he or she is welcome to write to the authors care of the publisher so that acknowledgement can be made in future reprints.
  This book should not be used by children without adult supervision. Parents and carers must assess each child's capability, as well as any particular food or plant allergies or sensitivities, to determine whether the activities and recipes are appropriate for the child.
  To the extent permitted by law, we, the publisher and the authors, disclaim any and all liability resulting from any accidents, injuries, losses or other damages resulting from the use of this book for play-based or related activities, cooking or eating.

5 4 3 2 1   09 10 11 12

Foreword

I'm a lucky person because my work is all play – in the ABC's long-running and ever-popular program *Play School*. But there's a message in the name. Playing may be natural and spontaneous, but there are skills in playing that can be nurtured.

For parents, one of the greatest gifts our kids bring with them is allowing us to experience some of our own childhood again. We re-read children's classics, and discover new writers – I'm not looking forward to the day my children don't want me to read to them anymore! By their delight in music, I've rediscovered the influence music had on me right from my preschool years.

As well as working to a broadcast audience and sometimes a live one, I've got the opportunity to revisit that period of awakening now through playing and making music with my own kids.

I'm doing what my mother did with me. She loved to play, and still does. She instilled in me a sense of wonder about life that I've carried with me to this day. Wonder is a great place to start learning. It ignites curiosity: the mystery and magic that is a part of childhood can be the greatest place from which to continue that learning process. And so it goes around …

My kids remind me daily that there's great freedom in letting your imagination lead you and getting totally absorbed in your play. And imagination is something that can be cultivated. Children just need a little spark to get them engaged and then they're off – on another great adventure that seems to have its own momentum.

Sometimes us parents forget that we can play too. We get wrapped up in responsibilities and miss out on the fun. The day gets long; as adults we need order. But sometimes the most refreshing thing to do is just to get down on the floor and play. Even if it means more mess, I know it'll mean good memories. I come home from work and get down on the floor with the kids and encourage them to lead the play. It takes us on many adventures … I love to join in with them as they play a spy game or make a cubbyhouse in the lounge room. I observe how calming it is for them to be engaged in an imaginary world, either alone or with a friend or sibling – and how long it keeps them occupied!

Sometimes it's about connecting with the kids after a day away from them. It could be as simple as singing a song or as complex as getting that 'useful box' out.

With *Small Fry Play*, Sue, Susie and Katrina have given us the inspiration we need to get started. Let your child's imagination do the rest.

Justine Clarke

Preface

Welcome to the third book in the *Small Fry* series, *Small Fry Play – Creative Play with Kids*.

What a joy for us to spend time considering the magic of play – not just for our own precious children (and yours), but for adults too!

While writing this book we had the delicious excuse to travel down memory lane to our own childhoods where we'd spent many hours engaged in simple play: splashing through puddles, hanging from the branches of trees, skipping and playing elastics. We devised potions, rode our bikes down muddy lanes and searched for crabs hiding under seaweed on warm summer days. We made countless cups of 'tea' for our parents, constructed fantastic rockets and cars out of cardboard boxes and drove them around the house for hours. Little did we know that every hour we spent playing was teaching us important foundation skills for life.

Why write a book about play, you may well ask?

Simple, unfettered play has so many benefits. It builds resilience and creativity and cultivates the imagination. Play encourages problem-solving skills; it nurtures independence; fosters self-worth and a sense of place in a sometimes bewildering world. The difficult art of sharing can be encouraged through group play, social outings and play dates with friends.

Like our first two books – *Small Fry Cooking* and *Small Fry Outdoors* – we hope this book will inspire parents, grandparents and carers to reveal the magical world of play to the children in their lives. Most importantly, all the activities and ideas are practical and cost-effective.

We are grateful to early childhood educator Sue Cant for sharing with us her wealth of knowledge which we know will be as inspiring to you as it has been for us.

Small Fry Play is a resource Katrina and I would have loved to have had at our fingertips when our children were small. Playing with kids sounds so simple and while we recognise that not every parent or carer will need this book, we've found it's always helpful to have additional ideas to get us through those times when we come up blank!

We'd love your feedback on this or any of our books. Contact us at info@smallfryfun.com or visit our website www.smallfryfun.com for updates, offers and more fun stuff for kids.

Susie and Katrina

SIONEN CANT

Introduction

How often have you told your children to 'go and play'? Such a simple childhood activity is fundamental to the way we develop and engage with the world through the whole of our lives. Play is vital for both children and adults. It is the way children learn skills, shape understanding, discover how to interact with others, learn to relax and energise, and make sense of the world and their place in it. For adults, play becomes leisure and is a way of escaping from our everyday routine. Through it we make connections with people, recharge our batteries, learn something new and create experiences to make our lives more meaningful. There won't be many people who will say, on their death bed, I should have worked harder! Play is vital for us all to grow and develop as human beings from cradle to grave.

Play is as natural to children as sleeping and eating. Think back to your own childhood and the way that you played. Remember how you used all your senses. Can you recall the smell of backyard cricket on a summer's day; the colour of the rock pool at the beach; the feel of mud between your toes at the creek behind your house while you collected tadpoles? Do you remember the sheer joy of being alive, of bursting with wonder and curiosity? Every one of those experiences, good and maybe at times not so good, added to your experience, knowledge and skills, and helped make you the person you are today.

As both a parent and an early childhood professional, I don't believe that childhood is a preparation for life; it is the life your child is living right now and you are living it with them. By creating an environment in which your child can play, develop and learn to relate to others, you are making the most of every opportunity to help them grow into their potential. You are creating a space within which your children can develop the skills, passions and interests that will give their lives meaning, and create family bonds and friendships which will sustain and support them throughout their lives.

Having said this, there is no doubt that a parent's role is tough. We want to love and nurture our children, pass on our values and beliefs, and give them every advantage. In today's competitive world, we feel an overwhelming responsibility to provide our children with everything they need to have a successful life, but 'everything they need' will already exist in a home that provides time, opportunities and resources to play.

This book is not an academic text dispensing expert information about how to encourage your children to play. Nor could it possibly cover every aspect of play. There are many wonderful books that analyse play. Rather, I hope this book will give parents an opportunity to relax and see that they are doing a great job.

I also hope it provides ideas on how to be involved in your children's lives, to build connections and celebrate family and friends.

Most of all, I want it to inspire you to create an environment for your children that is filled with wonder and curiosity, to stimulate their play time and help them achieve their unique potential while having a wonderful time together along the way.

Sue Cant

Kids and play

ENCOURAGING PLAY · PLAYING IT SAFE · DEVELOPMENT · LIMITS TOYS · CHILD'S EYE VIEW

Play is vital to a child's development. Through play, children build thinking and social skills, develop the ability to support their emotional wellbeing and also practise and build physical competence. Even more significant is the opportunity that play provides for parents to fully connect with their children in an increasingly hurried and pressured world.

Encouraging play

Children are naturally drawn to play. It is part of the process of expressing ideas and understanding, experimenting, exploring and socialising with others.

Getting started

There are some important things to know:
- Play is intrinsically self-motivated. A child will freely invent and engage in different plots, scripts, ideas and choices. Their likes and dislikes will be evident from their choices and play should not be imposed from outside.
- Children need opportunities with different types of play to enhance their development across a range of areas: active play to stimulate the intellect and body, and quiet play to recharge or when focusing on a complex task.
- Sometimes children will play in groups and sometimes, alone; sometimes they prefer to watch, or to be around other children while playing their own game.
- Younger children may prefer one playmate or an adult and might not be good at sharing. Even for some adults, sharing can be tough, so be patient.
- Older children will have developed cooperative skills and will invent games with rules.
- Children are unique and develop at their own rate; they have their own interests and passions. We all have talents, as well as skills we are working on.
- Different environments can stimulate different types of play. Children need access to a range of environments and spaces to explore different types of play.

HELPFUL CODES

Level of difficulty
This is a number out of five that we feel reflects the level of difficulty of this activity or recipe. One is the lowest and five the highest level.

Mess factor
A number out of five that we feel reflects the level of mess this activity/recipe will generate. One is the lowest and five the highest level.

Preparation time
A general idea of how long this item/dish will take to prepare.

Feeds/Makes
This is to give a general idea of how many people this dish will feed or how much it will make. We are catering for a family of four – two adults and two children, in most recipes. Of course, if you are feeding children, it will go much further and may feed up to eight.

Age levels
A guide to the age of the child we feel these activities are best suited to. Be guided by your child's abilities; every child is different!

- Children need large blocks of time to play, free from adult-imposed restrictions.
- Children need access to bought, borrowed, collected, made and recycled resources to explore their play fully.
- Children need limits to keep them safe and to help them interact and play with other children.
- Children need caring adults to keep them safe, help them negotiate difficulties, and facilitate ideas to extend their play.
- Play needs to be stimulating and it needs to be fun; otherwise children will vote with their feet.
- It's okay for children to be bored. Children don't have to be entertained by adults all the time. Being bored will often stimulate children to think of new and interesting things to do and encourage them to be resourceful.

Playing it safe

While bumps and bruises are part of growing up, no parent wants to see their child hurt. Preventing injuries while children are playing is an important part of creating an environment in which your children can play freely and safely.

SAFETY TIPS

After reading this section you may feel like wrapping your child in cotton wool, but most of it is basic common sense. In a safe, well-maintained environment, with good supervision, play and imagination should flourish.

- Supervise your children. Don't hover over them, but know where they are, what they are doing, and keep a weather eye and ear out so you can intervene if necessary.
- Make sure you have a well-maintained first aid kit or box to deal with bumps, bruises, splinters etc.
- Keep a list of important numbers handy – the Poisons Information Centre, Kidsafe, your GP, the local hospital etc. You will want to find these immediately in an emergency.
- Do a first aid course and keep your skills up to date. No one wants their child to have an accident, but having the skills to deal with injuries, if they arise, can save a life. This is not a time to be squeamish!
- Introduce the concept of 'stranger danger'. Define a stranger as anyone the child does not know and teach them that strangers come in all shapes and sizes and can be older children as well as adults. Set boundaries about talking to strangers – on the phone, the computer or in the park. Explain that there are no secrets in your family; they can tell you anything, no matter what.

OUT AND ABOUT

- When you are going on an outing discuss where you are going and what you are going to do, so children are prepared – and understand the limits in advance.
- Teach road sense by using Commentary Walking as advised by the RTA (Roads and Traffic Authority) website. This helps children absorb good practice. For example, 'Okay, now we are at the corner, we are going to stop and check for traffic, push the button and wait for the green light to cross the road'.
- Children cannot judge distances accurately. Peripheral vision, and the ability to judge depth of field, do not fully develop until the age of ten or eleven. NEVER let them cross a road without supervision.
- Remember, even with the best of intentions, when faced with the excitement of being out, children WILL forget. Set limits and stick to them.
- Choose your times to go out. Try to make sure your children are not tired or hungry.
- Know where the toilets are! No matter how many times you went before you left the house, SOMEONE will want to go.
- When travelling in cars and taxis children should ALWAYS get out on the kerb side, NEVER onto the road.

IN THE HOUSE

- Chemicals, cleaning fluids, household and kitchen implements should be stored out of children's reach.
- Make sure cupboards that store household chemicals and medicines are fitted with approved childsafe locks.
- Ensure that curtain and blind cords are well out of reach and that loop cords are cut to prevent injury.
- Mats and rugs should be secured with non-slip matting underneath.
- Kneel down and look at each room from a child's perspective. Where are the hazards? Remember to remove, repair or restrict access.
- Ensure that toys are stored for easy access and storage and to prevent injury from tripping.
- Toys that require batteries or cords need to be checked regularly and supervised when used.
- Check toys regularly and repair or discard broken toys.
- Limit younger children's access to electrical items such as TVs, CD and DVD players, unless you are sure they are capable and responsible. Make sure these items are securely anchored so children cannot accidentally pull them down on themselves.

IN THE BACKYARD

- NOTHING can replace effective adult supervision. This is an art form and you can supervise your children without them feeling that you are breathing down their necks. Be aware and available, listen and keep your eyes open.
- Get down to your child's level and examine the yard. Where are the hazards? Remove, repair or restrict access.
- Clean and make sure the yard is free of rubbish that might be harmful to your child.
- Boundaries and fences should be well maintained.
- Where there are no fences children should be supervised and know the limits of their play area. Keep an eye on them and enforce the limits.
- Make sure their play equipment is well maintained. Check swings and trampolines regularly to ensure catches, ropes, chains and springs are strong and in good order. Check wood, metal and plastic for cracks, rust and splinters that might cause injuries.
- Ensure that equipment is appropriate to the child's size and skills.
- Some clothing is potentially hazardous. Hoods and cords can snag on equipment and branches and cause nasty neck and head injuries; remove cords and choose jackets, jumpers and beanies or hats instead of hoodies.
- Prevent access to driveways, particularly for small children who cannot be seen by reversing drivers.
- Swimming pools and outdoor spas must have a childproof fence around them. This is a law in all Australian states and territories. Your fence should meet Australian Standard 1926 (AS: 1926) safety requirements.
- Garden tools should only be used when there is an adult present. You can teach your children how to use tools appropriately and safely or prevent access to them and lock them away.
- Chemicals, paints and fertilisers should be locked away.
- Check equipment for insect and spider infestations.

This is not a definitive list. You know your home environment and what your child is capable of doing. Prevention and planning will ensure that children can play happily and you can relax and know they are safe.

FAMILY PETS

Pets are a great addition to any family. Remember, always supervise animals when they are near children and check play areas for pet contamination. Ensure that your children treat animals with respect and help to feed and care for them. No matter how well trained a family dog is, it is still a dog and will act like a dog when confused, excited or threatened.

Development

Even with the ongoing advances in medical science, having a child is still a bit like the toy that comes out of the cereal box. It's exciting, waiting and hoping, but you never know what will fall into your breakfast bowl! Each child's emerging personality is part of this unique, wonderful, frustrating, lovable individual who is now part of your world.

In the beginning

The person who is developing before you will, in part, be influenced by the experiences they have, which will in turn, impact on how they see the world and interact with it. While parenting books tell you that child development occurs in a nice logical sequence, and to some extent it does, they cannot take into account your child's individual progress. Influences like illness, medication, special needs, nutrition, education and sibling relationships may have an impact on how your child develops. One of our guilty secrets, as parents, is that we all check out and compare our child with those of our friends, just to make sure that they are 'normal'. Well, here's a newsflash: defining normal is almost impossible! Each child has abilities, skills, talents and needs which are unique and may affect how they grow and connect with the world.

There are lots of ways to define 'normal'. Just because your neighbour's four-year-old is trading on the stock exchange while yours is running around with his undies on his head making siren noises, doesn't mean he's not normal. It is true that some children do not develop as we expect, and this is why having developmental scales and definitions is important. Getting help early is vital if you are at all concerned about your child. So while this chapter provides an overview of children's development, it is a guide and is not definitive. Remember to read between the lines and discuss your concerns with your GP, paediatrician or your child's early childhood teacher.

TWO – GROUNDHOG DAY

- For a two-year-old, every day is Groundhog Day. He is brimming with energy to face what the day brings. The 'wow' factor looms large in his existence as he discovers the extraordinary in the ordinary with an enthusiasm and zest for life that is exhausting to his parents.
- His natural curiosity will stimulate exploration of the world leading to great discoveries but also great disasters as he is still learning about his abilities and limitations.
- His responses will often be spontaneous. He will sing, dance, run, play, cry and sleep at the drop of a hat. Sunny moments can become stormy in seconds, as he learns to understand and manage his emotions. He is your own delightfully lovable Jekyll and Hyde.
- While he will respond to emotions in others, his world revolves firmly around 'Me' and his behaviour, decisions and choices will reflect this.
- He can kick a ball, but is still learning to jump and skip. He can manage the stairs, slowly; he will begin to use a push tricycle; he enjoys creating, painting, pasting, playing with sand, water, mud, dough and building, but may not always manage the 'tools' and is generally more interested in the process than the outcome. He loves to run, but doesn't think about how to stop and often crashes into something, someone or falls over.
- 'Messy' is his middle name and he will leave a trail of clothes, food, toys and games in his wake. He may move between play experiences, appearing to have little concentration, but then focus on things that interest him.
- He will play simple pretend games often choosing Mum and Dad as his playmates. He will probably enjoy the company of his peers but play alongside other children rather than with them most of the time. Oh, and watch out, he will see you as a role model!
- One minute he will want you close by and then he will play happily by himself, but may become distressed if you are not where he left you!
- A budding entertainer, he can recall simple rhymes and songs and will develop strong likes and dislikes in music. His vocabulary, around 200 words, will start to expand as he begins to explore and ask questions.

- He may begin to identify colours and shapes, start to sort and match and identify simple concepts like big and small, today and tomorrow.
- He may try to dress and undress with mixed results. He may not yet be toilet trained, but will move towards being day-dry as he approaches three.
- Everything belongs to him. He is not ready to share and may appear defiant and use his hands to express himself by pushing or hitting.
- He will develop rapidly in this period, but remember that there may be big differences in development between individual twos.

HE NEEDS

- Every shred of United Nations-style diplomacy you can muster to help him navigate his world and his emotions.
- Consistency, patience and understanding to accept the limits you set for him.
- More challenges and opportunities to practise – with safety – as his mobility and strength increase.
- Opportunities to play with other children in new and challenging environments.
- To be introduced to other children and the concept of the play date, but he will need you, or a trusted carer, to stay with him. Find a good play group nearby so he can practise new skills.
- Space, time and resources to create, sing, dance and explore.
- Play time where he can experiment with craft materials like paint, clay and dough, and scribble with simple crayons.
- Easy-to-manage, nutritious food and snacks. You may need to apply the 'grazing' rule – eat little and often – to meet his requirements. Make sure he gets plenty of sleep and keep an eye on his TV habits – 30 minutes twice a day is enough.

THREE – TAKING ON THE WORLD

- She is a budding chat show host as her vocabulary increases and she talks about what she is doing, or has done, and asks endless questions in her efforts to build her knowledge of the world around her.
- She will enjoy and seek out the company of other children and might develop a 'grand passion' for a particular friend. She will begin to engage in games that require simple negotiation and cooperation skills, but may easily be frustrated and leave the game when it doesn't go her way. She may spend time watching others at play before choosing to join in.
- She is still getting used to using her body as she learns to run, jump, skip, catch, throw, climb, ride, swing and use craft tools and implements to cut, roll and paint. Don't expect her to get it right all the time.
- Her understanding of concepts and colours increases and she will enjoy simple puzzles, construction toys and blocks of various sizes, as well as games that involve basic logic skills and sequencing activities.
- She will enjoy creative experiences whether it is building with blocks, drawing, sand play or dough. She will develop preferences for certain activities and often seek to return to and repeat or extend these.
- She is still very self-focused but is beginning to understand that other people have feelings and needs and that sometimes she has to wait her turn. She may be helpful and want to be with you or you may be summarily dismissed if she has something more important to do.
- Her competency grows daily and she will be able to manage simple dressing but will still need help and reminders.

SHE NEEDS

- Patience when enthusiasm outstrips skill and ability, leading to tears and frustration when things don't go just as she planned.
- Your help to negotiate to resolve conflict with other children.
- Simple responsibilities with your support, role-modelling and reminders to follow tasks through. She also needs limits to help her learn to take responsibility for her behaviour.
- Tolerance. Remember only to give her one or two directions at a time. Any more and she is likely to forget.
- Lots of opportunities to use her developing muscles and practise hand-eye co-ordination skills: playing with balls, bikes and on swings; in the garden or walking to the park.
- A variety of craft resources so she can paint, use scissors, glue, tape, roll etc.
- Time to listen to different kinds of music and share them with you; to express her responses through singing, dancing and movement.
- The chance to read and be read to, as well as time to chat with adults and peers.
- Opportunities to meet other adults and children through your social networks, playgroup, preschool, day care and play dates. These provide occasions to play simple cooperative games.
- Play to encourage her independence.
- To watch her food intake as she develops likes and dislikes. Encourage and model good eating and activity habits; keep TV and computer time to a minimum and vet what she watches. Install internet-filtering software on your computer and monitor her use.
- Make sure she gets adequate sleep. She still needs at least nine to ten hours a night for optimum health.

FOUR – BLASTING OFF

- Your increasingly confident and skilled four-year-old is bent on exploring and experimenting. He can generally manage his own dressing and toileting but may not yet be night-dry or able to manage complicated fastenings and shoelaces.
- He has developed skills which enable him to engage in progressively complicated play. He is competent at running, climbing, jumping, balancing, swinging and riding, as well as active and dramatic play which can be sustained and revisited over days and sometimes weeks.
- His concentration is improving and he approaches tasks and activities using problem-solving strategies; he is also more able to see tasks through from beginning to end.
- He is showing more confidence and initiative in play, often seeking out the resources he needs rather than using what is on offer. He may show an interest in making things and want to learn and use adult 'tools' to get the job done.
- He may take on different roles as leader, follower or negotiator, and will use language to manipulate games in which he is a participant. His language becomes more complex as his vocabulary grows.
- He is better at managing his own behaviour, at taking turns, following limits and responding to other's needs, but may still express frustration and anger with his hands and angry words. He will have a strong sense of justice, particularly when it applies to himself, and will see the world of right and wrong in terms of absolute black and white.
- He may copy the behaviour of others and not always use the best judgement.
- He will build more complicated constructions and engage in more detailed puzzles. His constructions may be part of a larger dramatic game and involve more than one child.
- His drawings will become more detailed and realistic, and often include a story but he will still experiment with, and manipulate, new materials. An increasing knowledge of shapes, colours, letters and numbers may be evident and an interest in reading and writing may emerge. He will start to understand the concept of counting but may not always count in sequence or get the amounts right.
- He will remember and want to read familiar and favourite stories by himself or with a group and may be able to recall words from memory.
- His knowledge of songs and rhymes increases and he will attempt to incorporate them with play for pleasure or act them out for an audience.
- He will enjoy outings outside the home and activities such as dancing, swimming lessons and visiting friends. He may be happy to stay and play for a short period at a friend's house without you and to go to preschool with confidence.

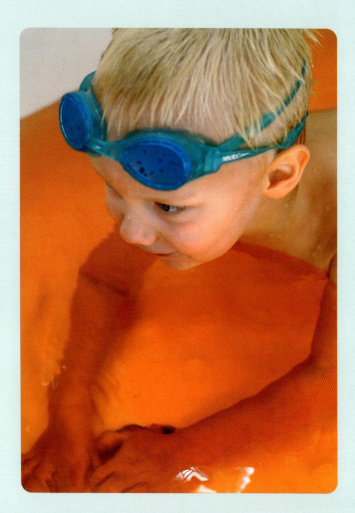

HE NEEDS

- Opportunities to engage in complex play experiences alone and with other children. He needs time to go back and revisit experiences.
- Time, space and resources to match his interests and needs.
- Clear and simple limits and guidelines to encourage responsibility, initiative and independence. Assistance to negotiate difficulties, but he will increasingly show himself able to negotiate outcomes himself.
- Support and encouragement to continue, when he is unsuccessful or frustrated by his lack of ability.
- Independence and the freedom to choose the peers he plays with and to extend his play experiences.
- Guidance in the appropriate use of TV and computers. Limit TV to one hour per day. Allow appropriate games and TV programs and balance this with play and activity away from technology.
- Help with his diet, to make sure he's getting adequate protein, carbohydrates and vegetables to fuel his active body. Encourage him to drink lots of water so he's well hydrated. He still needs nine to ten hours of sleep a night.

FIVE AND BEYOND – UP, UP AND AWAY

- Moving from early to middle childhood, your child is suddenly no longer a baby. This resourceful, capable individual may leave you feeling both nostalgic for the infant she once was and amazed by what she has learned in five short years.
- She is becoming increasingly independent in managing her own needs and tasks like dressing and self-care.
- With a vocabulary of 5000 to 8000 words, she is a capable communicator. Language will play an increasingly significant part in imaginative games, negotiating, facilitating, arguing, organising, telling jokes and stories, or being part of her peer group.
- She completes tasks happily and is competent at organising play and activities with her peer group. She will express her needs and wants clearly, but still needs assistance to manage the difference.
- She is more confident and aware of her body. As her shape changes and becomes longer and slimmer, she constantly refines her physical skills. Her play will extend these skills while she climbs trees, hangs upside down, rides and runs with speed and control, jumps, hops, skips, bats, bowls, throws and balances.
- As she becomes more dextrous, she will manage more complex and creative drawing and writing tasks.
- She will start to develop hobbies and interests and will show pride in her achievements.
- What she visualises may still not match her skills, and she may become distressed by what she perceives as her failings when she compares herself to others.
- While she is physically skilled, she still cannot judge distance well and will need an adult present when negotiating traffic.
- She may become besotted with the latest fad and desperately want to be part of the 'in crowd'. This may create rivalries and fights and cause drama and conflict within the home as well as with her peer group.
- She will start to read and recognise letters, symbols and numbers. She will enjoy simple maths – counting,

sequencing, number correspondence and activities involving mass and length.
- An appreciation of writing as a form of communication develops; she can differentiate between drawing and writing. These skills will grow with knowledge and opportunities to practise. By now, hand preference will be established and she will start to use her dominant hand for most tasks.
- Strong attachments to friends can develop and significant adults such as teachers may become more important. You will constantly be told, 'What my teacher said', till you could happily wish him elsewhere!

SHE NEEDS

- Lots of time to play. Large chunks of freedom and time to explore that will promote health and wellbeing, particularly as she heads off into the world of school.
- Support to learn and refine new skills. Basic knitting, sewing, woodwork, gardening, painting, collage, clay work, cooking and anything that involves building and creating, may be attempted.
- Tolerance and respect, as she learns to develop her talents and understand her limitations, and encouragement to build on her skills when she feels like giving up.
- Opportunities to play and spend time outside the home as her independence and confidence grow.
- To be involved in group activities and sport as she reaches the ages of six and seven. These will develop her social skills and interests.
- Limits on TV and computer time. Keep these items in the shared areas of the home, so you can check on what she is watching. It won't take long for her skills to outstrip yours!
- Good nutrition. This is vital to support her growing body and mind. Encourage her to make good food choices and balance snacks and treats with healthy active play. Try to make eating a shared family experience.

Limits

Let's face it, parenting is a tough job, and as full of frustrations as fantastic moments. Managing a child's behaviour causes more angst than just about any other area of parenting. The point here is to teach children the skills they need to manage their own behaviour so they can face the challenges when you are not there.

I'M YOUR PARENT: THAT'S MY JOB

No one is perfect, neither you, nor your children. Through play, we can help children learn to take responsibility for themselves and others. With guidance, they can begin to see that they are part of a larger family and community, as well as being individuals with rights and responsibilities.

Sometimes I think when your child is born, someone, somewhere, triggers a built-in 'guilt switch' so we spend the rest of our lives worrying about whether we were a good enough parent. Were we too hard, or too soft? Did we do enough or too much? Hours can be spent in self-reproach. Relax! Like all parents, we are doing the best we can with the resources we have. We are learning, too.

RULES FOR A PEACEFUL LIFE ... MAYBE

- **Remember you are the parent:** it's your job. This means having the power of veto. Use it fairly and wisely.
- **Love:** whatever his behaviour, your child should always feel loved and valued. Say, 'I love you, but this behaviour is not okay.'
- **Respect your children:** treat them fairly and help them to learn from their behaviour, rather than punish them. Punishment builds up resentment. Fair treatment teaches children skills to manage their own behaviour when you are not there.
- **Set clear limits and boundaries:** be prepared to change the limits as children's skills and abilities develop. Apply the 'Keep Limits Simple' principle and tailor it to your child's age.

- **Provide simple positive reasons for limits**: for example, 'When you kick the ball into the garden it damages the flowers; please keep it on the grass.'
- **Don't change the rules without warning**: if your child wants to change them, listen and negotiate. If you agree, review the rules. If not, acknowledge his input and be clear about why they will not change.
- **If there's no choice, don't give one**: if it's time to come inside, it's time. It is not a request or a suggestion. Prepare children for change and explain why.
- **Decoding the message**: behaviour is a response to the way we are feeling. Work out what your child is trying to say and it will give you the key to the appropriate response.
- **Consequences**: apply consequences for inappropriate behaviour. Don't threaten them if you are not going to follow through. For example, if she continues to fight with her sister over the TV, then it will be turned off until a suitable agreement is negotiated or peace is restored, NOT next Christmas!
- **Don't argue**: once conflict begins you have both already lost. Be calm, fair and firm. It's not always easy, but it's worth the effort.
- **Saying sorry and moving on**: everyone has bad days, makes mistakes. Help your child acknowledge her errors, make amends and accept responsibility.
- **Your turn to apologise**: if play gets out of control, take some time out, calm down and regroup. Go for a walk, breathe deeply, count to ten and start again. Apologise if you need to. It's important for children to know that we get it wrong sometimes, too. Show them how to recover and move forward.
- **When things get tough**: think about whether your child's behaviour is harming her, other children, or just driving you crazy. Act accordingly. Early intervention can make a big difference.
- **If her behaviour becomes overwhelming**: talk to your GP, paediatrician or local health centre if you feel her behaviour:
  - is harming her,
  - is harmful to other children or prevents her from playing and interacting with them,
  - is not what you would expect from a child of this age.

Toys

One of the really cool things about being a parent is having a legitimate reason to go back to the toy store! Your inner child itches to fill your trolley with treasures … for your child, of course!

THE GREAT TOY DEBATE

When my children were little, we didn't have a lot of money to spare. Buying toys was a constant dilemma between providing good quality multiple-use resources that would appeal to the children and resisting the lure of those sparkly new 'must-haves' that toy companies 'encouraged' us to buy. Before you add to the national debt, there are a few things to consider when choosing toys for your child:

- Choose toys that allow your child scope for exploration. Assess each toy in terms of what the child can do with it, rather than what it claims to do. Many an expensive toy has been abandoned for the cardboard box it came in or used in a way that would horrify the manufacturer and buyer.
- Assess a toy for safety. It needs to be well made, age-appropriate and able to survive the rigours of being run over, thrown off mountains, attacked by invading hordes, buried alive, drowned and played with, day in and day out.
- Expense does not equal quality. Sometimes simple is best.
- Recycle, borrow, share, collect and make toys. Organise a toy swap with your playgroup or preschool and swap or sell discarded toys to raise money for charity.
- Check out garage sales and your local council resource recovery service.
- Discover your local toy library. This can add variety and save money on items that your child may quickly outgrow.
- Buy for your child and not for yourself. Many toys are marketed to parents and have little lasting value to children.
- If you can't see a lot of purpose in the toy, it's probably a waste of money and will just create clutter.
- Build on toys and resources that interest your child.
- Build a collection that encourages all aspects of play.

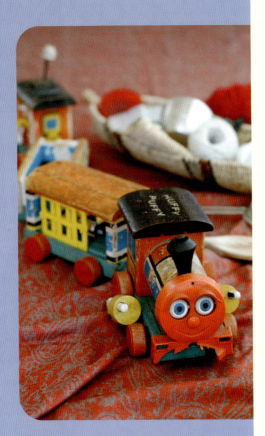

- Buy resources which encourage creativity like drawing, building, imagination and role-play. Toys that do this will be used over and over again.
- Delay gratification. Children, too, are seduced by advertising and fads. If your child really wants something that you feel they don't need, make a way for your child to earn it. This teaches the value of money and tests whether the interest is real or passing. Four-year-olds and up will understand this process, but keep the goal simple and achievable. Five cents a week isn't going to cut it!
- On a serious note, before you buy a toy, think about its impact on the environment. What is the real cost in terms of our planet and its resources, fair trade principles and your child's future?

BE RESOURCEFUL – THINKING OUTSIDE THE SQUARE

Your home is a treasure trove of objects that will stimulate, inspire and extend your child's experiences. Items discovered at home often take on different uses according to the child's needs at any given moment. An old sheet can become a bridal veil, a knight's cape, a theatre curtain, a cubby house, a monster's skin, or somewhere to hide and cuddle up if it's cold. Making use of what you have to hand encourages your child to be resourceful.

AVOID FRUSTRATION

When considering toys, think about your child's skills level and interests. Children will have different needs according to their abilities and stage of development. Some have additional needs relating to health and wellbeing. You want to challenge your child and enhance his experience, but not create frustration or danger.

IT BEGAN WITH A SIMPLE WHEEL

An old boat's steering wheel has been used by two generations of children at my parents' home and is eagerly remembered and requested when the grandchildren visit. Many an around-the-world adventure has started with that wheel for children who have grown up to become teachers, cinematographers, models, sound engineers, historians, designers and electricians.

- **Think handmade:** what skills do you have? Collect materials and think about things you can make together – a bug catcher to a wooden aeroplane, a simple doll's house and clothes for a favourite teddy or even a house for a mouse.
- **Beg, steal or borrow and recycle:** what materials can be borrowed from the house? Blankets, sheets, cushions, bags, old clothes, hats and shoes, magnifying glasses, binoculars, pots, pans, simple tools (with supervision), trays, crates, buckets – the list is as long as your child's imagination. The carton the new fridge came in can make a cubby house to be decorated and painted or, flattened out, a wonderful slide. Washed-out cardboard milk cartons taped together make fantastic building blocks. Fruit or shoe boxes glued together make a stage, a doll's house or shelves to store treasured items in the cubby.

Old plastic yoghurt pots and food containers make buckets and moulds for sand and mud or to carry, tip and pour water. Cardboard rolls make terrific telescopes and, with a bit of tape, binoculars, petrol pump hoses, tree trunks – whatever your child wants. When your child has finished with them, recycle. Perfect!

- **Tinker with spare parts:** consider a box of old radios, walkie-talkies, tape decks, old phones, and bits of machinery that have been checked and assessed, after removing batteries and other non-child-friendly parts, to add another dimension to play.
- **Use offcuts:** planks, odd pieces of timber and offcuts, that have been checked for nails and splinters, make seats, stages and planks to be walked, sat on or acted on. That old fallen branch may end up as a shark, viewed and fought from the safety of a washing basket boat in a wild sea adventure.
- **Something old:** used wheels, tyres and paddles can be used to make something completely new.
- **Mess is good:** make space for natural elements like sand, water, clay, wood, dough and even mud. These materials provide endless opportunities for creativity and yes, mess. Glorious revolting, gooey mess. Make sure there's a bubble bath waiting at the end of the day.

Child's eye view

Everyone's idea of beauty is different. Inside, outside, big or small, this diversity is what makes the world interesting. Celebrate and enjoy the wonderful variety of spaces and places life has to offer.

BEAUTIFUL SPACES

Children will create their own special places and spaces if we just provide the right starting point. Whether you live in an inner city terrace, an urban apartment or a rambling country house, spaces encourage and stimulate vital play or quiet introspection and reflection. If we want our children to develop respect for their environment we need to create beautiful spaces for them to play in.

Often our idea of beauty changes as we experience new and interesting spaces. The way environments are designed can dictate our response to them. Consider the stark fluorescent lighting in the supermarket; the shady green coolness of your street; the warm sand and cool blue of the beach; the vibrant colour and noise of the football stadium; the calm space and soft light of the art gallery. Each of these offers something different for children to experience and incorporate into their play.

YOUR HOME

The joy here is that each family's home environment, and notion of beauty, will be different. Your home is full of objects and spaces that say, This is where I belong, feel safe and comfortable. Its beauty will be experienced at a deeply personal level and will grow from your interests, passions, desires, and values, not necessarily from the pages of the latest home magazine. So whether your space is calm, quiet, organised, minimalist, eclectic, loud, bright, riotous or just plain crazy, it is your unique space. Enjoy it, and make the most of its beauty, so you can begin to share the world with your child.

THINK BEAUTIFUL THOUGHTS

Remember that beauty is in the eye of the beholder. Beauty means different things to different people and our likes and dislikes change and often develop over the years. Try to remember that children are often seeing and experiencing things for the first time and their responses will depend on you. Take time to talk with your child and introduce her to new ideas and places. Even the beauty of the humble caterpillar can be appreciated.

CREATING SPECIAL SPACES

- Think about the world through your child's eyes. Aim to create a feeling of freedom. Ask, 'Can I explore here and be safe?'
- Make space where children can be alone while you still keep an eye on them. Cultivate your inner CIA agent. Be alert and aware, but not visible all the time.
- Help children create spaces to enjoy peace and quiet. It can be as simple as offering a beautiful piece of material or coloured sheet to put over a coffee table with cushions underneath to make a reading nook, a cave, or a submarine.
- Have recycled and other objects on hand so children can make their own play materials. A wheel and a cardboard box can take you to the moon, over the sea or on a picnic.
- Make sure children have access to large spaces where they can run and use their bodies and expend their energy. If your yard is small, explore your local parks. Choose them because they make you and your children feel welcome. Public spaces should cater for both children and adults.
- Spaces should be child-friendly. This doesn't mean that your home should be one giant toy box, but you need places that are flexible so children can adapt them to their own needs.
- Does the space provide opportunities to explore and discover?
- Children should learn to respect shared spaces. This means learning that a particular space in the home requires a different approach when we play and that the needs of all the family must be considered.
- Put precious items out of reach or away until your child is mature enough to understand its value to you.
- Books and toys should be easy to access in attractive baskets and containers that are as easy to unpack as pack away or stored in containers in convenient cupboards and drawers. Finding the Lego® underfoot on a 2am trip to the kitchen in the dark is not pleasant!

- Think about colour. Do the colours in your home scream and shout, or do they welcome and invite? Is there sun in winter and shade in summer?
- Think about texture. Is there a variety of natural and man-made surfaces and objects? Is nature expressed in plants, flowers and trees, or sand and water?
- Is it a noisy, or a peaceful space? Are there both natural and man-made noises for the child to experience – traffic sounds, a water feature, a sound mobile or the crunch of autumn leaves?
- What does it smell like? Is there grass to lie on, an open window to bring in the breeze or to look at the view; are there interesting (safe) plants to crush, inhale and add to a mud or dough pie?
- Does it invite curiosity? Remember what it was like when going into the backyard was an expedition of discovery into the unknown?
- Are there different levels for children to play on; are there steps or a deck, a hill to climb? Are there things to crawl under?
- Ask whether the shared areas of your home convey the message that children are valued and belong. Does it say, We all live here?

Where the sidewalk ends

PRETEND・EXPERIMENT
LET'S COMMUNICATE・CREATE
MUSIC・LET'S MOVE・NATURE

To step off into the world of play very little direction is required to encourage children to think, pretend, create, imagine, dance and sing their way into a blissful day. With a little imagination, and some clever ideas and props, the stage is set for fun and adventure.

Pretend

In pretend play the child has the chance to put herself in someone else's shoes. She can be anyone or anything. She can fight lions, drive buses, care for a sick baby, go shopping or save the world … all before lunch.

I'LL TAKE TWO SUGARS AND A CAPE WITH THAT ...

As a parent and educator, I can't begin to guess how many imaginary cups of tea I've had prepared for me by small children. Each one serves to remind me that pretend play is a powerful activity in which children recreate the rituals of daily life, as well as develop their own rich, imagined inner worlds.

Initially inspired by the real world, children will play at what they know and the daily drama of the home will emerge as burnt toast and cups of tea. As your child grows, and her imagination develops, pretend play roles will increase in complexity, and imaginary people or storybook, TV and movie characters may emerge. Play will often be complex and governed by unspoken rules as children become deeply engrossed, returning to the game over days and weeks as the story unfolds. They will step in and out of roles as they extend and negotiate the plot and props.

The biggest contribution you can make is the provision of unstructured free time and space to allow the plot to develop, and resources that set the scene, enabling children to enter the world of their characters. You'll also need to provide occasional assistance to solve problems and calm arguments, or even to play an extra when there are too many roles for them to manage.

At home you can facilitate this type of play by being prepared and providing treasures stored for when the occasion arises.

CRAFT CRATE

Keeping a container filled with craft items may be useful when your children are making objects to extend their play. Include things like paper, pens, glue, scissors, sticky tape, old material, cardboard rolls, recycled plastic food containers of various sizes, plastic lids, bits of foil, leftover wrapping paper, wool, old greetings cards, one or two interesting magazines, stickers, whatever you can find and add that may be of interest. This is also a great way to give items a second life before recycling.

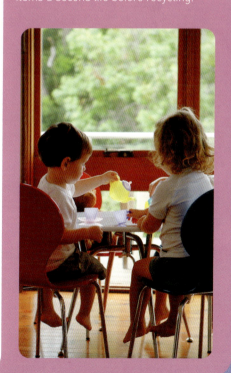

PROPS BOX

A plastic crate, woven basket or old suitcase full of dress-up items is like a treasure chest to explore. Jackets, boots and shoes, scarves, bags, hats, costume jewellery, small sheets, a blanket, some interesting pieces of material etc can be included. You can add finds from junk sales and charity shops such as a plastic sword, an old mobile phone or stand-alone telephone, a typewriter, sunglasses, or old frames (glass removed) and wigs (wash in washing machine before use). Use these to supplement what children borrow from around the house to extend their imaginations. Dig around in your closet, or even see what's hiding in Grandma's cupboards, for interesting items like shawls, caps, gumboots, raincoats, knitted or homemade blankets. These items will add a new dimension to your children's play and can be used to represent characters in their games.

MASKS AND HATS

Simple masks and hats can be made with very few resources. Paper plates or bits of cardboard and elastic, decorated with paper and pens, can create lions and tigers or superhero masks. Decorated ice-cream containers can become workmen's hats and space helmets. You just need glue, felt-tip pens, cellophane, materials and foil. When children make their own items, they are learning new and vital skills.

PUPPET THEATRE

A simple puppet theatre can be made out of boxes, large or small, with a section cut out for the 'stage' and a scrap of material glued or stapled for the curtains. Children can paint and decorate and make their own hand or finger puppets or use toys. This is a great rainy day activity and the box can be folded flat and stored for next time.

BORROWED ITEMS

Many things needed for pretend play can be borrowed from around the house. Plastic containers, wooden spoons, cups, plates, sheets and blankets, buckets and jugs, washing baskets, the esky, or even the picnic basket, can be used and returned to wherever they came from.

Experiment

Through trial and error, children learn to solve problems and predict outcomes in their drive to learn more about how substances interact with each other and how things work.

WHAT WOULD HAPPEN IF…?

Learning to reason and think logically are the outcomes of observing, experimenting and achieving. Children's capabilities increase as they learn from their mistakes, challenge what they know and generate new understandings.

It's easy for parents to fall into the trap of providing all the answers, but it's much less satisfying than seeing the joy of discovery on your child's face when he finds things out for himself. It's important that children understand that we don't have all the answers.

Children love to explore their surroundings. Learning by doing is part of the process of acquiring knowledge.

We are only expert at what we have been trained to do so take the opportunity to learn something new with your child, cultivate your own curiosity and share your newfound knowledge. Watch carefully to see where your child needs assistance, support and resources, so that he can move forward.

THEY WILL NEED:

- Puzzles of varying ability and interest as well as sorting, sequencing and logic games.
- Building and construction toys. Blocks of various sizes which stack, stick and press together.
- You to ask questions that encourage him to think about alternatives.
- You to use language to help solve problems. For example, that shape has a round smooth edge and is coloured blue. Can you see a place where it might fit?
- Real-world building projects like woodwork and 3D collage activities.
- Resources to help him explore and record such as magnifying glasses, bug catchers, and containers to keep collections in.
- Assistance to research subjects that interest him at the library and online.

Experiment 51

EXPLORER'S KIT

They will need an easy-to-carry container such as an old basket or backpack. Add a magnifying glass; bug catcher; some see-through containers with lids for his specimens; a camera; paper and pencils to record and draw what he finds and sees; a tape measure; compass; small binoculars; string; a small trowel or fork; a couple of small zip-lock or brown paper bags; a small unbreakable mirror; a torch.

Pack a hat, a snack and a bottle of water and away he goes.

UNDERWATER MAGNIFIER

Whether swimming at the pool, having a bath or playing at the beach, children love to explore the world under water. This simple magnifier can be made at home and used to enlarge objects so children can study things they find in the water up close. Use it at home in the bath or take it to the beach and explore the rock pools at low tide.

You will need: a wide waterproof cylinder, either a 30cm (12") length of PVC plumbing pipe or a large disposable soda bottle (it needs to be approximately 10cm (4") in diameter); cling wrap; a wide rubber band or strong waterproof string to fit around the container and hold the cling wrap in place; medium and fine grade sandpaper; a utility knife.

If using the soda bottle cut the top and bottom third from the bottle so you have a hollow cylinder or ask your friendly hardware shop to cut you a length of plumbing pipe and use sandpaper to smooth any rough or sharp edges. Use the rubber band or string to attach a sheet of cling wrap tightly across one end. Use the magnifier by placing over an object in the water and pushing down gently. The pressure of the water creates a concave lens. Experiment and see how the magnifier increases the size of the objects and talk about what you can see. Have extra cling wrap to hand for damage control.

BALLOON ROCKETS

DIFFICULTY **2**   MESS FACTOR **1**   PREP TIME **20 MINS**   AGE **3+**

Children love speed and this experiment lets them explore propulsion and the effect of air. This is a good collaborative task.

You will need:
- **enough cardboard cylinders (15-20cm long) so each child has a 'rocket', or an empty tin foil or cling wrap roll, cut in half**
- **strong string**
- **masking tape**
- **balloons (have extras in case they burst)**
- **felt-tip pens, pencils**
- **scissors**

- First, find a place where you can tie the string between two objects. They need to be about 5m apart. The string must be really taut.
- Get the children to make their rockets and decorate the cylinders. Slide the rockets onto the string and then tie up. Keep them above children's head height to avoid accidents.
- Blow up a balloon, hold end closed and carefully stick to the underside of the rocket with two pieces of tape.
- When ready, commence the countdown, let the balloon rocket go and see how far it travels. The children can organise races and see whose rocket propels the furthest.

Experiment 53

CHILDREN'S TOOLKIT

Play tools are great fun for 'under threes' who like to pretend to be Mum or Dad. Once they reach about the age of four, children need a small toolkit to help them with explorations and investigations. While many of these can be found in shops it's simple and easy to create one yourself. Before you decide to set up a toolkit, make sure that you think your children have developed enough to understand some simple limits based on its use. For example, don't unscrew the coffee table or dismantle the sound system! Buy the best quality tools you can so the tool does the job and doesn't frustrate your children or you, by breaking or bending things out of shape.

For a small toolkit include some or all of the following:
- Small hammer; Phillips head screwdriver and straight slot screwdriver; a small torch; tape measure or rule; small steel or plastic ruler; carpenter's pencil and eraser; pliers; magnifying glass; sheets of sandpaper; a soft paint brush; a small spirit level; glue; electrical tape; safety goggles; perhaps a simple fret saw – but only if you are sure your child is able to manage and use the tool appropriately.
- Make sure tools are appropriate to the size of your child's hands.
- As they grow older and more competent, you can add items when they require them.

DIY BOARD GAME

DIFFICULTY **4**   MESS FACTOR **2**   PREP TIME **1+** HOURS   AGE **4-6+**

Playing games with your children is a great way to spend an afternoon when you have a bit of free time. Board games help them to exercise their problem-solving skills and imaginations.

You can create your own game around an aspect of your family or community – base it on people and places she knows and enjoys.

Play one-on-one with your child or with a group of children during a holiday play day. Remember to let her guide your involvement.

You will need:
- **one sheet of cardboard or white foam board**
- **felt-tip pens**
- **construction paper**
- **contact paper**
- **'theme' stickers to suit your game**
- **dice**
- **game tokens**
- **camera and or magazines to find useful pictures**
- **glue**
- **scissors**

- Draw a pathway or track on the construction paper and divide into sections or squares that you will later move along.
- Create some squares that introduce barriers such as 'lose a turn, waiting to cross the road'; create squares to jump ahead such as 'take a shortcut to get to the next section quickly'; 'move forward two places'. Look at other board games for inspiration.
- Decorate your board. Take photos or draw pictures of places you want to represent that relate to the theme in your game and glue them onto the board.
- Glue the construction paper to the cardboard or foam board. You can cover the board with contact paper to protect it if you wish.
- To make the game pieces, glue photographs or pictures onto lightweight cardboard, cut them out and cover them with contact.
- Talk about the rules of the game and list them.
- Get your family or children's friends together, pick a game piece and let the game begin.
- Remember, your child may want to alter or change the rules. This is a very fluid activity and children should be encouraged to think and make changes as the game unfolds.

SPUR THE IMAGINATION

Design your game around something that interests your child. The object of the game might be to get from your house to your holiday destination or Grandma's house.

Or you could build a car racetrack or create a journey to a fairy castle. A photo of your house could be used for the 'start' square if you are making a 'journey' game. You could draw the starting flag and grid of the car racetrack, or a house to start the journey to the fairy castle. Barriers could include 'stop to buy Grandma some milk'; 'fight a dragon', 'flat tyre' etc.

You could make cars for the racing game, fairies for the journey to the castle, or use photos of your family for the trip to Grandma's house — the possibilities are endless.

GAMES TO MAKE AND EXPERIENCES TO SHARE

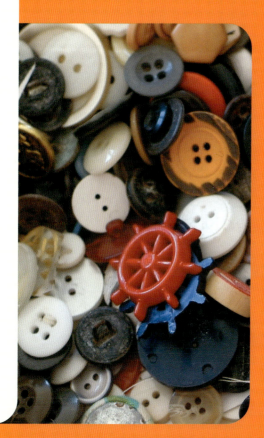

- Make a kite, pinwheel or whirligig to explore the properties of the wind and the air.
- Watch the wind direction with a homemade windsock.
- Put in a rain gauge and check it together.
- Watch clouds and talk about their different shapes and note the changes in the weather.
- Take a 'listening' walk - no talking unless absolutely necessary; or go to the park, lie in the shade and listen to the sounds of nature.
- Take the time to listen to a sea shell.
- Fill old glass bottles of different sizes with water and make your own bottle xylophone.
- Play hide-and-seek inside or outside.
- Colour the world with cellophane glasses.
- Blow and pop bubbles for fun.
- Make your shadows long and short, draw around them with chalk or on paper.
- Make binoculars out of a cardboard roll.
- Make sorting games out of natural, collected or recycled items. A basket of colourful buttons or pegs to sort and thread, a container of different textured stones or seedpods, can provide an afternoon of fun.
- Make a map with your child and head off on an adventure.

EVERYDAY EXPERIMENTS

Many routine activities at home provide opportunities for children to learn about and engage in basic maths and science. What's ordinary for adults can be wonder-filled experiences for children.

In the kitchen: counting, stacking and sorting cutlery and crockery, exploring the tastes, and textures, of food; washing-up to learn about concepts of hot/cold, wet/dry, dirty/clean.

Laundry: counting and sorting pegs, socks, clothes; the concepts of inside-out and back-to-front; ordering, sorting and remembering what belongs to whom and the shape and feel of different materials.

Shopping: good for the memory; find items and count them into the trolley, follow a sequence as you go down the aisle and use a list; concepts of big/small, soft/hard, cold/hot and rough/smooth as we choose fruit and vegetables, dairy and freezer items.

Washing the car: changing the nature of water as you add detergent; the properties of water as it flows and beads, drops and dribbles; concepts like warm, wet, cold, frothy, soapy, full and empty; sponges and their water-retaining properties, floating and sinking. Children can also learn about the environment and ways to conserve water – using a bucket instead of a hose.

Explore: have boxes of 'tools' handy to explore scientific concepts. Add thermometers, jugs and beakers, clear plastic tubes, magnets, string, tweezers, scales and safety glasses, measuring spoons, eyedroppers and straws. A kitchen timer will help monitor the time spent on important experiments.

SALAD DRESSING

DIFFICULTY **1**   MESS FACTOR **1**   PREP TIME **5** MINS   AGE **3+**   MAKES **1 cup**

Making a salad dressing is a great introduction to the properties of different liquids. You can explain that no two liquids are the same and watch as the liquids separate into layers. Note that the finely chopped garlic will float in the middle of the liquid layers. Your child can help collect the ingredients from the pantry, then pour, with you guiding the amounts required.

You'll need measuring cups and measuring spoons – which are useful tools to help explain liquid amounts – and a jar or bottle with a lid.

- ⅓ cup olive oil
- ⅓ cup grapeseed oil
- 3 tablespoons mirin
- 2 tablespoons balsamic vinegar
- 1 tablespoon soy sauce
- 1 garlic clove, finely chopped

- Let the children measure and add the ingredients to the jar or bottle.
- Let them help to secure the lid of the container and then shake it vigorously – watching the change in consistency as the liquids combine.
- As the dressing settles, again watch the different layers appear.

The liquids separate because some of them are lighter, or less dense, than others. A lighter liquid will float on top of a heavier, or more dense liquid. This is a really delicious dressing, just perfect for salad.

RAINBOW SALAD

Making a salad with as many different coloured vegetables as possible is a good way to learn some basic science. Observe the colours of vegetables and discuss how they occur as a result of the amount of chlorophyll they absorb. You can also discuss what parts of the vegetable you are going to eat, whether it is the fruit, leaves, flowers, stems or roots of the plant.

Choose vegetables from a wide variety of sources. You can try:

Red: cherry tomatoes, red capsicum (pepper), radishes;
Green: avocados, beans, lettuce, broccoli, green capsicum (pepper), herbs, snow peas (mange tout), spinach, rocket (arugula), celery, asparagus;
Yellow: yellow capsicum (pepper), corn, yellow beans;
Orange: carrot, kumara, pumpkin;
Purple: beetroot (beet), red onion, red cabbage;
White: cauliflower, fennel, mushrooms, daikon radish.

- Let the children help to peel, chop, grate, shred and tear and taste the vegetables as you add your selection to an attractive bowl or plate. Your children might like to sort them by colour or type, or create a salad theme of leaves, fruits, roots or stems.
- Add the dressing, toss your salad, and share.

Experiment

SCRUMPTIOUS SPROUTS!

DIFFICULTY **1**   MESS FACTOR **1**   PREP TIME **15** MINUTES TO SET UP/OVERNIGHT TO SOAK AND FOUR TO FIVE DAYS GROWING TIME   SERVES **4**

Sprouting seeds – sprouts - are healthy and very easy to grow. They will grow in any climate, in any small space indoors, all year round. Sprouts are the perfect example of a 'living' food and from a scientific point of view, demonstrate in a short space of time how to grow something edible from seeds. Concepts like germination and photosynthesis (the conversion of light into chemical energy), and the identification of plant parts may interest older children.

Best of all, eating sprouts will help boost your nutritional intake. Sprouts are rich in antioxidants, vitamins and minerals, high in fibre and easy to digest. They will spruce up any salad, sandwich or stir-fry.

You will need:

- Two or three tablespoons of seeds for sprouting. I like a combination of red and brown lentils, alfalfa or cress seeds and mung beans. You can buy your own seeds from the local health or organic shop and some nurseries sell packets of sprouting seeds. Don't use other nursery packet seeds as they have been treated with chemicals and are not suitable or safe to sprout. Remember that the smaller the seed, the more volume it will create as it grows and that seeds grow at a faster or slower rate, depending on the temperature.
- A jar sprouter (available from health food stores) or a one litre plastic or glass jar with a wide opening.

- Some large, wide rubber bands.
- A clean, washed pair of stockings. Cut a double section of a leg to lie easily over the jar opening with about 2 to 3 cm overhang or a new, washed, open weave disposable kitchen cloth.
- Inspect the seeds and remove any that look old or broken and check there are no small stones or other foreign materials.
- If using a jar sprouter follow the manufacturer's instructions or;
- Soak the seeds in ¾ of a cup of warm water in your sprouter or jar overnight to speed up germination.
- Next morning place the cut stocking or kitchen cloth over the mouth of your jar and secure with a couple of rubber bands. This creates a sieve for draining your seeds.
- Rinse the seeds with cold tap water twice and drain through the stocking or cloth covering opening.
- Stand the jar on its end at a 45 degree angle on the kitchen bench. A half-rolled hand towel will help to stabilise your jar and absorb any water that drains out or you can balance it, stocking side down, in your dish drainer if water collects in the neck of the jar. Excess water sitting in the jar will cause bacteria to grow and ferment and ruin your seeds.
- Rinse the seeds two or three times a day with cold tap water and after draining, gently rotate the jar to loosen the seeds and prevent them from bunching together. It is important they stay moist but not too wet.
- You can chart or photograph the sprouts each day with your child as you discuss the changes as they occur.
- As a rule of thumb when the sprouts are two to three times the length of the seed, they are ready to eat.
- Wash and store the sprouts in a container in the crisper section of your fridge and add to salads and sandwiches, or eat by the handful.
- For maximum freshness, eat within three days.

Let's communicate

Interact, read, respond ... The ability to communicate through language, storytelling, music and dance not only connects us to each other but allows the spirit to soar

MAKING CONTACT

There are so many ways to communicate with others. More than just talking, interaction through story, drama and music adds richness and depth to our experience.

Have you ever wondered how many times a day we communicate with our children? Thousands of small verbal and non-verbal interactions occur. Every one of these creates an opportunity to learn or practise a skill, feeds the spirit, creates shared experiences and gives a child just that little bit more information about the world.

Make time to communicate and talk to your child every day:

- Share a family dinnertime; chat over a snack or game after school or before bedtime.
- Encourage her to express herself through stories, music, singing, signing or art.
- You can support her learning your home language if it is other than English.
- Help her to express her thoughts and feelings and to read the way others are feeling, for example, 'I can see you are feeling sad, because you have lost your teddy'; or 'Cinzia is upset, because she hurt her leg when she fell.'
- Show her you are listening to her by sitting or kneeling down and making physical or eye contact.
- Listen, not just to her words, but to what she is trying to tell you. 'Mummy I have a fire engine in my tummy', is a child making a powerful statement about an upset stomach that should not be treated humorously or ignored.
- Communicate with other adults and children, for example, a phone call to Grandma to tell her about the bird you saw on your walk; say hello to a favourite aunty by helping your child send an email; choose and send a birthday card to a cousin with her own special message.
- Talk about the signs you see when driving in the car or walking together and what they mean to help build an understanding of communication through print.
- Play with language. Make up silly songs and poems, tell jokes and stories, share things that may interest her and listen to her jokes and stories in return.

JUST ONE MORE ... PLEASE!

Storytelling is one of the oldest art forms. It is used not only to entertain, but to pass on culture and history and teach values and beliefs. Storytelling and reading build vocabulary and language, introduce new ideas and provide information and knowledge where first-hand experiences may not be possible.

Reading to, and sharing books with your child is a daily joy! It brings you closer together, not only through physical touch and bonding, but by creating a shared experience to sustain and maintain your relationship. My children still remember and quote poems I read to them when they were small children and they discuss books and stories we shared.

Good books and literature for children abound. Buy or borrow books for your children to challenge and interest them as they grow up. Here are some tips for choosing books, but first, some ideas to get you going:

- Please, please, please read to your child every day!
- Make sure your child has access to a range of reading material – from alphabet, counting and story books to poetry, reference books, fiction and appropriate non fiction to fuel his imagination and knowledge.
- Be guided by your child's interests and let them be part of the process of choosing books as soon as possible.
- Use your local library. Story sessions are generally available and borrowed items can extend home resources at minimal cost.
- Tell stories. Make them up, retell favourite stories from your childhood or tell stories about your own childhood adventures.
- Teach your child to care for his books and store them in easily accessible containers or on low shelves.
- Read aloud to older children or share a book as a family.
- Model good habits by reading where your children can see you.
- Encourage your child to make up and illustrate his own stories and publish these by hand or on the computer.
- Create spaces that encourage reading. A comfy chair or beanbag or a book nook invite the child to read and are also spaces for quiet reflection.
- Tapes, DVDs and CDs of favourite stories can enhance the story experience. Make your own recordings as you read the book.
- Use expression when reading and storytelling. Give characters their own voices to create mood and build the plot.
- We don't always have to read 'good stuff'. Everyone likes to indulge in a comic, magazine or light read once in a while. It's okay to indulge. Magazines can be useful non-fiction resources on topics children are interested in and comics can be fun and provide an entry into the world of literature for the reluctant reader.
- Share interesting, relevant bits from the newspaper and retell them in words your child can understand.

BUYING BOOKS

When purchasing books, think about what each book will add to your family library. Ask yourself:

- Does the story have an appropriate theme and a logical ending that will make sense to the child?
- Do the layout, illustration and text work well together to create the story experience?
- Is there too much or not enough text for your child? Is the language developmentally appropriate?
- Are there positive role models and is there gender equality in the story?
- Does the story reflect positive images of characters from different and diverse backgrounds?
- Is the book easy to manage for small hands and fingers?
- Is the book sturdy enough to stand up to regular use?
- Does the book include familiar events and people as well as new and interesting ideas.
- Is the book worthy of your child's intelligence and time?
- Is it worth the investment?

Let's communicate

READING TO YOUR CHILDREN

- **Be comfy:** make sure you are comfortable. Whether you are inside or outside, in a chair, on a couch, lying on the bed or cushions on the floor, everyone should feel relaxed.
- **Remove distractions:** if possible, find a quiet place to read together. Turn off the TV, computer and radio.
- **Prepare:** make sure you have read the story first. This helps you to concentrate on your 'audience' in the telling.
- **Be joyful:** you are sharing this moment with your child. Let your wonder and pleasure show.
- **Use your voice:** small eyes will widen in wonder if you use your voice to build suspense, create characters and evoke emotion and action.
- **Use your eyes:** make contact with your children while telling the story. Half the story's joy is in the connection between those sharing the moment.
- **Respond:** let the words determine the way you tell the story. Make the words shout and whisper according to the text.
- **Rhythm:** allow the natural rhythm of the story to emerge. Fast, slow, bumpy, smooth – let the words sing with their own music.
- **Sound effects:** create your own with your voice, or get the children to join in and make crickets chirrup and bears roar.
- **Build mood:** the ending of a good story needs to be deeply satisfying to the reader and listener. As the resolution or climax is reached, don't hurry the last page of text, but pause to allow the story to resonate before moving on to what is coming next.
- **Discuss:** if the child wants to talk about the story, allow time to consider his thoughts and ideas about the book.
- **Repeat:** be prepared to read it again and again and again!

Create

'Some painters transform the sun into a yellow spot, others transform a yellow spot into the sun', PABLO PICASSO ... Dream, Represent, Express

FEEDING THE MIND AND SPIRIT

No one would argue that we want our children to grow up with the skills required for a successful life. True intelligence, however, requires imagination – the ability to both create and express ideas, to break the boundaries of convention and to bring new meaning and understanding to everyday experiences. Painting, drawing, sculpture, collage, music, dancing and movement provide opportunities for children to share their developing understanding of life.

Being creative allows your child to see things in a new way and to express her ideas in a manner that's sometimes unconventional and unique. Children can express their creativity through art, music and dance to explore ideas, push the boundaries of their knowledge, understanding and imagination and to feed their spirit.

Support your child's creativity by:
- Developing a warm and trusting relationship which lets your children know it's okay to be themselves.
- Creating a spirit of acceptance for their ideas and creative pursuits.
- Showing them that as adults we celebrate creativity and individual expression.
- Providing toys and resources that can be used in new and creative ways.
- Creating opportunities for them to be creative, to paint, to build, draw, dance and sing.
- Visiting and sharing creative spaces like galleries and sculpture gardens and attending performances such as plays, musical events and puppet shows to open the world of individuality and creativity to them.

MAKE YOUR OWN ART BOX

You will need:
- Different textures of paper, cardboard, corrugated paper and card.
- Brushes of different shapes and sizes. Buy them cheaply at discount shops.
- Glue sticks, liquid and model glue for the tough jobs.
- Eye droppers, plastic syringes (without needles, of course), spray bottles, improvised brushes such as nailbrushes, toothbrushes, paint rollers, cotton buds, paddle pop sticks and sponges.
- Crayons, pastels, chalk, pencils, water-based felt-tip pens, children's scissors, pencil sharpeners, sticky tape, masking tape.
- Adult scissors, pinking shears, utility knife and extra-strong glue or a glue gun. (ONLY UNDER ADULT SUPERVISION)

ART

Every child loves to have an art space. Whether this is a box or basket full of pencils, paper and crayons; the bottom kitchen drawer willingly sacrificed to glue, scissors and paint; a shelf in the hall cupboard or a permanent space in the child's room, the home study, garage, shed ... wherever children need space to create.

I could fill this section with lots of art activities for you to do with your child, but this would defeat the purpose of encouraging true creativity. What we want to do is encourage self-expression not just rehashing more of the same, so here are ideas, tools, resources and recipes to help you create space for open expression and creativity:

Here goes!
- Make art and craft materials freely available to your child.
- Encourage her to use a wide variety of materials, paint, pencils, crayons, clay, dough, paper and glue.
- Keep some recycled material such as cartons, boxes, washed-out containers, leftover materials and birthday/Christmas papers, cards, cardboard cylinders, yoghurt containers, old buttons, wooden pegs, pipe cleaners and anything else interesting on hand for building and making.
- Encourage her to find her own solutions to problems when she's painting or creating. Instead of stepping in the minute she asks for help, say, 'How do you think you could do it?' or 'I wonder what would happen if you did?' Try to let her arrive at her own solution and help her to complete the task, rather than doing it for her.
- Celebrate her work and comment on the colours and shapes and if she wants to discuss it do so, but remember having completed the project she may be finished with it and not want to talk about it. Respect this.
- Make a space to display her art. Send pictures to family members and keep some stored for the future.

PAINT

DIFFICULTY **2**   MESS FACTOR **3**   PREP TIME **15** MINS   AGE **2+**   MAKES **4-5 cups**

Buying paint can be expensive. This simple recipe can provide a cheaper alternative than bought paint and making it is a fun activity for your children. They can help collect and measure the cold and dry ingredients. Older children can help stir the mixture and add a few drops of their chosen food colouring.

Make the paint thinner or thicker by altering the amount of water. It can be used with brushes or for finger painting.

You will need:
- **2 cups cornflour**
- **1 cup cold water**
- **4-5 cups hot water from the jug or kettle**
- **soap flakes**
- **food colouring, optional (gel and powder colours are available from kitchen and cake decorating shops and give really rich, vibrant colours)**

- Mix cornflour and cold water in a bowl.
- Heat other water in a saucepan until very hot.
- Take off the heat and stir in cornflour mixture.
- Put the mixture back on the heat, stirring constantly until it thickens and is smooth.
- Add colour if desired, or pour into 4 cups and colour each differently.
- Cover with cling wrap and store in the fridge when not in use.
- Adding soap flakes or a little detergent can help to minimise staining on clothes.

SOAP CRAYONS

You can make your own crayons with this simple recipe.

You will need:
2 cups soap flakes
2 tbsp hot water
food colouring, paint or dye

Mix ingredients together to form a thick paste. This takes time. Press mixture into moulds, such as ice cube trays, or form into small 'sausages'. Leave to set for two days. They can be used on paper or in the bath.

COLLAGE

Paper, glue and sticky tape fascinate children. They can see limitless possibilities in what the rest of us would call a load of old junk. Opportunities to cut, paste and stick encourage thinking, problem-solving and stimulate the imagination.

A couple of cardboard boxes and a yoghurt container can become a jet plane or a dog. Two tissue boxes make wonderful and challenging shoes to play in. Paper can provide endless opportunities to tear, scrunch, twist, snip as 2D and 3D creations emerge.

Younger children may be happy simply to spread glue all over the paper or stick endless pieces of sticky tape on everything, but older three-and four-year-olds will want to make and create independently.

SIMPLE STICK & FINGER PUPPETS

DIFFICULTY **2**   MESS FACTOR **3**   PREP TIME **10** MINS   AGE **2+**

A wonderful activity that develops out of collage. Children will delight in making a creature that can have its own voice and personality. Younger children may not be interested in performing yet, but older ones will enjoy putting on a show. Be prepared to be entertained, again and again and again!

You will need:
- **cardboard**
- **range of coloured and textured papers**
- **old magazines**
- **wool, cotton, material and felt remnants**
- **paddle pop sticks and/or chopsticks**
- **glue**
- **sticky tape**
- **scissors**
- **stapler**
- **felt-tip pens, crayons, pencils**

‣ Encourage your child to draw and invent his own puppet creatures on the card.
‣ You may have to model this initially to show him how to make the puppet.
‣ Encourage him to cut out, draw or even sew clothes and hair for the puppet.
‣ Add the hair, eyes, clothes etc, and then either glue or sticky tape to a paddle pop stick, or chopstick, or glue a ring of cardboard to the back, through which the child can slip his finger.

See *Pretend* play, page 49.

CLAY

Clay has been used for centuries as a material for domestic pots, plates, storage containers and for decorative purposes. It is still used to produce both serviceable and artistic products throughout the world. As a natural substance, clay comes in a variety of colours and textures depending on its origins and is reasonably cheap to purchase. Clay hardens when exposed to the air but it can be reused and rejuvenated even when dry. Children can gain satisfaction and pleasure breaking it up with small hammers and putting it in water to reconstitute it for further use. This helps to develop an understanding of the scientific properties of clay as well as making it a fabulous and engrossing medium for creative activity. While playdough has its place I would choose clay any day for its rich and varied potential in play.

You will need:

- Clay from a reputable art supplier. It must be soft and malleable. Try to buy it in small amounts as it tends to dry out quickly once it's opened. Or buy a packet and divide it up between friends.
- A piece of strong string to cut the fresh clay slabs into workable pieces.
- An apron or old clothes.
- Paddle pop sticks, toothpicks, rolling pins (don't use your kitchen one, buy a cheapie from the discount shop).
- Containers to keep your clay in.
- Interesting natural and man-made items to make patterns and textures.
- Cling wrap or wet cloths to keep clay damp.
- Clay can be used indoors or outdoors. It is important to have a good surface underneath to work on, such as a heavy duty plain, plastic cloth, a vinyl place mat or an old cake or bread board.

GETTING DIRTY

- Offer your child a ball of clay and encourage them to explore it with their hands, pounding, pinching, flattening, squeezing and poking. As children start to see its potential, show them how to roll it and make coils, roll it flat into a slab with a rolling pin, cut it into tile shapes, and join it together with paddle pop sticks and toothpicks.
- As their skills increase add interesting objects to make textures and patterns in the clay such as seeds, stamps, textured cloth and shells.
- Teach your child to make a cream-like slurry of clay and water to join pieces together or to smooth the surface of the clay.
- Make a coil or pinch pot. Let your imagination guide you.
- When your child has finished with the clay, leave her creations in the sun to dry or roll it into balls and push a finger into the middle to create a hollow. Put the balls into an airtight container and fill the holes with a little water to help keep the clay moist. Store in a cool place.
- When dry, your children's creations can be painted and displayed in your very own art gallery. Invite family and friends to the opening ceremony.
- Take the opportunity to visit a pottery or potter's studio, watch the potter at work, and talk about what kind of items the potter is making and their uses.

CLAY FACES

DIFFICULTY **2**   MESS FACTOR **4**   PREP TIME **15** MINS   AGE **2+**

Your children will have lots of fun making individual faces. They will develop their fine and motor skills as they manipulate the clay and create a unique face.

You will need:
- clay
- small rolling pin or short lengths of dowel
- apron or old clothes
- paddle pop sticks
- plastic forks
- roll of cling wrap
- heavy plastic tablecloth
- small mirror
- non-toxic acrylic paint

▸ Give children a lump of clay about the size of an orange and a rolling pin. Encourage them to thump or roll the clay until it is reasonably flat, round or oval. If children have not used clay before they may simply want to play and experiment. If this happens go with it and leave clay faces for another day.

▸ Encourage children to look in the mirror or at other people's faces and to add eyes, hair, ears, mouths and noses by moulding and rolling extra clay or glueing bits of clay inplace with slurry and toothpicks. Younger children can draw on the clay with their fingers, or a plastic fork or paddle pop stick.

▸ Use a stick to push a hole in the top of the face.

▸ When complete put the faces in the sun to dry.

▸ When dry, faces can be painted and hung up using the hole through which you can thread a piece of ribbon or string.

For more craft activities and recipes, read *Small Fry Outdoors*

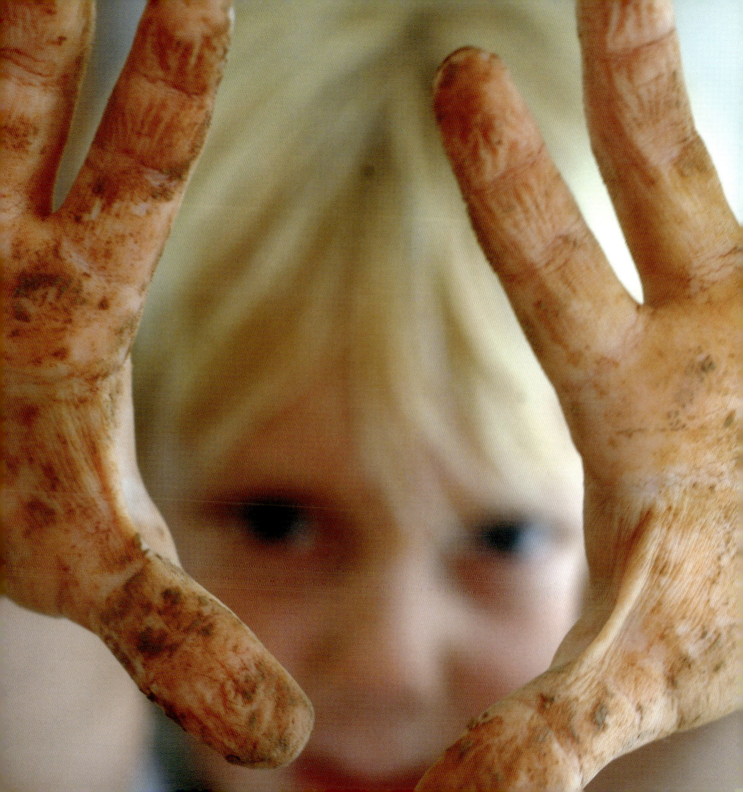

Music

Children are naturally drawn to music. At a deep level music feeds the spirit and allows them to express their emotions and ideas. It builds both physical and intellectual skills as children use their bodies and minds to make music and express themselves through song, dance, making and playing musical instruments.

TURNING THEM ON TO MUSIC

Children will love to spend time with you making music in any form.

Here are some things you can do together:
- Provide access to many types of music. Classical and modern music both have their place, as does any music from your child's culture and ethnic origin.
- Sing to your child. Your child doesn't know the meaning of tone deaf and won't care if you sound like a cat stuck in a drain. She will love the chance to share songs together. Sing to your child from birth or even before. Sing for her and sing with her. Sing the songs you love and the songs she loves. Sing the songs your parents sang for you. Just sing!
- Share the music of your childhood and family.
- Make the effort to watch people sing and play instruments at festivals, on the street, at concerts, ballet, opera, jazz in the park.
- Let children create their own music with props and instruments.
- Make singing before bedtime a daily ritual.
- Relax the mood in your home through appropriate music at special times or when sharing a meal.

- Encourage play and exposure to real musical instruments and noise makers. Let your child play and handle them. Join in.
- Explore found objects such as seed pods, shells, sticks, bottle caps etc to explore making sound.
- If you play an instrument make it something you do together.
- Avoid background music on all the time. It dulls the senses and eventually your child will stop tuning in.
- Put on some music and dance. It's great fun, reduces stress and is good exercise, too. Encourage your child to move, sway, tap and dance to music and join in.
- Children love action songs, for example, songs where they have to point to parts of the body, such as Heads and Shoulders, Knees and Toes.
- When you sing, take your cue from your child for the pitch of the song. The golden rule is, 'no strain'. If she appears to be straining her voice, stop and try again a little lower or higher. Continue with this process until she seems comfortable.
- Remember that singing is a developmental process. Children will take time to grow confident and sing with the right pitch.
- Singing songs in a second language can introduce children to new cultures and experiences.
- Check out your local early childhood music groups where you can socialise and gain confidence in your own musical abilities as well.
- It is always nice to keep a recording of your child as her singing and talking progresses. Use a simple tape recorder or go all out with an MP3, 4 or 5 and computer technology.

Simple musical toys, like a xylophone or some maracas, can be useful and fun. Younger children will begin to experiment with the sounds that different instruments make, while older ones will use instruments to copy the rhythm and beat of the music they are making or listening to.

MAKING MUSIC

You and your child can make simple instruments at home. This is inexpensive and great fun. Lucy Bainger, early childhood music expert and the author of *Music Magic,* suggests some of the following ideas for creating simple musical possibilities.

FOUND SOUNDS

Pick out some kitchen utensils: an old egg beater, a pair of spoons, barbecue tongs, old saucepans, etc, and sit down with your child and sing a song like *Old Macdonald Had a Band*, beating out the tune as you go.

MAKE A SOUND BAR

Stretch some twine between two trees and hang different objects from it, at a height your child can hit; things like saucepan lids, old CDs, a cup, a box, any old children's instruments you have, an empty plastic bottle.

MUSICAL PAUSE

Play some dance music and bop along. Every now and then, pause the sound and freeze – have fun striking different poses. It's great for balance! Let your child be in control of the remote next time.

SHAKERS

Find some film canisters or small jars with lids. Go outside with your child and half fill the containers with anything you can find – gravel, sand, stones, leaves etc, or things from the pantry – sugar, rice, lentils, chickpeas etc. Seal with glue or tape and explore the different sounds.

BALLOON DRUMS

One cleaned-out tin can or infant formula-style container (make sure it has no sharp edges); heavy duty tape or string; balloons; chopsticks or a wooden spoon

Make sure the tin or container is well washed and dried. Your child might like to decorate a sheet of paper, cut to size, to glue to the outside of the drum. Cut the end off a balloon and stretch tightly across the top of the container and secure with tape or string. Add chopsticks or a wooden spoon for drumsticks. Different-sized containers will create different sounding drums.

PROPS FOR DANCING

Children respond spontaneously to music with their bodies, swaying and moving to the rhythm. It's a great idea to provide some props so they can extend their bodies. Fill a box with scarves, lengths of wide ribbon with a circle of elastic sewn on the end to attach around children's wrists, lengths of feather boa, shimmy belts, small finger cymbals, castanets, a tambourine and a few hats. Tuck in some face painting crayons for that rainy day.

Let's Move

Run, jump, roll, swing, dig, wonder ... children's play will naturally involve physical activity. In an increasingly sedentary world children need to discover the joy of movement if they are to stay healthy and well.

GET PHYSICAL!

There is no denying that childhood obesity and related illnesses are on the increase. This problem is so serious that internationally, many governments have developed physical activity guidelines for young children. Activity is vital for the growing mind and body. It helps to develop connections in the brain, improves self-esteem, helps children create friendships and sets a habit for a healthy life.

Unless health problems restrict exercise, it's recommended that children have at least sixty minutes of unstructured active physical play every day. In addition, some fun 'planned' physical activity, in the form of a walk, a game or singing and dancing, should be added to stimulate and extend children's developing skills. It doesn't have to happen in one session. Activities can be accumulated through the day. In fact your children should not be sedentary for more than hour at any given time. So why are you still sitting there? Grab the children and get moving!

RESOURCES FOR ACTIVE PLAY

In most cases parents don't need to do anything more than provide the resources and space for children to be active. Your backyard or the local park is perfect. Most children love to get going and run, somersault, stand on their heads and climb trees. It's part of an innate desire to test out and use their bodies. If your child is a reluctant starter the best thing you can do is to be active yourself and to build activities into the day that the whole family can participate in and enjoy. Yes, some of the activities below will require you to assess the risks and ensure your child's safety, but they are so much fun to do together and the skills they learn will increase their competence and confidence.

BALANCE, BOUNCE, JUMP AND ROLL

Children show a sense of achievement and pride as they develop control over their bodies. The first time your three-year-old somersaults on her own you'll think she's won gold at the Olympics. Provide hoops, balls of different sizes, beanbags, Frisbees®, and planks to walk along or stepping stones to jump between. Find a soft grassy hill and roll down together. Roll other things down hills and ramps. Climb appropriate rocks or boulders in the forest or bush; walk around rock pools at the beach when it's low tide, or step across the stones in the shallow part of a river or stream. If the budget permits, provide a trampoline. Jumping is such a joyful and powerful activity. Your child will be too busy having fun to know that it's also doing her good.

RIDE, TRANSPORT AND BUILD

Opportunities to ride, push, pull and build are important for coordination and developing strength and muscle control. Wheelbarrows can be used to push things around or to be pushed in, cars and trucks provide occasion to play and pretend while crawling and crouching. Blocks can be bought, or created out of recycled objects and then used to make cubbies, forts and walls. Bicycles, scooters, tricycles can often be obtained cheaply at local resource recovery centres or garage sales. A bit of work and you have the perfect vehicle for learning about balance, control and speed, as well as a resource to move you through space in new and interesting ways.

RUN, THROW, KICK AND SWING

Put a child in an open space and most will naturally want to run around. There is great freedom in running. It uses all the large muscle groups and builds aerobic fitness. Go to the park or play chasing games in your backyard; run down a hill at the park or a sandhill at the beach (and climb back up again!). Provide balls to kick and throw; play simple football with a single goal where everyone wins; introduce backyard softball, basketball or T-ball for older children, or throw balls or bean bags through hoops or into buckets. Teach your child to skip stones on the pond, float sticks down the river; build and fly a kite together; blow bubbles on a breezy day and let your child chase them. Purchase a swing or if you have the skills, make a tyre swing in your backyard, or go to the park and let your child pump his legs and swing.

DIG, GROW AND NURTURE

Digging the garden or sandpit is great exercise for building upper body strength and coordination. The experience of growing and caring for a living thing, and anticipating what will happen, extends children physically and intellectually. Gardens can be created in pots on the veranda or patio, or you can find spaces for children to grow a small vegetable garden in your yard. Make places where children can bury things in the sand or mud and make mud dams and ditches to drive their trucks around in.

SMALL WONDERS

Children love to get into and out of things. Make spaces where children can get away from it all. Lying under the branches of a green tree, a small nook or little table and chairs in an out-of-the-way place can create a little oasis of calm for children. Cubby houses make great places where children can pretend and develop their imaginations. You can build a permanent cubby or a temporary one out of a cardboard box, or put an old blanket or sheet over the outside table.

Nature

Letting go into the natural world is like a sigh of relief at the end of a busy week. There is something relaxing, familiar and welcoming about the feel of natural elements that eases the mind and spirit, encourages creativity and invites exploration.

Children have an affinity with nature and the elements and they enjoy incorporating them into their play. Natural elements have a living, breathing, sensory quality that invites exploration and experimentation. Some of my earliest memories include making mud pies, and as a parent I can recall watching my children revel in building dams in the rain and sailing homemade boats made out of sticks and leaves.

Sand, water, mud, natural materials, the weather and green spaces offer opportunities to investigate nature first-hand. Children can learn about texture, mass, the changing properties of elements as well as developing language to describe and identify the world around them.

SIMPLY SAND

A sandpit or sand tray is a great addition to any backyard. Dry sand has wonderful qualities for tipping and pouring. It can be used in imaginative play to make tea or a cake or build into roads, hills and mounds. Wet sand can be patted and moulded into shapes for tunnels and structures. Keep to hand a gardening trug or washing basket with old pots and pans, an unbreakable teapot and cups; include plastic containers as well as spades, a bucket or two, a watering can, a plastic trowel, a child's wheelbarrow, some cars and trucks and your child will be happily entertained for the afternoon. Make sure it's covered when not in use, to keep it clean.

For more adventurous sand play, head to the beach and make sandcastles or sand sculptures that can be decorated with shells, seaweed and driftwood. Dig holes near the water's edge and watch what happens as the tide comes in; bury your children's legs or your legs (if you're brave) and make a mermaid's tail. Remember to make it easy to get out again and don't dig holes too deep.

WONDERFUL WATER

Children love water. It can be splashed, tipped poured, used to create mud puddles and dams, used to float boats and to watch things sink. It changes the colour of rocks and is very calming, particularly on a hot day. At home you can fill an old plastic washing tub and put it on a low table or a wading pool for children, but water play needs to be supervised – particularly when younger children are present. Add plastic bottles, lengths of plastic hose or pipe, funnels, jugs, an old colander, sponges and items that will float and sink. Remember to tip it out when the children are finished.

NATURE'S BOUNTY

Rocks and mud, grass, shells, leaves, wood, seedpods, vines and flowers all stimulate children's imagination. Rocks and shells can be sequenced, stacked and sorted. Mud makes an interesting change to wet sand for digging and building. Seedpods, leaves and vines can be examined and investigated and then used to sort, make patterns, decorate outdoor play spaces or make things. Wood can be used to hammer, saw and glue into useful and interesting objects and shapes. Always check the safety of plants with your nursery.

WHATEVER THE WEATHER

Rainy days don't necessarily mean staying indoors. Pull on your gumboots and a raincoat and head out to explore the puddles, watch the way water falls, drips and runs. Make a paper boat and float it down the gutter. On sunny days take a walk, play chase your shadow, look at how the light shines and sparkles on water. Make the most of the weather as an opportunity to learn about the environment.

THINGS TO DO

BIRDBATH OR FEEDER

Buy a simple birdbath and install it on your balcony or in your garden. Alternatively buy a bird feeder from your local pet shop. Discuss and identify from books or the internet the birds that use the water or feeder.

GROW A GIANT PUMPKIN

Pumpkins are very satisfying to grow, because the vines develop and grow almost overnight. Atlantic Pumpkin seeds, the giant variety, are really fun to grow, as the pumpkins will be enormous. While they are inedible, their sheer size and speed of growth will fascinate children. You can measure and record the pumpkin's growth daily and chart how it changes.

WALK BAREFOOT

Take your child to a variety of different places where he can walk barefoot. Include the beach, a pebbly river bed or a leafy park. Let him make different sounds walking in the grass over dried leaves, mud or in shallow puddles. Encourage your child to describe what he heard and felt.

MAKE A DINOSAUR TERRARIUM

Using a large clear plastic PET or glass container with a lid, create a terrarium. Lay small pebbles on the bottom for drainage and cover them with a layer of moist seed-raising mix. Wipe the sides of the container before adding small plants such as ferns, small flowering annuals or moss. Leave a little room for growth. Place a few plastic dinosaurs into your landscape. Mist gently with water and then seal and put in a warm, light place out of the direct sun. Watch your prehistoric garden grow! The terrarium maintains the temperature and keeps moisture levels even. If the weather is hot and your container sides are misty, lift the lid a little to release the moisture and then seal again.

WILD WEAVING

DIFFICULTY **3**   MESS FACTOR **3**   PREP TIME **30** MINS   AGE **4–6+**

Children love using their fingers to join things together and create something unique from ordinary garden and special found objects.

You will need:
- **secateurs, long-nose pliers; garden twine or fuse wire (for grown-ups only)**
- **gardening gloves**
- **passionfruit, wisteria and/or grape vines; flax and palm leaves for the basic frame. You need to make sure the leaves and vines are safe to handle without spikes and not poisonous. If in doubt, don't use.**
- **leaves, feathers, seed pods and soft paperbark strips; found objects, old rope, ribbon, strips of material, clay, wool or felt.**

- Make a loop of strong vine about the size of a dinner plate and tuck in the ends. Secure with garden twine or fuse wire.
- Wind another two to four vines through the loop to make a star pattern in the middle of the loop and secure.
- Let your child weave and tuck in more vines, leaves, feathers, bark, or seed pods to fill in the space, folding and pushing in the ends as he goes. You can use clay to secure items. Some vines and leaves will be more pliable if soaked in water for a short while.
- Encourage their creativity and see what happens.
- Hang your woven sculpture in the house or garden. Add items as you find them and continue to build on your basic pattern or start anew.

Technology

TUNINGIN·TUNINGOUT

Technology is now an integral part of our lives. Used well, it has the potential to extend children's creativity and learning. It's a wonderful resource to help them connect with others and learn more about the world.

'Going on a Tiger Hunt' Digital photo story by Aiden, age 5

Tuning in

Used in the right way, cameras, computers and the internet open up whole new areas of creativity for your child. Before you know it, your children's digital literacy will far outstrip your own, so get in early and set good habits.

COMPUTERS

Supporting your child's developing computer literacy is a new skill for many parents. Promoting and encouraging his interest, while setting appropriate boundaries for the use of the computer, requires thought, but can offer a whole new set of challenges.

Each family will have had a different experience with computers. Many parents will already have embraced this technology, while some will feel it is not yet appropriate for them or their child. There are many benefits to being able to access computers, but as parents, we must establish some ground rules that allow our children to explore the wonders of the digital age, while maintaining a balanced life. Building appropriate skills will benefit your child when he starts preschool or school, where computers are part of the modern learning toolkit.

- Right from the start, protect your children. Install internet-filtering software and keep an eye on what's going on.
- Teach your children not to give their names or personal details to anyone online.
- Model good habits; remind your children that the computer is a tool.
- Monitor the time spent on the computer. Thirty minutes to one hour per day is adequate. After that, switch it off and encourage active play.
- Watch those ergonomics and make sure the screen is positioned to prevent neck and eye strain. Make sure your child's feet are placed on the floor or on a box. Encourage your child to take a break from the screen every fifteen minutes.
- Spend some time playing with your children on the computer so you become aware of their interests and what they enjoy.

The internet brings the whole wide world into our living rooms in a way never seen in the past. As parents, the days when we knew everything we needed to know to help our children grow and thrive are gone. Access to the worldwide web can bring real benefits into your home to build knowledge, explore our interests and search for activities and games that can extend and enhance play. Just remember it's a tool and 'real life' is just outside your door.

BUILDING COMPUTER SKILLS

EMAIL

We all love mail, and snail mail will always have a special place. Encourage your children to keep in contact with family and friends via email. Write messages with them and scan in their pictures or photos to send and read the return messages to them.

COMPUTER-TO-COMPUTER VIDEO AND PHONE

We take so much new technology for granted, but this particular technology has many wonderful applications. Imagine the joy of talking to Mum, Dad or grandparents on the other side of the country or world with video phone when they are away. Children are concrete thinkers and will love to show whoever is on the end of the computer what they are doing, or have Mum or Dad read them a bedtime story. This type of interaction is priceless.

CHOOSING SOFTWARE

Choose software that is open-ended and has lots of different applications. Good children's software should encourage creativity and support learning by allowing your child to explore by himself and with others. It should allow him to make choices, extend his ideas, and solve problems. It should contain attractive visuals, sound and music that appeals to children. Good software should also encourage children to work together and not compete. Always preview software before use.

STORIES

Use the computer to write and record stories, photos and scanned pictures. Print and bind them to add to your child's book collection.

ONLINE COMMUNITIES

There are some excellent protected online communities where children can socialise, make new friends and share ideas and games. Do some research and find a good age-appropriate community. Remember, though, that nothing replaces vigilance. Always keep an eye on what is happening and report any problems to the service provider.

PHOTOGRAPHY

Photography is a fun art form that offers instant results. It encourages children to be observant and to record and revisit events that interested them. In this way it extends their creativity. Cameras have the added benefit of being portable so you can take them with you wherever you go.

Many families will have an old camera at home that their child can use, or you could consider buying a good, cheaper alternative. The camera should be light as well as tough. Look for one with automatic settings and a basic zoom setting. It doesn't matter whether it's film or digital, but digital provides instant feedback and there is no additional cost for film or processing.

Explain the camera's functions, such as zoom, and the way light affects the photo. Talk about how to care for and handle the camera. Remind your children to loop the handle around their wrists and not to touch the lens.

Once you have shown them how to use the camera, try not to stage-manage their efforts. Among the pleasures of photography are the unexpected results that come from experimenting. The beauty of a digital camera is that you can retain some photos and easily delete others. Help your children to develop their computer skills with photo editing and printing software. Make folders and files to keep their photos and print and display their work.

PHOTO DISCOVERY WALK

Pack up your camera and head off to take photos of things you see along the way. You might suggest subjects such as flowers or shapes or together make up a list of things to photograph. Use the photos later to remind yourselves of the walk and discuss what you discovered.

Things to do with your photos:
- Make a book and create a story to go with it. This makes a great gift for a favourite friend or family member.
- Make a collage of your photos for a wall display.
- Make a secure family blog site and upload the photos to share with family and friends.
- Use a favourite photo as the family computer desktop image
- Laminate your photos and use them as placemats or as luggage ID tags.

Tuning out

As children and adults in an increasingly busy and complex world, making time to reflect, take a breath and sift and sort the mind is important for our mental health and wellbeing.

REALITY CHECK

As parents, we often feel time-poor. Life is busy and stressful, as we try to juggle our responsibilities and commitments. The world can also be a stressful place for your child. Weeks filled with play dates, pre-school, day care, school and extracurricular activities such as music and sport, access to world events via TV and computer, as well as all the other activities in your family's routine, can add up to your child feeling overwhelmed or fearful. Let's be honest, most parents feel snowed under as they try to negotiate the family's activities each week – so what hope has your child got!

Children need time to relax and unwind, just as their parents do. Taking the time to gaze out of the window, daydream or engage in simple relaxation or meditation can not only provide them with strategies to cope and feel good about themselves now, but set down healthy habits for coping with stress as they become adults.

Do a mental check of your child's activities and see if you think he needs more time to relax.

Relaxation exercises can help to release muscle tension, improve posture and breathing and increase energy. They can also help your child learn to understand and manage his emotions, recognise when he feels stressed and provide a means of coping.

- Is your child doing too much? If you need a diary to keep track of all his engagements you might need to rethink what is important.
- Does he look forward to the activities he is involved in?
- Does he complain about headaches, stomach aches and body aches and pains regularly?
- Is there time each day for unscheduled play and relaxation?
- How much time is spent in front of the TV and computer? While this may provide respite for us, it is not quiet time for children!
- What other responsibilities and engagements is he involved in that are part of the family schedule?
- Is there time to just chill out with friends without you being involved in a planned activity?
- Is he cranky and uncooperative about participating in family activities most of the time?
- Does he experience trouble sleeping, or appear tense and tired or tearful more often than not?
- Check yourself. Where are you on the stress scale this week? Children take their cues from their parents. If you are unduly stressed, this may be having an impact on your child.

WAYS TO CHILL OUT

- Lie on the grass and watch the sky.
- Swing in a hammock.
- Take a walk in the bush or by the sea, get in touch with nature and breathe it in.
- Make a cubby to hide in.
- Let your child have free time each day to explore his own hobbies and games.
- Let him lose himself in a story tape or book.
- Make a nap or rest as a regular part of your family's weekend routine. Great for everyone's mental health!
- Create peaceful and beautiful places in your home. A vase of flowers, a shallow stone bowl of water with some interesting rocks, a wind chime or garden sculpture, a poster or painting that depicts a relaxing scene.
- Put a giant cushion or comfy chair near a window in your child's room and create space for a moment of peace and reflection.
- Make time to exercise. Put on your shoes and walk your stress out.
- Limit your child's access to TV news and frightening events. Even though you cannot always protect him from finding out about wars and disasters, try to ensure he gets information in a calm, age-appropriate and factual way from you, or a balanced source for children. Give him lots of reassurance.
- Make it a family ritual to share time each day, perhaps over dinner, to talk about what has been happening in your child's life.
- Organise sensible routines for your child to follow to help him manage his activities, so he knows what is going to happen and when.
- Eat well. Particularly at times of stress, good nutrition is important.
- Create a bedtime routine to calm the mind before sleep.
- Hug him EVERY day, no matter what.
- If, after making some changes, you feel your child is really not coping, seek help from your GP or paediatrician.

CREATIVE VISUALISATION EXPERIENCES

There are lot of good books and tapes with ideas for 'creative visualisation' techniques (where we create images in our minds to help us relax), but you can save money and make them up yourself.

LETTING GO

- Have your child lie down somewhere comfortable without distractions.
- Make sure she is warm or cool enough and that her clothes don't constrict her movement.
- Encourage her to close her eyes and take a few deep slow breaths in and out.
- Encourage her to feel her toes, legs, torso, hands, arms, neck and head and to relax as she imagines each one.
- Once she has begun to relax, start to tell a story with a relaxing theme – perhaps a walk in the bush or a swim in the sea – and talk about the animals she meets. Perhaps she can imagine she is a leaf floating down a stream or a marshmallow in a giant mug of hot chocolate!
- Keep your voice calm, soft and low as you tell the story. Create a space of complete quiet in the story, for example, time to watch the sea animals swim.
- Finish by bringing the story to a positive end, by swimming back to the surface, walking back home and then encouraging her to take a few deep breaths and S-T-R-E-T-C-H.
- Allow her to lie quietly for a minute or two before she resumes her activities.

Playing away

**OUTDOORS·MYCOMMUNITY
PLAYDATES·HOLIDAYS**

Children benefit from time spent apart from their families so they can spread their wings and learn to cope with their peers and the other adults in their lives. This helps them to build resilience, confidence, self-respect and self-esteem.

Outdoors

Children need to develop confidence in their ability to manage the challenges that come their way. The outdoors offers opportunities to investigate and try out new skills, engage in physically active play and helps them develop persistence and find out what they are capable of achieving.

BUILDING RESILIENCE

The world our children inhabit is different from the one we experienced as children. Increasing urbanisation, traffic, greater work commitments for parents and even fears for their safety have led to many children having less opportunity to play outside the home.

Children need room to run around and to learn how their body moves in space. The self-assurance that comes with this will reap benefits as they develop resilience and grow stronger – physically, emotionally and socially – and begin to believe in their own abilities. Outdoors provides an ideal context in which children can play in a less controlled environment to gain these skills.

Despite our best efforts to protect our children, it's important to remember that many of them naturally seek out challenges and play activities that overextend their skills. In general, most children's early vocabulary includes those famous, determined words, 'I can do it!' well before they learn that some skills take time to learn. You only have to look at the scars on your own knees and elbows to realise that some of your best childhood memories involved getting into and out of scrapes. This kind of risk-taking is normal and should to some degree be encouraged. When we take risks, we test ourselves and learn what we are capable of achieving.

Now, before you send your child to bungee jump off the closest bridge I am not advocating a free-for-all. As a parent I want my children to be safe. I have spent my fair share of time in the emergency unit of the local hospital, while chins were stitched and arms plastered, but I also wanted them to develop determination, resilience and self-assurance.

I think the trick is to manage risk while still allowing children to be enthusiastic and inventive in their play and not allowing our fears to impede the wonderful gains that can be made in the relative freedom of the outdoors.

EMBRACE THE NIGHT

The world outside changes at night. Take a walk in the evening or on a moonlit night and explore your environment.

- Have dinner or a BBQ outside and let your children play in the yard as evening descends.
- Try to tell stories around an open fire and toast marshmallows.
- Use candles or fairy lights to create a magic mood, or let children make pictures with sparklers as they swirl them around in the dark.
- Use a torch and go spotlighting to find what's hiding in the trees.
- Make time to gaze at the night sky and identify star formations and constellations such as the Southern Cross.
- Check out what the Man in the Moon is up to in your part of the world.
- Let your children stay up late on special occasions such as New Year's Eve, or camp in your own backyard.

KNOW YOUR ENVIRONMENT

Where possible, walk or cycle to preschool, school, the shops, or the park. This helps to familiarise your child with the local area, increases her fitness and confidence, and creates opportunities for her to learn how to manage road safety.

PROVIDE CHALLENGES

Find opportunities to experience new environments that require a new set of skills.

- Ice-skating or walking in the snow requires different muscles and lots of concentration.
- Try to stand up in the waves at the beach
- Climb and scramble over rocks at the seaside or in the bush.
- Climb up and roll down hills at the park.
- Check out interesting outdoor play equipment. Many cities have interactive fountains and water features that are designed for people to explore. Seek these out and investigate them.

My Community

Learning who they are and where they fit into their community is an important part of growing up. Children need to be given the chance to get to know the place – and the people – where they live.

WHERE I LIVE

Each type of urban or rural environment offers its own special experience. It invites the child to engage with the community, the larger world and his place in both.

Whatever your budget, there are many ways to surround your child with beautiful, interesting places, in and around your community which will ignite his curiosity and enhance his play.

- Leave the café and shopping centre behind. Fill your backpack or esky with delicious snacks and drinks and head off in your car, on the train or bus, on your bikes, or use your feet and investigate what your community has to offer.
- Once a month, go on an adventure that doesn't cost any money. It's great for the family budget! Local community newspapers are often a good source of ideas for free activities in your community.
- Go fishing, walking, swimming, or canoeing. Investigate the inner city, gaze at art, interact at the museum, or spend time at the zoo.
- Discover parks and gardens, feed the ducks, visit the beach and find other natural or manufactured environments that invite exploration.
- Travel beyond your local area. Allow one and a half to two hours travel out of any major city and it will bring you to a beach or river, a farm, a national park, or if you live in a remote area, consider a weekend or holiday in the city, or a visit to your closest regional town.
- Share these experiences with friends and family. Organise a weekend of camping, an overnight visit to friends or family, stay up late, sleep in a tent, a cabin or on a boat.
- Support your favourite football, cricket, soccer, netball or other sporting teams or get involved with a local one and join the fray.
- Get involved in a community event or charity fundraiser with your children. This creates opportunities to meet new people and develop an understanding of how other people live.

Play dates

All children need the opportunity to experience time away from home and family, playing with other children and developing relationships outside the home.

Creating social networks and friendships allows your child to practise social skills learned at home and provides an opportunity to develop independence and self-reliance. It teaches skills in collaboration and negotiation, and introduces them to new experiences. It's sometimes hard to know when it's time to let your children spread their wings a little and trust that other people have their best interests at heart. This is the most precious person in your life and you should plan for their wellbeing at all times.

PLAYING AWAY TIPS

- Your two-to-three-year-old child is probably not ready to spend time away from you other than with close family, trusted carers and friends. Arrange a play date where parents are also invited or attend a local play group and connect with other parents in your area while your children play.
- When your child is ready for play dates, get to know their friend's parents. You don't have to have them home for dinner but be interested and create a relationship to support your child.
- Always make sure you know the place and family where your child is going and who is going to be home. Go inside with your child and make sure he is settled and you feel comfortable before you leave him.
- Be clear about the details of what the children will be doing. Are they planning to go out, stay home, and will there be older children etc.
- Exchange contact numbers.
- If your child has allergies or special needs make sure the other parent is clear about both needs and the consequences. Does he need an Epipen®, have a special diet, mobility or language issue that needs to be explained.
- Plan play dates around your child's routine and schedule.
- Encourage your child to think about what they might like to do before their friend arrives. Make sure both children know and understand the limits in your home. Be gentle, positive but firm.

BEWARE! THE LAWS OF ATTRACTION

When it comes to friends, you have little control over who your child chooses. If you are unhappy with your young child's choice of friends stop and think for a minute. Why? Are you concerned for your child's safety? Are you worried that the other child may be a bad influence? Is it because you don't warm to the child's parents? Be careful that your reasons have a logical basis, and tread carefully before limiting contact, as your child may see her friend as even more attractive because of your response.

Be pleasant to the child but if you decide that there should be no contact outside preschool or school, be fair and honest and acknowledge why you have made this decision to your child. Remember that some friendships can be fleeting, and within a short space of time your child may come to see that this person is not really for her and move on without your intervention.

Always try to encourage your child to have a wide range of friends and play opportunities. Talk about your expectations and limits and stick to them.

PLAY DATE IDEAS

- Ask your child to choose some toys and games and have them ready when her friend arrives. Discuss sharing.
- Choose a simple cooking activity, such as making scones, pikelets or a muffin pizza.
- Spread a blanket out under a tree in your backyard and arrange games for children to play.
- Set up a table outdoors or inside with interesting paper, pencils and your craft crate on it to stimulate a collage or drawing activity.
- Go for a walk to the local park and play on the equipment or kick a ball around and have a picnic afternoon tea.
- Make a puppet.
- Get out the dress-up box and the face paints.
- Throw a sheet or blanket over a table and add some cushions for an instant cubby house.
- Let children socialise and invent their own games rather than watch TV or play video games.
- Give your child's friend something you've made together to take home so they will remember the playdate.

Don't over-manage the children's play, but be ready with ideas and have an activity planned to settle them in or distract them if their play becomes overly enthusiastic. Playdough, or a simple cooking experience can be an easy and soothing activity. Making a collage or doing some drawing can help a shy child break the ice.

CREAM CHEESE FROSTING

250g (9oz) cream cheese
60g (2¼oz) butter, softened
2½ cups icing (confectioner's) sugar
2 tablespoons of milk

- Beat the butter and cream cheese in a bowl, add the icing sugar and milk and beat until smooth.
- Spread the frosting on the cooled carrot cake and serve.

CARROT CAKE

DIFFICULTY **2**   MESS FACTOR **3**   PREP TIME **40** MINS   COOKING TIME **35-40** MINS   FEEDS **8**

Play dates are a chance for a treat. Carrot Cake is a reasonably healthy choice and also delicious. The children can help collect, measure and mix the ingredients and crack and beat the eggs . They can pour the mixture into the greased and lined cake tin – and finish with that much-loved childhood treat, licking the spoon and bowl!

2–3 medium carrots, grated
1 cup walnuts
3 eggs
1 cup caster (superfine) sugar
½ teaspoon ground nutmeg
1 teaspoon ground cinnamon
¾ cup vegetable oil
1 teaspoon vanilla extract
1⅓ cups self-raising (self-rising) flour
1 level teaspoon bicarbonate of soda

- Preheat the oven to 180°C (350°F/gas mark 4). The children can grease and help to line a 20cm (8in) springform cake tin.
- Combine the carrot and walnuts in a bowl.
- Beat the eggs, sugar, nutmeg, cinnamon, oil and vanilla until pale. Stir in the carrot and walnuts. Sift in the flour and bicarb soda. Mix lightly. Let the children help to spoon the mixture into the prepared cake tin.
- Place the cake in the oven to bake for 35–40 minutes or until a skewer inserted in the centre comes out with only a few crumbs attached.
- Turn out, allow to cool, then spread with frosting.

SCONES

DIFFICULTY **2**   MESS FACTOR **4**   PREP TIME **30** MINS   COOKING TIME **12** MINS   FEEDS **12**

Scones turn out to be lighter the more the flour has been sifted, so let the children keep sifting for as long as you want! They can help collect the ingredients and measure out the flour, with adult help.

3 cups of self-raising flour
1 cup of lemonade
I cup of pure cream
Pinch of salt

- Preheat the oven to 220°C (425°F/gas mark 7). Children can grease a baking tray.
- Sift the flour and salt into a bowl.
- Pour in the cream and lemonade and mix into a soft dough.
- Place the dough on a lightly floured work surface and knead very gently.
- Pat the dough out to a thickness of 3cm (¾in).
- Dip a small glass or a 5cm (2in) cookie cutter in a little flour and cut out rounds from the dough. Try to cut as many rounds as possible from the first pressing as the extra kneading can make the remaining scones tough.
- Place the scones on the prepared tray and dust with a little flour. The children can sprinkle the flour over the top of each scone.
- Place the tray in the oven for 10–12 minutes or until lightly golden.

HOMEMADE BUTTER

1 cup of cream (the higher the percentage of butterfat the better)
Pinch of salt
A glass jar or plastic container with a tight, well-fitting lid (or one small jar per child). If using plastic, make sure it's clear to you can see the butter form

- Pour the cream into the jar/container and secure the lid.
- Now it's easy – just shake the jar vigorously for 10–15 minutes. Share the job and make it fun by singing silly songs or dancing to a good beat while you shake.
- Stop and check the cream every two minutes. It will start to thicken and then yellow butter will start to clump on the sides of the jar. Once you have a good clump of butter, pour out the remaining liquid. This is buttermilk and is great for making pancakes so don't throw it out!
- You need to 'clean' the butter. Run cool tap water into the jar and whirl it around to remove the last of the buttermilk and tip out. The butter will remain in the bottom of the jar.
- Scoop the butter out with a spoon, mix with a tiny pinch of salt if required and spread it on your freshly made scones.

Play dates

Holidays

Does the thought of packing up the car and children and heading off on a family holiday fill you with dread? Before you run screaming from the room, consider the benefits.

WE'RE ALL GOING ON A FAMILY HOLIDAY

Holidays mean time to spend relaxed moments together. They offer opportunities to ease back and throw our routines out the window. They provide the chance to stay up late, take naps in the afternoon, eat and drink when we're hungry and thirsty, read and relax; and that's just the adults! For children, holidays present new and interesting places to play, resources and treasures to discover, people to meet and a chance to spend unpressured time with their favourite person ... you.

Now whether you choose to travel by plane, train, car or bike, a little forward planning can make all the difference between a great time and a disaster.

Keeping children occupied while you travel requires strategies and forward planning.

CHILD PLANNING

- If you travel by car, make the back seat a comfort zone. Add pillows, padded seat belt covers to make long journeys more comfortable and seat pockets to store drinks, snacks and activities. Think about screens to shade the windows but don't totally block access to the view. Watching the world go by is fun.
- Whether you go by train, plane or car, make sure there is some leg room for wriggling.
- Plan your stops around places where children can run their wriggles out.
- Use the onboard DVD player as an activity – not a babysitter. While this technology is a wonderful asset to the travelling parent, set some boundaries about its use. This is a time to be together and share the travel experience.
- Make sure you pack 'cuddlies', comforters and teddies in easily accessible places. Think about having a back-up for emergencies if you are going a long way from home.

TRAVEL PACK

This is a must-have item for any parent travelling with young children. Find a backpack that is easily identifiable and easy for your child to carry himself. One that has a couple of easy-to-access compartments helps to organise things for the trip. Fill this with things to do on the journey – games, paper, pencils, an MP3 player with his favourite music and songs. Put in his cuddly and teddy if needed, a small inflatable pillow and a jacket or an adult wrap or shawl that can double as a blanket if it gets cool. Include a change of clothes in case of accident or emergency. Add a few surprises at the bottom, in the form of unexpected activities or toys to distract him when things get too much. Include a few healthy snacks or even a treat.

EMERGENCY PACK FOR PARENTS

While travel is fun, it is always best to follow the Scouts' rule and Be Prepared! Pack a bag or zip-up travel sack with the following items: washcloths or wipes, a couple of plastic bags, child and adult pain medication, medication for diarrhoea and constipation, earplugs, sticking plasters, sunscreen, antiseptic wipes or gel, tissues, rehydration salts and jelly beans. Add a few extra small surprise items or games for those times when overtiredness, long waits or drives start to make the world spin out of control for your child. This is not bribery. It's survival!

PARENT PLANNING

- Research your destination. Get on the phone, the internet and email, ask your friends. Find out about the place you are going to and what will be available for children.
- Plan your route. Allow for well-spaced breaks and snack times to help minimise boredom and overtired children and adults.
- For big or extended trips, talk to your children about where you are going, how you are getting there and what you will be doing when you arrive. Tell this story over the week or two leading up to the travel. This could be done as part of a bedtime story routine, so they become familiar with the travel schedule and sequence of events, and help them to cope with rigours of the trip and unfamiliar places and events.
- If travelling by air, seek help from airline staff. Most airlines will allow children and families to board a little early so they can get settled. This is not a time to be stoic. Ask for help with food and drinks or anything else you need. Order children's meals in advance. Other passengers will thank you and in my experience will be more than happy to help you have a calm and relaxed flight.
- If you are heading off to a resort and plan to put the children into a crèche or holiday program there, check it out first! Many overseas child care facilities and crèches may have few or no regulations with which they must comply. Ask about the program, how the staff are hired and assessed and what activities are offered. Meet the staff who will be caring for your child when you arrive.
- Check it out for yourself. Before you leave your children, make sure it's safe. Check out your government travel website before you travel.

TRAVEL GAMES

FINGER PUPPETS

These are easy to make with a little preparation. Buy a pair of large rubber gloves, cut off the fingers and discard the hand section. Put the finger sections together in a plastic bag with a couple of felt tip pens and toss in the glove box. Your children can draw on the finger pieces and create puppets. You can make up a story or recreate a known story and everyone can join in (well, maybe not the driver!). Just a word of caution, this is not an activity for under-twos who may want to put the puppets in their mouths.

OBJECT I SPY

This is an easier version of the famous I Spy game and is suitable for children who are not familiar with the letters of the alphabet. A child or adult chooses an object – and tells the players. It might be a yellow truck, a red car, a black and white cow, whatever you like. Start the game with: 'We spy, with our little eyes, a ... yellow truck/short man, black sheep, big banana ...' You can make this as silly as you like. The first person to 'spy' the object wins and chooses the next object. It pays to know the territory with this game so you can choose items children are likely to see.

JUMPING WORDS

This is a word association game where one person starts with a word and the next has to say the first word that comes into their heads. For example, you might start with frog-jump-pond-water-swim-goggles and so forth. If you repeat a word, or have a brain freeze and can't think of one quickly, you are out. The last person to think of a word is the winner.

THUMB WRESTLING

It's really silly, but it's fun. Two people lock right hands with all fingers except their thumbs which remain free. The players call out, 'one, two, three, four, let's have a thumb war!' On the word 'war', each player tries to pin down the other player's thumb. Players can't unlock their hands or move them around.

MUSIC MEMORY

Sing or play a CD of favourite songs that your children know. As the music plays encourage your child to singalong, then stop or pause the CD and see if they can complete the next line of the song. Take turns, so all the children get a go. The person who can remember the most song lines gets to choose the next CD to play.

SHHHHH!!!!

A great game to restore peace in a noisy car. See how long everyone can maintain silence. You may need to offer a reward to encourage children to play seriously as there will always be someone who wants to push the envelope by making a silly noise! The reward could be to choose the next snack stop, a CD or a treat. At the word 'Go' everyone should stay quiet for as long as they can. The winner gets the prize and the parents get five minutes' peace ... maybe!

SURPRISE BOX

Prepare ahead and fill a shoe box with items to be given out every 50 or 100 kilometres. Fill it with small wrapped items, usually a toy, stickers or interesting things to do. In some of the packages, add a juice box or a snack. Let the children choose an item at the appointed time.

Family

WEAREFAMILY
PLAYINGTOGETHER

Families are central to children's lives. It's where they learn about life, learn to love and to fight, to make up and feel strong and confident as they grow up. The family is a powerful force that nurtures, teaches and extends a child's experience and gives them the courage and strength to be themselves.

We are family

Through play and ritual in our family we create memory and experience. We learn about the power and security that comes from belonging, from being loved and loving in return.

RITUALS

We come to our families in different ways – eagerly planned and anticipated, chosen with love, by surprise and sometimes default. Whatever way we arrive, we are there warts and all. In our families we see the world in microcosm. Home is the place where we learn to love, negotiate, cry, manage conflict, learn compassion and tolerance. We also discover that relationships are not perfect, life is not always easy and we don't always get what we want. We come to understand what it is to be loved and valued for the people we are.

As a family unit we celebrate our uniqueness and individual family culture; we develop our identities and mark the special and significant events that are important to us. We create memories and build experiences that influence our relationships with others. Our extended families – grandparents, aunts and uncles, cousins, whether through blood or chosen – expand our children's experience of life and serve to protect them as they grow and develop.

Whether you are a group of two, twenty-two or two-hundred-and-two, you are a family and will have your own distinctive way of celebrating events. Do you play post-lunch cricket or a football match on Christmas Day? Do you have a special birthday plate you get once a year or do you make a ritual of sharing the evening meal together? Is there an Easter Egg Toss or a Boxing Day water fight that is legend in your family? The key is to go with it and celebrate.

Many children will experience the rich and diverse traditions that come with a migrant history or through links to Indigenous culture. Consider the rituals in your home. Do you leave carrots out for Santa's reindeers and attend midnight mass at Christmas? Do you light candles at Diwali, the Hindu Festival of Lights? or light the Hanukkah candles? Do you play a part in NAIDOC Week? Does your family celebrate Eid-ul-Fitr to break the Islamic fast at the end of Ramadan? Or recognize Trung Thu, the Vietnamese Mid-Autumn Festival, or the Chinese Ching Ming Tomb Sweeping Day in honour of your ancestors? Does your family take part in an annual tomato passata-making day? These are a few of the cultural and religious traditions that families mark to create links to their past and their culture to pass on to their children.

Encourage your child to be part of each celebration. Give her a role or a job to show her she is valued. She may not be good at it yet, but it is an important part of belonging.

Create a journal to record your rituals. Add to it each year with photos and written or oral memories. As your family grows, share it together.

Playing together

Developing a sense of playfulness and curiosity helps build lifelong relationships and understanding.

PLAY AND LEISURE

Play and leisure are two sides of the same coin. Many of us develop interests and passions through childhood that become pleasurable leisure pursuits later on. These allow us to take time out, de-stress and enjoy adult company. Sharing these pleasures with your child helps her to develop interests of her own, but more importantly, helps her understand who you are and where you all belong in your family. It is a first step into the life of their community and an opportunity for your child to begin to develop tolerance, autonomy and independence.

They say children and grandparents have a common enemy! Oops, that would be parents! Whether this is true or not, grandparents can offer new experiences for your child, provide pampering and spoiling and time for you to relax. If possible, encourage your child to keep in touch with her grandparents – by phone, email, or paying a regular visit. It can be a great support for parents to have another adult that your child loves and trusts and is happy to be with.

Visiting grandparents, cousins and friends provides opportunities for your child to expand her horizons and enjoy herself in a safe, supportive environment. It also creates time for parents and children to be apart so they can recharge their batteries. While parenting is fundamentally one of the most important roles you will ever fulfil, it's important to maintain your identity and foster your relationships with partners and friends. This makes us better parents in the long term.

IDEAS FOR OUTINGS

At times, life will be deliciously frustrating as this small trusting person wants to do more than she is capable of; or becomes tired before you've even warmed up. But relax, be patient, go with the flow, and enjoy the world through new eyes as you spend time together.

- Go to the museum and look at the dinosaurs.
- Gaze at art and then go home and paint a picture.
- Ride your bikes or scooters to the park.
- Attend a concert and introduce your child to your love of opera or jazz.
- Go to the fish market or the fruit and vegetable market and cook a meal together.
- Go fishing, boating or camping.
- Sew something.
- Build an object out of wood.
- Work on the car.
- Go to the footy and barrack for your favourite team.
- Spend time in the garden.
- Swim, surf, canoe, or take a walk in the bush.
- Ride a horse, or care for animals at the local shelter.
- Visit a folk festival.
- Go to the car races.
- Visit a poultry show.
- Go skiing.

PARENT PLAY

While families benefit from time together, they also benefit from time spent apart. It's important we spend a little time restoring mind and spirit. This is the time to call on your network of family and friends to support you and your children. Most friends will love to help you out and most children enjoy having a break, too. If you don't have family close by, create a network and take turns to look after each other's children.

What to do:
There are only two rules:
1. This is 'you' time and involves no housework, family tasks or shopping, unless it's indulging in a little retail therapy.
2. No children, of course.

Spend time on a favourite hobby; make a cup of tea; read the newspaper; take a bath; join an evening class; have coffee with a friend; make a date with your partner; plan a weekend with friends; snooze the afternoon away; go to a movie; read a book uninterrupted; do the garden; meditate; have a massage.

The aim is to relax and recharge. Go on, you know you want to, and whether you can snatch five minutes' peace or have the luxury of a night, a weekend, or a week away, make the effort. You will all benefit.

DAILY PARENT TIME

Make time each day for yourself and your partner, even if it's as simple as having a cup of tea together. It's a good habit to cultivate early on, once your child is old enough to occupy herself for a short period. Over time, she will understand that this is 'grown-up time' so Mum and Dad can catch up on the day. Reinforce this habit gently, but remind her you are there if there is an emergency and keep an eye on her.

In the end

At the end of the day, rosy from the bath, fed and read to, kissed and cuddled, your own special person can be tucked into bed to dream of new adventures ahead. Sigh and relish that warm glow as peace descends upon your home and adult needs take priority for a brief time. Make the most of it, because in a couple of hours he's going to get up and do it all again!

REFERENCES

Books

Bainger, L, *Music Magic: a music teaching resource for ages 3-6 years*, Inscript Publishing, NSW, 2007

Blakey, N, *More Mudpies: 101 Alternatives to Television*, Tricycle Press, Berkeley, California, 1994

Cameron, S and Crook, K, *Small Fry Cooking*, ABC Books, Australia, 2006

Cameron, S, Crook, K, and Webster, Caroline, *Small Fry Outdoors*, ABC Books, Australia, 2008

Clark, H, *The New Useful Book: Songs and ideas from ABC Play School*, ABC Books, Australia, 2001

Crees, G & C, *Yoga Play & Relaxation for Young Children*, Manly, NSW: G & C Crees, 2005

Curtis, D and Carter, M, *Designs for Living and Learning: Transforming Early Childhood Environments*, Redleaf Press, St Paul, MN, 2003

Elliott, A, *Learning with Computers*, Early Childhood Australia Inc. Watson, ACT, 2003 (2nd edition)

Greenman, J, *Places for Childhoods: Making Quality Happen In The Real World*, Exchange Press, 1998

Greenman, J and Stonehouse, A, *What Happened To The World? Helping children cope in turbulent times*, Pademelon Press, 2002

Kolbe, U, *Rapunzel's Supermarket: All About Young Children And Their Art*, Peppinot Press, 2001 (2nd edition)

Matterson, E. M, *Play with a Purpose for Under-Sevens*, Penguin, 1975 (3rd edition)

Muldoon, Michell, *Re-Thinking Toys: the Plastic-Free Way*, *PlayRights*, The International Play Association (IPA), Oxfordshire, UK, (Vol 29, Issue 4), 2007

Richardson, C, *Do and Learn: A Book of Early Childhood Play Activities*, Sydney Day Nursery & Nursery Schools Association (Inc), 1979

Shipard, I, *How Can I Grow and Use Sprouts as Living Food*? Queensland Complete Printing Services, Nambour, 2005

Silverstein, Shel, *Where the Sidewalk Ends*, Jonathan Cape, London, 1984

Thomas, P, *The Magic of Relaxation: Tai Chi & Visualisation Exercises For Young Children*, Pademelon Press, 2002

Thomson, J. B, *Natural Childhood: A practical guide to the first seven years*, Hodder & Stoughton, 1995

REFERENCES

Internet sites

Kidsafe NSW (Child Accident Prevention Foundation of Australia)
Tel: (02) 9845 0890

Raising Children Network Australia
Australian parenting website

Reverse Garbage
(Not-for-profit co-operative that sells industrial discards, off-cuts and over-runs to the public)
Tel: (02) 9569 3132

Freecycle: free community network organisation which distributes unwanted household contents, etc
Australian recyclers community website

Roads and Traffic Authority NSW
General enquiries: Tel: 132 213

Smart Traveller
Includes tips for travelling with children
Tel: 1300 555135 (helpline)

Kids and traffic (Early Childhood Road Safety Education Program)
Tel: (02) 9805 3200

Kidzwelcome
Includes tips for travelling with young children
Tel: 1300 130 161

BBC – Parents' Music Room
BBC Radio website about the benefits of music

Young Media Australia – information about the media and children
Tel: 1800 700 357

Child Development Institute
US parenting website

Australia's Physical Activity Recommendations for 5-12 year olds (Department of Health and Ageing)
Government website/Physical Activity section

ACKNOWLEDGMENTS

Wow! Book number three in the *Small Fry* series ... and the same group of wonderful people, who formed our support teams for the first two, are to be warmly thanked.

Special thanks to our children Aiden, Saskia, Oliver and Phoenix for their constant inspiration and enthusiasm in all our madcap ideas. We love you to the moon and back. The *Small Fry* series is dedicated to you all.

Thanks to our families, the Camerons, Pascoes, Crooks and Emerys for their encouragement in getting these books out! Thank you all, especially David.

Thank you from Katrina to her wonderful partner Ross. Thank you for your love and encouragement and for being a very patient sounding board.

Nuncio D'Angelo, our 'rock' and fountain of legal knowledge – your guidance, support and availability leave us speechless! Heartfelt and endless thanks. How do we ever thank someone for a lifetime of friendship and unwavering support?

Thanks to the families and friends who have helped out with the photography:

Aiden and Saskia Emery; Oliver and Phoenix Pascoe; Robyn Latimer and Aja Elshaikh; Caro, Angus and Grace Webster; Kristy, Ruby, Ava and Ginger Fogerty; Leigha and Isaiah Broad; Rebecca Steele, Jed and Amelia Munro Justine, Finn and Isla Skogstad; Julianne and Lucinda Pascoe; Lynny Wheeler and Mia Vivien; Elizabeth Enahoro and April Elleston; Lynne Bennett and Molly Cheney; Christine and Alexia Ryan; Oswald and Cynthia Emery; Reika, Harry and James Roberts; Sandra and Flynn Jowitt; Fiona, Geena and Eloise Reeves; Cinzia and Alessia Ascani; Fiona and Lara Barraclough; Sally Dettmann-Hughes and Alicia Dettmann-Hughes; Nicky and Lucy McColl-Jones; Helen and Hannah Rodrigues; Angela and Aliya Barrett; Melissa, Molly and Maggie Megan; Lydia, Will and Sophia Feely; Elise and Judy Lockwood; Matilda and Ripley Voeten; Olivia Spears; Lisa and Paige Morris; Jacqueline and Ashley Saric; Anne and Emilie Harrison; Juliet, Phoebe, Sam and Archie Lawson.

Thanks Sue – for sharing your wealth of knowledge and for being brave enough to walk this path with us.

Our love and thanks to our friend and *Small Fry Outdoors* co-author Caro Webster – your generosity of spirit continues to amaze and inspire us. Our girlfriends Cath Stace, Michelle Richmond, Margie Greenup, Linda Garske, Danielle Ainsworth, Elise Lockwood, Robyn Latimer, Juliet Lawson, Liz Seymour, we love you and couldn't do this without you – thanks for letting us bounce ideas and frustrations off you all!!

Thanks also to farmer Kevin and Joy Roberson of Memundie for making the most incredible treehouse with the kids ... we all adore it!

Many thanks to Belinda Bolliger and Penny McDonald at ABC Books – as always, your guidance and support is so valued. We also look forward to a long relationship with our new friends at HarperCollins Publishers. And the lovely Liz Seymour (who is also our designer), thanks again for being part of our team.

Susie and Katrina

ACKNOWLEDGMENTS

Writing a book about children and play is a bit like distilling the contents of an encyclopedia into a pocket edition. Where to begin? Where to end? My thanks go to the many people who have generously shared their own experiences and ideas which have helped to guide and direct the content of this book: colleagues Lucy Bainger, Alison O'Hea, Sandy Quine, Anne Royds and Sharyn Baker deserve particular mention for their support and professional input.

My thanks also to TAFE Illawarra for creating an opportunity for me to pursue this project and to the staff at ABC Books for their commitment to this project. Of special mention is editor Penny McDonald. I think she has learned more about play than she thought possible!

I first discussed the idea of *Small Fry* in Susie Cameron's lounge room several years ago and was excited by Katrina and Susie's enthusiasm to create wonderful play experiences for children and families to share. The opportunity to be involved with *Small Fry* has been both a joy and pleasure. Thank you.

My parents gave me the blessing of a magnificent, play-filled childhood brimful with siblings and friends. There were always exciting experiences and opportunities which encouraged growth and development. Words cannot express how much I love them and my eternal gratitude for their support, which has allowed me to fulfil my own passions and dreams.

Best friend and 'parent-in-crime' is my partner, Russ, who continues to fill our lives with play and laughter. None of this would have been possible without his love and support. Thanks for the endless cups of tea when you were here and the encouraging Skype calls at midnight when you weren't.

My children, Jonathon and Sionen, are now grown up with partners of their own. I stand in awe of all they have achieved in their lives so far. I have learned so much from them and I am proud to be their mother. I could ask for no greater gift than the joy they bring me every day.

To all the children and families with whom I have shared the highs and lows over nearly thirty years in this profession, heartfelt thanks for the gift of time with your children which has increased my knowledge and enriched my life, professionally and personally.

My final thanks go to the many, many early childhood professionals, teachers and students with whom I have worked over a long career both at home and overseas. Too many to mention here but never forgotten. Their shared passion and commitment to children and families is awe-inspiring. This collective knowledge, about the importance of play, is truly a treasure, and the generosity with which it is shared brings richness and depth to the lives of children every day.

Sue Cant

INDEX

art 72

balloon drums 87
balloon rockets 53
beach activities 95
birdbath 97
books 67
building activities 90

chilling out 107–9
clay 78–9
collage 76
communication 65–9, 104
community awareness 117
computers 103–5
craft activities 47

dancing, props for 87
dinosaur terrarium 97
DIY board game 56–7

environmental awareness 39, 96, 114
experiments 51–63
exploration 52, 60, 95

family activities 133–7
friendship 120

games to make 59
garden activities 92

hats 49
holidays 125–9

jumping 90
jumping words game 128

kicking 92
kitchen activities 60

language play 65
laundry activities 60

masks 49
music 83–7
music memory game 129

nature 95–9
night time activities 114

object I Spy game 128
outdoors 95–9, 113–14
outings 136

paint recipe 75
parent planning for travel 126
parent play 137
photography 105
physical activities 89–92
play dates 119–23
pretend play 47–9
props box 48
pumpkin growing 97
puppet theatre 49
puzzles 51

reading 66–9
recipes
    carrot cake 122
    cream cheese frosting 122
    homemade butter 123
    rainbow salad 61
    salad dressing 61

scones 123
relaxation exercises 107
resources for activities 36, 49, 51, 90
routine activities 60
running 92

sandpits 95
shhhhh!!!! game 129
shopping activities 60
songs 83, 84
sound bar 86
spaces 41–2
sprouts, growing 62–3
stick & finger puppets 77
stories using computer 104
storytelling 66
stress 107
surprise box 129
swings 92

throwing 92
thumb wrestling 129
toolkit, children's 54
toys 33–7
travel games 128–9
travel pack 125

underwater magnifier 52

visualisation experiences 109

washing the car 60
water activities 96
weaving, wild 99